God Emperor of Didcot

Toby Frost

MYRMIDON

Myrmidon Books Ltd
Rotterdam House
116 Quayside
Newcastle upon Tyne
NE1 3DY

www.myrmidonbooks.com

Published by Myrmidon 2008

A catalogue record for this book is available from the British Library.

ISBN 978-1-905802-24-1

Set in 11/14pt Sabon by Falcon Oast Graphic Arts Limited,
East Hoathly, East Sussex

Printed in the UK by CPI Mackays, Chatham ME5 8TD

1 3 5 7 9 10 8 6 4 2

God Emperor of Didcot

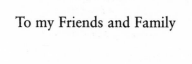
To my Friends and Family

Also by Toby Frost:

Space Captain Smith

Contents

PART ONE

URN, 4th planet in the Didcot System: Type 72 Civilised World

Population: 4,600,000

Notable Settlements: 'Capital City', capital city of Urn

Alien Natives: None

Climate: Clement to rather sticky

Notable Game: Sun dragons. Specimens up to 100ft long observed. Recommended for the experienced hunter

Principal Land Usage: 4% Urban, 96% Agricultural (plantation)

Principal Export: Tea

Encyclopaedia Imperialis, Volume 43 (Tiffin – Vindaloo)

1

A Deadly Mission!

Isambard Smith ran ten yards before the jungle burst open behind him and a mass of tentacles the size of a house threw a tree-trunk at his head. The tree flew past, throwing up earth like a bomb, and he swerved and headed east towards base camp. He glanced over his shoulder and shouted, 'You didn't give me an answer!' A second Thorlian broke out of the greenery to his right, honking and bellowing, and Smith ran headlong for the bridge.

His boot caught on a protruding vine and he stumbled and lurched upright to hear the forest erupt in roars and the flapping of frightened birds as he raced on down the path.

His earpiece crackled. 'Smith! What the devil is going on down there?'

'Minor problem,' he panted. 'They seem to want to murder me.'

'Hmm, that's not good.' A tentacle swept into view, glistening like an anaconda. Smith ducked as it whipped overhead, and he plunged off the path and weaved between the trees.

On the other end of the line, Hereward Khan struck a match and lit his pipe.

'So I suppose they don't want to join the Empire,' Khan said.

'Well, they didn't actually say no,' Smith replied. Fronds snagged his coat; branches and trunks splintered and fell behind him. 'But to be honest, they don't seem very keen.'

The ravine was in view. Smith broke from cover and sprinted to the rope bridge. The Thorlians howled. He bounded across, wood and hemp swaying under him, reached the other side and drew his sword. Smith cut once, twice, and the rope-bridge fell across the gorge to slap against the rock beneath the aliens.

As Smith dusted himself down Khan emerged from the undergrowth with a mug in either hand. 'Hello, Smith. Tea?'

'Good idea, Sir.'

They drank, watching the Thorlians make threats across the gorge. 'Typical aliens,' said Khan. 'Always making a fuss.'

'It's as though they think space belongs to them by rights,' said Smith. 'Shame, really. They'd have made useful allies against the Ghast Empire. I suppose someone will have to civilise them now.'

'I doubt the Navy can spare a destroyer. Besides,' Khan added, and he smiled, 'a message has come through from my contact in the Service. You're to fly to the Proxima Orbiter at once. Top Secret stuff, apparently. Very dangerous.'

'Excellent!' Smith finished his tea and wiped his moustache. 'My crew will be delighted, once she knows. She's always saying how she needs to get more action.'

*

There was light: painful light. Dimly, voices seeped into Polly Carveth's mind and she realised that she was still alive. Debris crackled under polished shoes. A man's voice said, 'My God. What a hell-hole.'

She muttered, rolled over and sat up in bed. She was still dressed, although her boots were gone. The stripes on her socks made her eyes hurt. 'My skull,' she moaned. 'What did I pour into my skull?'

'What didn't you?' He was young, dark haired, in a Royal Space Fleet uniform: very dapper and very handsome.

'Hello,' she said, and she frowned. 'No, I don't know your name. But you look nice.'

'You look like you had a hard night,' he said. He was holding one of the empty bottles he'd encountered beside the bed.

'I'm sure you helped,' she said coyly. Then she winced as she rubbed her face. 'Oh my God, I've got boils!'

'It's all right,' said the officer. 'You fell asleep with your face in a box of Milk Tray.'

Puzzled, Carveth prised off one of the boils. It was a blob of chocolate, slightly melted. 'Gross,' she said, looking at it. 'Well, waste not want not. Mmm, praline.'

A second young officer stepped out of the bathroom and adjusted his hair. 'Whoa,' Carveth said. 'There's two of you?'

'You're not seeing double, no,' said the first man.

'Two. Bloody hell.' She rose uncertainly to her feet. 'Look, um, I'm not feeling too good. I'm sure you're both really nice blokes, but two. . . I feel really bad. I honestly have never done this before. This isn't the sort of thing I'd normally even dream of doing on a night out, even with one of you. I feel low, slutty and really ashamed of myself. Last night was not typical of me.'

One started to say something, but she raised her palm like a saint and trudged into the bathroom.

She closed the door, slid the bolt and did a dance. I scored twice, I scored twice, she mouthed at the mirror, look at me cos I scored twice. She did several pelvic thrusts, but stopped when her brain started aching. Grimacing, Carveth stepped into the shower, annoyed that her memories of the night were so dim.

When she came out, the nearest of the two said, 'Fleet Command sent us with orders to collect you, Miss Carveth. You're needed for a mission: Base wants the *John Pym* to travel to the Proxima Orbiter this morning, and you're to go as ship's simulant.'

'You didn't sleep with both of us last night, if you were wondering,' said the other officer. 'Or either.'

Carveth felt that it was only force of will that stopped her shrivelling up like a salted slug.

'I don't know where you got that idea,' she replied, rising to her full height of five feet four. 'I am a Class Four synthetic with precision piloting capacity, not some sort of cheap harlot. Now, I have work to do. A chance has arisen to serve the Empire, and I welcome it with open arms.'

'And legs,' one of the men muttered. She ignored him and proceeded to the door with haughty regal dignity. It would have been a perfect exit had she not tripped over a Bacardi bottle on the way out and nearly brained herself on the doorknob.

*

The car's engine echoed off the walls of the huge, vault-like hall that held Valdane Shipping's selection of spacecraft. The great nose-cones jutted out of the dark like a row of missiles, shining and white. At the end, the *John Pym* stood, looking like a missile that had bounced off its target and come back for a second go.

Smith had flown in it several times now, but the emotion he felt on seeing it was always the same: a mixture of affection and disappointment, like someone coming home from the wars and discovering that his wife was actually quite plain. Under the left back leg (the one that sometimes only folded out halfway) two men in overalls were working beside a van. He drove closer, wondering who they were. Technicians, perhaps, fine-tuning the thrusters? No, Pest Control.

Smith got out of the car and took out his bag. He adjusted his collar and stepped over to one of the exterminators. 'Hello. I'm Captain Smith.'

'Alright mate.' The older, squatter of the men pulled off a glove and shook Smith's hand. 'Mike Rudge, pleased to meet you. You had some vermin running around in the hold.'

'The hold? You, ah, didn't look in all the rooms, did you?'

'All the ones that were unlocked. There was one we couldn't get into.'

Smith breathed again. Suruk kept his favourite things in that room, which visitors unused to his lifestyle might have found unsettling.

The exterminator said, 'Don't worry, mate: it's all sorted out now. We killed 'em – very quick and painless.'

'What did you use? Traps?'

'Submachine gun. Normally we'd just put some stuff down, landmines, say, but this is a small ship, and you've got to remember that it's somebody's home.'

'Guns? What the hell was it?'

'Procturan black ripper. It's always a shame. Near-perfect organism, your Procturan ripper. Beautiful animal. A born predator, unencumbered by delusions of conscience or remorse. Its hostility is matched only by its physical perfection. . . we found him down the back of the fridge.'

'I didn't realise the fridge was that big,' Smith said, looking into the back of the van. A corpse lay in there, a wiry, bulbous-headed thing slightly larger than a man. 'Are you sure that's not a motorcycle courier?'

'Nope, genuine article. We'll fax the costs over to your boss. Got to get off,' the exterminator added. 'Flying up to the polar regions to deal with a metamorph. Best get up there before it turns into the bloke what's paying for our petrol.'

Smith opened his cabin and dumped his bag on the bed. The *John Pym* hadn't changed: the same posters were there, the same model space-fighters hanging from the ceiling. He brushed his hands together and smiled, then stepped out into the corridor.

Suruk's room was open now, but had been padlocked shut while the ship was empty: there was always the possibility that some busybody might report Suruk to the police for collecting human skulls. Smith was not greatly troubled by this: it was a little uncivilised, true, but the ones Suruk had told him about had been generally bad people: murderers, traitors, TV chefs and the like. Besides, Rhianna would have been impressed to see him respecting indigenous cultures. If only she were here.

'Hullo, Suruk,' he said. 'How's things, old man?'

The alien turned and opened his mandibles. He had been polishing the rows of skulls on his mantelpiece and still wore his apron. There was a duster in one of his hard fists and a can of Mr Shiny in the other.

'Ah, Mazuran. I greet you as a friend. Once again we step into this steel beast and bring the justice of the blade to our enemies. I hear the call of battle once more, and I answer it.'

'Ah, so they called you up as well, eh? One of those secret service chaps, I suppose.'

'Uh? Secret service, you say?' Suruk reached up and quickly removed a pair of sunglasses and a coiled earpiece from one of his skulls. 'Ah. . . Do you know, they never visited me. They must have got lost on the way or something. I, ah, had a mystic dream instead. Something of that sort.'

'Well, here we are again. How was your holiday?'

The alien shrugged. 'I don't know. It has become touristy. No eccentric locals in their quaint clothing, no pretty pictures on the houses anymore, no lively street parties: sectarian Belfast has really gone downhill. Ah well. Perhaps we shall get a few good battles in space instead.' He did his equivalent of frowning. 'I notice the little woman is here again.'

'Well, she *is* the pilot.'

'I shall greet her.' He left the room and Smith followed

him. Carveth was in the cockpit, having a last flick through the Haynes manual before takeoff. On the far side of the dashboard, Gerald the hamster toured his cage, sniffing. 'Ah, so you still live, puny one,' Suruk said.

'Hello, Frogboy. You do know that someone's stuck a dead crab to your face, don't you?'

'Now look,' said Smith. 'Let's try to be civil, shall we?'

'Of course,' Suruk said. 'Indeed, I am impressed that you are here, and from the smell of things have not yet shamed yourself at the prospect of danger. I expected you to be the sort of coward that whenever duty calls, nature calls louder.'

'No, no, glad to be on board,' Carveth said with a weak smile. 'Glad to be back in space. Just can't wait to face those hungry aliens. Super.'

There was an element of truth to this. She was indeed relieved to be away from Earth, largely because she had done little but embarrass herself since stepping off the ship. At the East Empire Company Christmas party, she had mistaken a Yothian trade delegate for a Christmas tree and tried to put a fairy on his head. Carveth was eventually removed, but by then the damage had been done, especially when she knelt down and tried to reach under the Yothian, repeatedly slurring 'Where's my pressie?'

'Well, excellent,' said Smith. 'Let's get this show on the road, shall we? Full speed to Proxima.'

'Right, Boss.' Carveth leaned over and knocked down two rows of switches with the side of her hand. From deep within the guts of the ship there came a coughing sound, then a steady hum as the engines fired up. Smith pulled on his seatbelt, hearing the growl of the engines creep up through the walls. In a dozen brass dials on the main console, the needles swung trembling into the red. The back of his chair began to shake. Suruk ducked into the corridor. Gerald took shelter in the bottom of his cage. Carveth wrapped her hands around the throttle and threw the switch and, with a mighty roar, the *John Pym* leaped four feet into the air and stopped.

'Whoops,' she said. 'Handbrake's on.'

Two hours later, Carveth knocked on Smith's door, and when he didn't reply she opened it. The Captain sat in his armchair with his back to her, headphones on, drumming his fingers on the armrest.

'Ah, ah woomaahn,' he sang, 'Woomahn, you hurt me deep inside. Woomahn, on the steed of Sauron you ride. . .'

Carveth leaned over him and lifted the headphones away. 'Pink Zeppelin?' she inquired.

'*Mordor Woman Blues*,' Smith said. 'How's things in the control room?'

'Dunno – I'm not there, am I?' She looked at the headphones. 'I never got prog rock. Can't see what's so progressive about singing about a wizard for half an hour, myself. If you ask me, anyone stupid enough to set the controls for the heart of the sun gets what he deserves. Fancy a look outside?'

'Yes, why not?'

Smith followed her into the cockpit and took his seat in the captain's chair. Carveth nodded at the navigation computer. 'I've plotted a course for the Proxima Orbiter.

Some idiot had set the Didcot system as our destination. We're bloody lucky I looked before I hit the switches, else we'd be going in the wrong direction.'

'Oh,' said Smith. 'Sorry about that. I was doing a bit of research, trying to see how far we are from things–'

'From Rhianna, you mean? We're about eight thousand million miles.'

'Eight thousand million and twenty eight.'

Carveth folded her arms. 'Boss, don't you think this is a bit sad? I mean, she's almost on the other side of the Empire. Not to mention her being part scary-psychic-alien-ghost-thing.'

Smith sighed. 'I know,' he said. 'I know. She might as well be on the moon. In fact, it would be a damn sight easier if she was. We could just drop round for the afternoon then. It's difficult to accept that she's gone for good. She's not an easy person to forget, you know.'

'Not if you've heard her playing Bob Dylan, she's not. Christ, she was lucky I didn't ram that harmonica down her neck.'

Despite himself, Smith agreed. Rhianna had once stood in for an over-medicated member of Spaceport Convention, a reasonably well-known folk band, which had left her with pretensions of musical skill. She had a rather operatic voice that tended towards the squeaky, which, if not actually awful, was certainly an acquired taste.

Carveth shrugged. 'She had her moments, I guess. She was clever, and good-looking, but on the plus side she was always good for a smoke. That woman had more grass on her than a cricket pitch.'

'I don't really know what to do, to be honest,' said Smith. 'I rather miss her, Carveth. Maybe she even liked me back.'

'That whole trying to have sex with you thing makes me think so. Too bad you offered her tea instead. In future, remember that if a woman asks you to debag her, she doesn't mean for you to put one less in the pot.'

'Carveth, is there a chance you'll ever stop banging on about that?'

'At least I would bang on if I got the chance.'

He glanced away, staring literally into space. 'It's very difficult to know what to do. She just seems so far away, even if she ever was interested. Whatever chance I had, I missed it. I almost wish I could forget about her and find somebody else, but I can't. Where else will I find someone like that again?'

'Why not just get another one?' Suruk said from the door. He stepped into the room and stretched his arms and mandibles and yawned.

'Get another one?' Smith cried, appalled. 'She's not a bloody cheese sandwich, Suruk. More like. . . a sandwich made of gold.'

'So, inedible,' Suruk said. 'Completely useless.'

'You know,' Smith said, 'it all reminds me of a song Rhianna once played. It said, "You don't what you've got 'til it's gone". It's only now I realise how true that is. I think it was by Motorhead.'

'Joni Mitchell,' Carveth said.

'Well, same section.'

'What, folk?'

'No, M.'

'Fair enough.' Carveth turned her attention to the controls. 'We're nearly there. Look.' She pointed to a speck in the left of the screen, gradually growing. 'That's it: the Proxima Orbiter. Funny how they all start to look like baked bean tins, isn't it?'

Smith nodded. 'Less 2001 than 57 varieties,' he said. 'It's easy to get tired of space. It's all rather black.'

'Don't feel bad, Captain,' said Carveth. 'I know it's hard about Rhianna, but you've got to keep trying. I've been waiting for fate to throw me together with the right man – or any man, for that matter – but I always try keep cheerful. You know, sometimes I think about Rick Dreckitt. I liked him. We went on a date and everything.'

'He only took you on a date in order to kill you, Carveth.'

'Yes, but he didn't, did he? That's a start, right? We could have had something there.'

'A gunfight?'

'Cynic.' She typed their co-ordinates into the navigation computer. 'Proc's picked us up and we'll come in on autopilot. We've got priority docking.' She spun around in her chair and studied Smith. 'Come on, Cap, put on a happy face. You're depressing me.'

'Just land the ship, would you please?' said Smith.

'Lady, gentleman and colonial life-form, you are clear to enter,' the computer said, and with a hiss the pistons drew back and the airlock doors rolled apart.

The station docking hall was full of soldiers, full of activity and talk. Armoured men chatted with Proxima's stevedores. Troopers carried boxes of equipment between them, jogging from electric trams to the airlocks that led into their own ships. Mechanical arms flexed from the wrought iron ceiling, loading and refuelling the vehicles. Three Conqueror landships waited by the far wall while their turrets were checked, occasionally letting out puffs of steam like agitated horses. In the corner, an NCO argued with a clipboard-wielding simulant.

'Convoy, from the looks of it,' said Smith.

Technically, the worlds of the British Empire were self-sufficient, but as the war against the Ghasts intensified the battlefront shifted, and one colony after another was equipped and fortified to become the latest outpost of the Pax Britannicus Interstella. No doubt these men would end up as the garrison of some highly-productive factory-world that the Empire could not afford to lose.

An electric car rolled up beside them and a woman in RSF uniform looked them over. 'Captain Smith?'

Smith felt the slight pang of annoyance he always felt when he saw RSF personnel. They had prestige, good pensions and, most importantly, access to Hellfire Space-Deployment Fighters, something of which he was secretly very jealous. 'Ah, yes, that's me,' he said. 'Here are my colleagues. We're here to accept a very important mission, the details of which I can't tell you.'

'Great. Hop on. Don't damage the suitcases.'

They climbed onto the back of the car and it rolled away down the long corridor to the docking offices. Smith pushed a rucksack off his lap and reflected that, although not a difficult man, he would rather have accepted the mission in something other than a luggage cart.

They passed little groups of dockers taking their second morning tea-break, as authorised by their guild. The cart rolled to a stop beside a metal door. 'Here we are,' the RSF woman said.

They dismounted. Abruptly, the door opened a crack and a gloomy oblong of a head was thrust into the corridor. It had a thin moustache and messy black hair, and belonged to W, the master-spy. 'Ah, Smith, it's you,' he said. 'Come on in.'

'You're just in time for tea,' W said, ushering them inside.

They stepped into a large, high-ceilinged room, perhaps once a store, now an office made cosy by the vast amount of junk and paperwork lying about. On the wall there was a bad picture of someone who might have been King Victor. The desk was hidden under files, several maps and a scroll-worked computer. Behind the desk, a Factual Information Bureau poster showed a knight with a pencil moustache marching at the head of a variety of stern-looking citizens. The caption read 'Forwards To Victory!' The oddest item stood against the wall: a wheeled tea-urn the height of a man, made of dented, shiny metal with a tap on the front.

A small group of people in caps stood beside the massive urn, dour and serious. They wore short black coats over blue overalls and solid boots: guild uniform. One grunted at the new arrivals; another gave them a sullen nod. A small, solid man stepped forward from the group. He wore the long brown coat and cloth cap of a high-ranking Union official. Behind his ear was a pencil of office.

'Isambard Smith, Polly Carveth and Suruk the Slayer,' said W. 'This is Wilfred Hebblethwaite, assistant advisor to the Ministry of Food and the Grandmaster of the Collective Union of Plantation Production Associates.'

'How do,' the small man said. He shook hands with Smith and Carveth and said, 'Does it bite?'

'Not with my hand,' Suruk said coldly, and they shook.

W nodded at the opposite wall. A simulant sat in an office chair, dapper and attentive. She had the refined, rather sharp features of a Type 64, one of the many models more advanced than Carveth.

'Well hello there!' she said, getting up. 'A pleasure, I'm sure. Call me Hattie.' She put out a hand. 'Captain Smith, Mr Slayer, Miss Carveth – always nice to see a fellow sim.'

'Hello,' Carveth said.

'Nice to see you again,' W said. 'Hope you're all well.' He coughed nastily into his palm, looked at it, thought better of shaking hands and sat down. 'I've called you here to discuss a rather difficult problem that's arisen of late. But first let's have some tea. There's some cups over there, Miss Carveth—'

'Right,' said Carveth. She stood up, picked a mug off the side table and put it against the urn and turned the tap.

'Get your hands off my nozzle!' said the urn.

'Bloody hell!' Carveth cried. 'There's someone *in* there!'

'Course there is,' said the urn, and with a slow creak it rolled into the centre of the room. She stepped back, astonished. 'I'm the Grandmaster,' said the Urn. 'Weren't you listening?'

'I meant for you to pass me the cups,' W explained. Carveth sat down, looking rather shell-shocked. 'I'll put the kettle on. It's important that these things are done properly.'

'Quite right too,' said the Grandmaster from within his urn. 'If I hadn't flooded my system with the stuff, I'd want a cup as well.'

'We could tip one in the top,' W suggested, filling the kettle.

'Thanks awfully, but no.'

'To business, then.' W brushed down the leather patches on his elbows and crossed his long, thin legs. He was a scarecrow of a man: bony and unkempt. 'Hattie. Perhaps you could give us a run-down of the situation in this sector?'

'Certainly!' she said, and a lens folded down from her Alice band and dropped in front of her left eye. A quick flicker of light burst from the lens and her features became hard and cold, the eyes a little distant. Hypnos, Carveth realised: the hyper-normative operating status of a top-range strategy synthetic. Hattie's voice was quick and precise.

'Status report, East Empire Company Sector Twelve. Full mobilisation. All available units diverted to front line to counter anticipated Ghast attack over sectorial edge. Six full divisions in immediate war zone. Fifteenth Fleet on full alert. Equipment and morale optimal. Sector defences graded A2, anticipated A1 in three standard weeks.'

'Excellent,' said Smith.

Hattie glanced round at Smith. 'All defences optimal,' she said. 'All regular units are diverted to the sector rim. Citizen Guard units are being trained to take up local defence in the event of unrest.'

W nodded. 'Unit strength of Citizen Guard?'

'Fully trained,' she replied.

'Well, that sounds splendid,' said Smith. 'Should Gertie put his big red arse over the border, we'll easily get him on the rim.'

W said, 'But this mobilisation leaves our internal defences weakened. Were a major fifth-columnist movement to arise, we could well find ourselves without the manpower to put it down.'

'Fifth columnists!' cried Smith. 'Those dirty traitors! Where?'

W raised a hand and coughed. 'All in good time, Smith. But first, a question. Our Empire hasn't lost a major war since the Imperial Revolution and the fall of the Over-empire. Despite being civilised and amenable, we have a reputation for military success unrivalled among the Great Powers. So, what makes the Empire so good at fighting?'

Smith frowned. 'Well, I'd say it was either a combination of superior equipment and training, or not being made up of foreigners.'

W stood up and poured the tea. 'Close, but not so.' He pushed their cups across the table, along with an extra one for Mr Hebblethwaite. 'Look at what's in your hands, and you will see the answer.'

'China?' Carveth suggested. 'Is it Chinese people?'

'No!' W's big hand slapped the tabletop. 'It's the tea! The tea is what makes us strong!'

There was a brief, not-wholly-comfortable pause.

'Are you *sure* it's not superior training?' said Smith.

'Watch,' said W. 'You, girlie. Turn the projector on, would you?'

'I knew there was a reason I got my pilot's licence,' Carveth said grumpily, and as a projector descended from the ceiling on an arm, she pressed the switch. The room lights dimmed.

Elgar played. In the centre of the wall, a Union Jack fluttered. The words 'Public Information Film – Private' appeared across the flag. W pointed at the centre of the image. 'Pay attention, everyone.'

The image of the flag cut to a desk: the desk in this room, in fact. W stood behind the desk. 'Pay attention, everyone,' he said. 'This is a film about tea, sponsored by the Combined Horticultural Amenities Regulator and the Factual Information Bureau. Many of you may be wondering why you are watching a film about tea.'

The picture cut to a street on what might have been Ajax Minoris. A reporter thrust a coffin-shaped microphone at an old man. 'What's all this about tea?' the old man said.

The film cut back to W behind his desk, lighting a roll-up. 'Quite,' he said. 'Today, I intend to tell you about the importance of tea to our culture and its role in defeating our alien enemies. But first, a little history. Tea was discovered by Chinese people many years ago.'

'See?' said Carveth. 'Chinese people.'

A picture of some ancient Chinese appeared on the screen. 'Soon afterward, tea began to be grown in what is now modern Indastan. In the seventeenth century, tea was acquired by British colonists and taken back to England. It was not long before the custom of adding milk to tea was developed, shortly before the spread of British naval power across the Earth. This is no coincidence.' The screen now depicted Nelson and his officers sipping tea on the quarterdeck of HMS Victory while, behind them, a rather disorientated cow was being winched aboard.

Scientists appeared on the screen, working in a cavernous laboratory. 'These are *boffins*. Boffins such as these have proven, through science, that the addition of cow's milk to tea causes a chemical synthesis, producing enzymes conducive to high levels of moral fibre. And we all know how essential moral fibre is in strengthening the morale, wisdom, bravery and downright decency of citizens everywhere.

'Following the discovery of the proper way of drinking tea, the First Empire remained unbeatable in battle, conquering a wide range of scoundrels, despots and foreigners with the help of unlimited tea. However, the golden age of tea was not to last.'

The music became sombre, and the screen now depicted a group of feeble-looking aesthetes sipping some sort of cream-topped, sprinkle-spattered drink, like an anaemic dropping in a cup. On the edge of the picture, a pot-bellied lout swilled pop from a can.

'During the period of decline leading to the tyranny of the World Government, tea was discouraged in what historians now see as a concerted and malign effort to poison the resolve of the Imperial People. Insidious corporations foisted unnatural drinks made of coffee and syrup on the demoralised populace. For that dark period the future of man was decided by others, until the Imperial Revolution and the fall of the Over-Empire. Now, we may rest assured that the strong arm of the honest tea drinker will never again be made skinny by the latte of foreign oppressors.'

The music changed again, this time to brisk Walton. A pair of citizens, a woman and a man, ran through a meadow hand in hand. 'This is the future,' W's voice said. 'Your future. The Empire lies in the hands of citizens like you, people ready to fight to defend democracy and decency from alien aggression.' The man and woman had climbed a small hill, now dawn broke over them. The woman was pointing at something out of shot, while the man poured from a teapot. 'We shall go forward and face our foes with weapons in one hand, mugs in the other. Let those who seek to oppress us remember that a storm is brewing.'

'Jerusalem' played, and the flag reappeared on the screen. Smith stood up instinctively, realised that no-one else was standing and sat down. The lights came up.

'Stirring stuff,' said Smith.

'It's consumption of tea that makes t'army strong,' Hebblethwaite said. 'And, I may say, what makes your British worker the finest int' Empire, if not int' whole galaxy.'

Hattie nodded. 'Statistical analysis of historical data indicates that moral fibre raises the efficacy of combat troops between twenty-four and sixty percent. Moral fibre is estimated as thirty percent more effective than numerical superiority, selective breeding, honour codes, religious fanaticism, and so forth.' Her calm, dead eyes fixed on Smith. 'The most effective factor in the development of elite troops is moral fibre.'

'And moral fibre comes from tea,' said W.

'Good lord. Well, I'll remember to have more of the stuff,' Smith said, uncertain how he could do this without wiring himself up to a drip. 'But where do we come into this?'

'You need to see how tea production is managed on a galactic scale,' W said, rooting about on his desk. 'We need to look at the Empire as a whole. There should be a holographic projector here somewhere. . . and I put a map under it. Here we are.'

He tugged out an Ordnance Survey map of Known Space and opened it up. 'Now, this large pink area in the middle is the Empire. At present, the main battlefront is down here, along these systems. Here, from Cerberus to Pleides, is where the main attack is expected to come, and where we've sent most of our heavy ships ready to meet the Ghasts head-on.'

'Splendid,' said Smith. He was familiar with the battlefront.

'And here, near the border, is the Didcot System.'

Smith was particularly familiar with this dot: Rhianna was stationed there. He knew the distance from Didcot to a variety of other places, just in case he was going past and could find an excuse to divert a few billion miles from his course and drop round to say hello. He found himself smiling at the prospect of being able to look her up. Unfortunately, he had no idea of where in the system she was stationed.

W frowned. 'The Didcot system has two settled planets: Didcot 6, which is used by Morlock settlers and, more importantly, Didcot 4. On Didcot 4, sixty percent of the Empire's tea is grown.'

'Can't say I know the place,' Smith said, surprised.

'You may know it by its other name. People call it Urn.'

'Urn,' Smith repeated. 'Yes, I've heard of Urn alright. Is that a force field around it?'

'No, that's where I was using the map as a coaster. Urn is a self-governing British Protected Dependency. It has a permanent contract to supply the Empire with tea. In return, we have supplied it with a missile grid to deal with orbital threats and have promised to protect its integrity.'

'Good.'

'It was indeed good,' W said. 'Perhaps too good to last. Recently, a rabble-rouser calling himself the Grand Hyrax seems to have appeared from nowhere. He's already gained considerable support on Urn. He's a cultist, probably a lunatic, and he claims to represent the Brotherhood of the New Eden.'

'Wait a moment,' Smith said, 'isn't that the same funny church they have on – oh, New Eden?'

'Quite. The same thing.'

'Gilead,' said Carveth.

New Eden was a league of human worlds allied to the Ghast Empire. They worshipped a god of their own design called the Grand Annihilator, a delinquent amalgam of the worst features of several of Earth's old gods. Smith had run up against the Edenites before, when the brutal, stupid Captain Gilead had tried to capture Rhianna, believing her to be an angel who could be forced to fight on his side. There weren't many people who could make the Ghasts look sane, but the Edenites were making a good job of it.

'The Grand Hyrax is a maniac,' W explained. 'His version of Edenism is even more extreme than the sort practised by Edenite High Command. He has amassed a horde of fanatical followers known as the Crusadist Cult, who have pledged to overthrow the democratic governor and make the Hyrax their divine emperor. We believe that, if this happens, the Crusadists will ally openly with New Eden and halt the export of tea. And you realise now what would happen to the armies of the Empire were they to be deprived of tea.'

'By God!' cried Smith. 'What an evil plan! We can't just sit here and let a man like that plot against the Empire! We should fly to Didcot this minute, settle his goose and cook his hash!'

'Sort of,' said Carveth.

Suruk had been sitting quietly, listening to the humans discuss a lot of stuff that did not greatly interest him. Now, however, the talk was taking a more appealing turn. He made a rattling noise at the back of his throat. 'Then, tea-makers, I will be glad to assist. My humans here will transport me to the world of Urn, and I shall confront this fool and chop off his head.'

'No,' said W. 'If the Grand Hyrax is to be stopped, it must be done with subtlety. The potential for civil unrest is too great.'

'I could creep up on him first,' Suruk suggested. 'Then chop his head off. How about that?'

'You're to fly straight to Urn,' W said. 'There you will meet up with our chief – and only – secret agent there. He's been instructed to make contacts with the Teasmen, the local settlers. From the amount of money he's been asking for, he should have built up some strong contacts by now. I will reach Urn a few days later, undercover as a journalist. I'll claim to be researching a story for the *Daily Monolith*. Together we'll work out what to do, and together we'll put a stop to this conspiracy against the common people of the Empire. For a plot against tea is a plot against the liberty of the human race.'

'Well said,' Hebblethwaite declared. 'Grand sentiments!'

From the side came the creak of wheels. Smith had forgotten about the Grandmaster of the Collective Union of Plantation Production Associates, as much as one could forget about a man who lived in a gigantic vat of tea. He looked around at the Grandmaster, and saw his own face reflected in the smudged, dented metal above the little tap: a mask of determination with a well-kept moustache.

'The tea *must* brew,' the Grandmaster said.

'We will go at once,' Smith promised. 'We will prepare for all eventualities and, if needs be, we will destroy this man. But we need to do this the Imperial way. First, before we kill him and take this planet for ourselves, we shall see if he will listen to reason.'

2

Casino Imperiale

'Crusade! Crusade! Butcher the unbelievers! Wade in their blood! Rejoice in the lamentation of their women and drive their children before you like lambs to the slaughter! Crusade!'

'So much for reasonable,' said Isambard Smith.

They stood at the back of a crowd that spread for a hundred yards in every direction from the front of the ex-warehouse that was now the Church of the Grand Annhilator. Above them, the sun of Urn had reached its peak, and the heat was remorseless. The combination of sun and shouting made Carveth slightly queasy and she felt grateful for her hat and ice cream.

On the balcony of the church, the Grand Hyrax was a flailing mass of beard, hair and wide sleeves. He looked like a battered wizard trying to summon up spirits.

'What do we want? Crusade! When do we want it? Now!'

'What's he doing?' Carveth demanded, jumping up and down. The crowd roared approval, a wave of sound.

'Not quite sure,' Smith said, struggling to lean around the tall man in front of him. The fellow wore a collapsible wire frame on his head, with a piece of cloth stretched over it to form a sun-shade. 'The tea-towel this chap's got on his head is spoiling my view.'

Carveth elbowed him. 'You can't say that!' she whispered hoarsely. 'That's, I dunno, racist or something? Rhianna'd have your knackers if she heard you going on like that.'

'Excuse me?' The man in front turned around. 'I couldn't help overhearing. This *is* a tea towel, actually,' he said, gesturing to his headwear. 'It's traditional on Urn: it bears the symbol of the collective plantation where I work. We Teasmen are a proud bunch, you see. Also,' he added, pulling the ends of the tea towel over his ears, 'it's good for blocking out all the noise made by that colossal tit up there.'

Behind the Hyrax, a row of robed, wild-looking men ran out like a chorus line and started battering themselves industriously with sticks. 'You've got to admit, he knows how to put on a show,' Smith observed. 'He's even got his own flagellants.'

'Indeed.' Suruk nodded. 'He seems full of hot air.'

'Flatulence, Suruk,' Smith said. 'Different business.'

'Forgive me, Lord, for I have wind,' Carveth added.

'Two, four, six, eight, what do we appreciate? Crusade! Give me a C! Give me an R!'

'Let's go,' Carveth said. 'We're not learning anything helpful here, and the mission briefing says that our contact has a swimming pool.'

They turned and slipped through the crowd, Suruk leading the way. People moved out of his path: although free citizens, M'Lak rarely came to Urn, and the sentient population was almost entirely human. Around them, the crowd still gawped at the demagogue.

'I wonder why anyone would listen to a load of arse like that,' Smith said.

Suruk shrugged. 'Humans are stupid.'

'Maybe, but not *that* stupid. You wonder what anyone could see in him.'

They emerged beside their car, a Crofton Imp that Smith had hired at the spaceport. Smith drove, Carveth sitting beside him and Suruk *stretched* across the back seats, next to Gerald's shaded, air-conditioned cage.

The landing on Urn had gone surprisingly well. The most notable form of local fauna, the allegedly man-eating sun dragons, had failed to appear. This was fortunate, as they were apparently invisible to radar and stored vast quantities of static electricity that they spat at anything passing through the stratosphere, which they clearly considered as their territory. Now the *John Pym* was tucked out of sight between two larger, better ships, which seemed to make up the entire Urnian merchant fleet.

Smith pulled out into busy traffic, and the sleek, dusty little car slipped between rows of domed office blocks. Carveth rolled her hat up. 'I don't like this place,' she declared. 'What kind of people call their capital city Capital City? That's the most stupid place name outside Thisland.' She looked over her shoulder, towards the Church of the Grand Annhilator. 'So, you religious, then?'

'Me?' Smith dialled up the destination on the onboard computer and typed in their course. He sat back, hands resting on the steering wheel in case their car changed its mind. 'C of E,' he said, 'I suppose. There might be something, but if it's anything like matey boy's god back

there, I'm not sure I'd want to be on its side. I just try to
be a good sort and hope I can talk it over with whoever's
on the other side, if there is one.'

'I think it's generally assumed that God's an alright
bloke,' Carveth said. 'As for me, though, I'm atheist. I
refuse to follow any god.'

'It is probably mutual,' Suruk observed. 'I doubt any
deity would want you traipsing after him, continually
demanding thinness and male concubines. It would lower
the tone.'

'That's rich coming from you. You worship a stick.'

'I do not "worship" anything. I honour my ancestors,
whose valour I see enshrined in the weapons I wield.
Anything else would be absurd, and my spear agrees with
me.'

'Well, I'm a free agent,' Carveth declared. 'I kneel
before no man.'

'I shall not lower myself to comment on that,' Suruk
said.

The Grand Hyrax closed the doors behind him and the
cheering crowd became silent. He took a handkerchief
from his pocket and wiped his brow. 'How was that?'

Two men watched him from the side of the room. There
were biscuits and coffee cups on the table. 'Not bad, not
bad,' said one of them.

The speaker was youngish and slim, neat and groomed
in contrast to the Hyrax's tattered robes and potent odour.
'I think you put up a strong performance there, Steve.
But you've got to remember that you're addressing
confirmed party stakeholders here. It won't be half as easy

to work a crowd that considers you a deranged tyrant.'

The Hyrax reached into his beard and rubbed his chin. 'Why not?'

'Focus groups suggest that the proles are going to want reassurance on key touchstone issues: health and schools, for instance, pensions too.'

'Well,' said the Hyrax, 'that's easy. Once we're in charge, God the Annihilator will provide us with health so we can fight his crusade. Obviously, schools won't be necessary, except to tell children to obey me, and to go on crusades. And as for pensions. . . some sort of crusade, maybe?'

'I think people are worried that we're a one-issue party,' Calloway said.

'That's the point,' the Hyrax replied. 'There won't be any other issues to worry about once everyone is dead. Or any voting. The unimaginable suffering I intend to impose upon mankind will make all other issues unimportant. Problem solved.'

Calloway frowned. 'That might take some spinning.'

'Hell, I like it!' the third man said. He sat in the shadows, a rug across his lap. He leaned across the table to the coffee pot, and the rug fell away.

His body was a robot's: the spindly, stripped-down body of an old-fashioned mechanical android, painted in army drab. The metal stopped at the base of the throat. From there, a thickly muscled neck led to a jutting slab of brutal, chiselled jawline. Above the jaw was a Caucasian face that cosmetic surgery had left angry and permanently surprised, the face of a beach-bronzed Adonis for whom kicking sand in people's faces had never been quite enough.

'You see?' said the Grand Hyrax. '*Gilead* likes it.'

'Oh, I like it alright,' Gilead said, his voice dreamy. 'Everything you say is right, especially the suffering bit. These people stole my body; they deserve to pay. Every day a hundred things remind me how much I owe the British Empire.' Out of instinct he scratched his crotch, leaving scratches in his paintwork. He glanced down. 'See what I mean?'

'I see,' said Calloway.

'Yeah.' Gilead paused, the coffee pot tilted at his cup. 'All I need is the call from my uh, sponsors, and we'll be good to go. And then this place will be ours.'

'Mine,' the Hyrax said.

'It will belong to the New Eden, with you as governor.' Gilead explained. 'This rock may not look like much, but it's the right hand of the British Empire. Once we've got control of it, we will squeeze – and squeeze – until we've choked the life out of these godless bastards and paid them back for what Isambard Smith did to me.'

'You choke someone around the neck, not the right hand,' Calloway observed.

'You choke them how I say,' Gilead retorted. 'When Johnny Gilead plays hardball, if you're not rolling with us, then you ask how high. Remember that next time you doubt the word of the Lord, because the word of the Lord is *strong*.'

He raised his hand and crushed the coffee pot in his metal fingers. From his metal chest a female voice said, 'Compression damage imminent.'

'We hit them very soon, and then they stay hitted,' Gilead said. 'Once our new allies are ready, all your people need do is take the missile grid and this planet belongs to us.' The pot buckled; coffee ran down his steel fist, onto the table and the cups. 'My cup runneth over,' Gilead said. 'It's a sign.'

'It's going on the carpet,' Calloway said coldly. 'Which is presumably a sign that you're a fool.'

'Still,' said Smith, as they turned into the suburbs, 'leaving aside these religious madmen and the coup they're obviously plotting, it is quite a lucky assignment because we'll be able to see Rhianna again. Once we've foiled the Crusadist uprising, I thought I might take her some flowers and see if she'd like to go out for dinner sometime.'

The car rolled past broad lawns and long, wide houses. Mowing machines slowly drew stripes on grass. The children of Imperial bureaucrats threw balls for retrievers, spaniels and fat Labradors.

'It's a good plan,' Carveth said. 'Of course, you'll have to find her first.'

'Oh, I'll find a way.'

She sighed. 'I only wish I could be so confident about my own situation.'

'I'm sure you'll meet someone sooner or later,' Smith replied. 'There's probably plenty of single men on a world like this.'

'Most of them have a pulse,' Suruk observed. 'You will be spoilt for choice.'

Something went *ping* on the dashboard and a needle sprang up in one of the dials. 'Looks like we're here,' said Smith, and he turned the car into a wide gravelled drive.

Ahead, shining in the hard sun, the front of a huge white house loomed up like a glacier. Long windows winked as the light caught them. A striped awning threw shadow across a pool. Wallahbots rolled across the lawn, clipping the hedges and plumping the pillows on the sun loungers.

'Well,' Carveth said, 'it's nice to know that the Security Service's budget is going where it's needed.'

Smith stopped the car and they got out. One of the wallahbots turned from its work and waddled over to them, gravel crunching under its stumpy legs. A little panel slid back in its domed head and a probe scanned them. It said, 'Wooty doot-doot?'

'I'm here to see the owner of the house,' Smith said. He glanced left and right to make sure that he was not observed, and added pointedly, 'Birds fly south for the winter.'

'Woo,' said the wallahbot. 'Woo doot doot Pimms?' it asked, and the dome flipped back to reveal an array of bottles.

'Bit early for me,' Smith replied, and the wallahbot's dome closed up.

'Fair enough,' it said. 'I'll just see if the master's at home. Wait here please. Woodle-oo.'

Smith watched it stomp into the house and said, 'How do I understand those things?'

'I've no idea,' Carveth said. 'I thought it was a flip-top bin.'

A sprinkler system hissed into life across the lawn. A small, weasel-like man strolled around the side of the house in a sports jacket. His eyes were half-closed, like a lizard's, and there was a cigarillo between his long fingers. If he got any more languid, Smith thought, he would fall asleep and topple into the shrubbery.

He smiled. 'You must be Smith. Pleased to meet you. James Featherstone.'

Smith shook hands. Featherstone nodded at Suruk.

'Is this your boy?'

Smith looked at Suruk. 'No,' he said, puzzled. 'Do we look similar?'

Featherstone said, 'Boy as in *servant*. Any decent spy has servants.'

'He's not a servant, he's my friend. I hope that's not a problem,' Smith added, giving Featherstone one of his hard stares.

'Not at all. I rather like the fellow. His mouth has a cruel twist. And I must ask, who's this perky young thing?'

'Hello,' said Carveth. 'I'm Polly. Nice house.'

'Polly Carveth, my pilot,' Smith explained.

'It's bad to have women on a job: they have to be kept in order. Women are always trouble to someone,' Featherstone said, with the air of one reciting a proverb. He raised an eyebrow and blew out smoke. 'The only question is, Miss Carveth, are you going to be trouble to *me*?'

Carveth grimaced. 'Which is more platonic: yes or no?'

Featherstone laughed lightly. 'Come with me, Smith. We need to talk about your being here. Your moon-man can bring in your things. In the meantime, your people are quite welcome to use the pool, so long as the alien doesn't turn it green. The little woman's *very* welcome.'

He turned and passed gracefully through the French windows. Smith frowned and glanced at his crew. Behind him, Carveth mimed nausea and Suruk kicked the suitcases over.

'As soon as this cretin is of no more use to us. . .' he growled.

'True,' said Smith. 'He seems a little on the, ah, louche side. Can't say I'm impressed.'

Carveth patted her pockets. 'Has anyone got the keys to the ship?'

'I thought you had them,' Smith said.

'I gave them to you.'

He sighed. 'You had them, Carveth. This is a professional mission, you know. We won't look like good spies if you lose the spaceship keys on our first day here.'

Irritated, he strode into the cool of the house. Featherstone was prodding buttons on an enormous machine as it coughed ice cubes into a cocktail shaker.

'Cocktails make a man keen,' Featherstone said. 'What do you take?'

Smith thought about it. He would have preferred a gin and tonic, or a pint of beer, but one of the most important arts of the spy was looking the part. 'The one with the little umbrella,' he said.

Featherstone's eyes stared at him from under their heavy lids. The exhaled smoke did not quite freeze in mid-air. 'They *all* have a little umbrella,' he said.

'One of those, then,' Smith said.

'I suppose you'll want it stirred next,' Featherstone said crossly, and he poured some liquid into a glass. Outside, Suruk had taken the champagne out of the ice bucket, filled the bucket with pool water and was enjoying a drink from it. Smith tried his cocktail. It tasted like the venom of an alcoholic snake.

Featherstone watched Carveth climb onto the sun lounger and wriggle about to get comfortable. 'That little pilot of yours,' he said thoughtfully. 'She's got an attitude on her. You know what you ought to do?'

Smith was too busy adjusting his face to his cocktail to reply.

'You ought to throw her across your lap, pull her britches down and thrash her bare arse till she squeals for mercy,' Featherstone said, with relish.

'She's only lost the keys,' Smith replied. 'Bit harsh, isn't it?'

'Nonsense, my dear Smith. Harshness is the only language women understand. My own wife was like that when I met her: a wild filly, secretly yearning to be broken, and then ridden. One night,' he smiled slyly around his cigarillo, 'I seized her roughly after dinner, threw her against the wall and told her I knew she longed to surrender to my manliness.'

'What happened then?'

'She hit me with a toaster. But that's not the point, Smith. A firm hand is the answer, preferably across the backside. They love it really. *Vae victis.*'

Smith frowned, sipping reluctantly at his cocktail, trying to work out whether Featherstone had just revealed a shocking truth, or whether he was just a sleazy little git.

'So,' he said, deciding on the latter, 'you've been watching things here for a while. What do you think of this Hyrax chap?'

Featherstone frowned. 'Well, there's no doubt that the fellow is well organised. He has a simple agenda, he promises all things to all people, and he has a large number of fanatical followers. In short, he's one of the chief political players on the colony – in fact, the *only* one other than the governor.'

'I see. I've just seen him give a speech, as a matter of fact. The man's obviously barking mad – but I suppose that's irrelevant, isn't it?'

'Quite. Who knows what a lunatic will do? To you or I, this cocktail and chat is quite pleasant – but a madman like the Hyrax might get exactly the same enjoyment out of exploring his back end with a garden strimmer. These people are not normal.'

Smith ventured to sip his cocktail again, which still tasted like antifreeze with an olive. 'So what would you suggest we do? I'm not used to all this cloak-and-dagger stuff.'

'Well,' said Featherstone, 'what's your gut feeling?'

'Hmm,' Smith said. 'I rather thought we might spy on him or something: you know, set up a chain of agents, infiltrate his organisation, dead-letter boxes, park benches, overcoats, that sort of thing.'

Featherstone laughed. 'Oh, my dear fellow, no,' he said. 'You've been watching too many films. Spying's moved on from those days. We're going down the casino.'

'The casino?'

'Of course. The heart of any modern spying operation is in the rolling of dice. Or, better still, getting a dolly bird to roll them for you. This isn't the dark ages, you know. You see, the Hyrax himself lives a life of simple purity, but his men don't. His PR guru is a hired gun called Calloway. He's the one who helps the Hyrax answer questions that aren't about crusades. Thing is, he spends a lot of time playing cards. If we can get close to him, we can learn a lot about how to get to the Hyrax himself.' He finished his drink and turned to the ice machine. 'Do you know baccarat?'

'Only *Raindrops Keep Falling on my Head*. Did he do that thing about the cake left in the rain?'

'Well, this is the life,' Carveth observed, three hours later. She had moved straight from the sun lounger to the bathtub, and had spent nearly an hour there. Now she stood in front of her open suitcase in her dressing gown, trying to decide what to wear.

In the next room down, Smith was ready to go. He wore his red fleet jacket with black trousers and shiny shoes. He was not looking forward to this.

Suavity was not one of Smith's strong points. He was not stupid, but he was not good at assessing other people; he could not tell jokes, impress or look clever. That was for other men, men who got girls without trying, and who inevitably treated them badly and were loved all the more because of it. Perhaps Featherstone was right and that was the way to success. Surely not. Rhianna would never embrace a philosophy like that. Depression welled up in Smith. How long would it be before some smoother, less sincere operator got Rhianna instead of him?

He stood up and checked his moustache in the mirror. It was inevitable that she would belong to someone else soon. A woman like that couldn't stay single for long. Forget about her, he told himself again.

'What the hell's happened to my fishnet tights?' Carveth cried from across the hall. 'There's a massive hole in the crotch!'

Suruk peered out of his room. 'Apologies,' he said. 'I used them as a T-shirt.'

'Thank God for that. I thought I'd done some kind of gigantic fart. Has anyone seen my boots?'

Smith strolled into the corridor and Carveth stepped out to meet him. She was wearing her blue dress, which made her look like Alice in Wonderland.

'Hey, Boss, looking very dapper there!'

'Thanks, Carveth. What's that stuff on your face?'

'Lichen-based facial cream. The pack says it'll make you look five years younger. Which, seeing how long I've been functional, should give me a visual age of about minus three, but what the hell.'

'It looks like a clown hit you with a pie. Step in here a moment, would you?'

She followed him into his room. 'What's the prob?'

'I want you to look out, Carveth. From what I've heard, this Hyrax is a serious chap to have as an enemy.'

'Huh. I'll be fine. Besides, isn't a hyrax a girly bit?'

'I really wouldn't know. Now look, this casino sounds like neutral ground. Chances are that no weapons will be allowed inside.'

'I see.'

'I want you to go in our car, with Suruk. Stash the Civiliser somewhere out of sight, and if there's any trouble, be ready to go for it. Understand?'

Her small face became serious, under the cream. 'Loud and clear, Boss. When it's time for action I grab your rod.' She saluted.

Suruk wandered in. 'How do I look?' he asked.

'Threatening, verging on macabre,' Carveth said.

'Excellent.'

Smith examined the alien. 'Any chance you could ease off the skulls a bit?'

Suruk untied some of his more impressive trophies. 'Cannot handle a few severed heads? Very well, if I must. La-de-da puny humans.'

'Mr Featherstone?' the barman asked.

'White Russian in a tall glass,' Featherstone replied. 'Single cream.' He pulled a scrap of paper out of his pocket and sighed. '. . . And a pint of mild in a jug. . . two pints of forty percent sucrose solution and. . . God almighty, "something that doesn't taste of alcohol but will get me well wrecked".'

It was half nine and Casino Imperiale was in full swing. On the verandah, knots of drinkers watched a hundred people lose money. Businessmen and plantation officers mixed with policemen, criminals and servants of the government, and the air rang with the rattle of roulette wheels, the chink of glasses and the strident ringing of haughty laughter. At the head of a huge staircase, a man in a Nehru jacket stood quietly behind two bodyguards, his face in shadow, studying his domain.

Smith felt uneasy here, far from deep space. He looked around the room, with its dapper inhabitants, and realised that he would have been happier in the void, or creeping through the jungle of some alien world with his rifle in hand, looking for artefacts to send back home. Odd, he thought: for a civilised man, he felt more comfortable in the wild than pretending to be a sophisticate.

That's where I should be, he thought, on the frontline, blasting hell out of Ghasts instead of swanking round like a particularly effete swan. I should just grab this Hyrax fellow, give him to the law and take the fight back to Gertie.

'No sign of Calloway yet,' Featherstone said at his elbow. 'Here's your beer.'

'Thanks.'

'I'll keep watch. If he arrives, I'll let you know.'

Smith left the mezzanine and strolled between the card tables, feeling lost. The crew were seated a little way off. Carveth was drinking one of her noxious not-proper-alcohol drinks and eating a toasted sandwich. Suruk was halfway through a pint of sucrose solution. Smith sipped his drink and sat down opposite Carveth. 'On the hard stuff, Suruk?'

'I will say only one thing for this palace of folly, Mazuran: it serves a good snack. Would you like the roasted flesh of a peanut?' he added, holding out a little bag. 'Hunt well and you might even catch the one with the monocle.'

'No, thanks.'

'As you wish. I think I may chance my skill at the card games.'

'Well, just remember to lay off the Tizer.'

'I do not touch it. Fizz-water is the ruin of many braves and the cause of much tusk decay. Ah, human females have arrived. Rutting time for you, Isambard Smith.'

'We're finding you a wife,' Carveth explained. She nodded at the doorway, where two pretty girls had just arrived. 'Blonde one might do you.'

'I'm really not sure,' Smith replied. He was not keen on entrusting the selection of his future wife to Carveth and Suruk, especially if this involved his future wife ever meeting them. Who knew what kind of misbegotten creature they might dredge up?

'I reckon you should get yourself one of those rich RSF girls,' Carveth said. 'I'd have thought you'd be the right sort for a posh space-fleet girl.'

'Ladies who launch? Ugh. I don't know, Carveth. It would be settling for second best. I'd far rather have someone like Rhianna over there. Bloody hell! Rhianna's over there!'

They looked around, following Smith's outstretched finger. 'Nah,' said Carveth, 'it can't be.' Then: 'Bugger me, it is.'

She stood on the far side of the hall, by the doors. Rhianna was slightly taller than average, pale-skinned, with dark hair in dreadlocks that nearly reached her waist, held back by a cloth band that, for once, matched the rest of her clothes.

She had dressed well, Smith thought. Rhianna wore a high-collared crimson jacket which struck him as vaguely Chinese, a skirt decorated in a way reminiscent of a sari, platform sandals like a geisha girl, and a scarf thrown back over her shoulder which made him think of Biggles. Smith had not seen the Indo-Oriental aviator look before, but he thought it suited her very well.

Someone was offering Rhianna a drink, presumably made with non-organic grapes, and she smiled politely as she refused it. She looked so graceful, Smith thought, so refined – and so completely out of his league.

'Good Lord,' he said. 'She looks ever so different to how I remember her.'

'That's probably because she's had a wash,' Carveth said. 'Go and talk to her.'

Smith pinched the bridge of his nose. 'I don't know. I feel light-headed. I think the alcohol's gone to my head.'

'That's the blood going somewhere else,' Carveth said. 'You'd better go and see her before you have to sit down.'

'That's quite enough of that,' Smith retorted and, feeling obliged to shut Carveth up, he straightened his fleet jacket, stood up and strode across the room.

'Excuse me?' he said. 'Miss Mitchell?'

She turned away from the bar, saw who it was and smiled. 'Hey, Isambard! How's things?' she asked, leaning in and kissing him on the cheek. '*Namaste*, Isambard. Is that jacket new? You look very smart - given that you're wearing the trappings of an Imperialist aggressor, of course.'

'You look super too. How did you know I'd be here?'

'Your friend told me – the journalist. Tall man, kind of gloomy, drinks a lot of tea.'

'Ah.'

She glanced around the room. 'So, how's it going on your ship? Is Suruk still, um, keeping to his indigenous customs?'

'Oh yes, he's fine. The police tend to turn a blind eye.'

'And has Carveth found a man yet?'

52

'Well, she's found loads – she just hasn't run any to ground yet. But she's not doing too badly.'

'That's sad,' Rhianna said. 'She should realise that as a woman she shouldn't feel obliged to define herself by her relationships with men. Many of the women I respect the most never married at all.'

'But not you, surely,' Smith said quickly. 'I mean, you'd want a decent chap at the end of the day, right?'

Rhianna laughed. 'I'm staying with the alternative lifestyle for now, Isambard.'

Smith wondered if this involved other men, which would be despicable and morally wrong, or other girls, which would be smashing. Whatever it was, it didn't sound like it included him. He felt depressed which, he knew, would make him less attractive because women liked confidence, which in turn made him feel more depressed. Business as usual, then.

'So. . . um. . . all this top secret training you're involved with,' he said. 'What's it like?'

'I can't really tell you that,' she said, running a hand through her dreadlocks. 'It's top secret.'

'I suppose,' Smith said. He was pissing this up, he realised.

'I can tell you about where I'm based, though,' Rhianna added, seeing that he was unhappy. 'Not locations of course, but it's disguised as a convent school run by the Order of Saint Carmilla the Tactile.'

'Oh, right. Is that good?'

'No, it's terrible. I have to stay in cover, so I have to wear this ridiculous uniform all the time. I'm over thirty, and I have to dress like a sixth form schoolgirl so as to stay incognito. You can imagine what *that* looks like.'

Smith found that he could imagine it quite well.

Rhianna turned and stared down the length of the casino, past the slot machines, card games and roulette tables. 'I really feel that a place like this, with its rampant capitalism, really. . .' she waved her hands vaguely, 'oppresses the soul. Don't you think?'

'Well, quite. Absolutely. Tell you what,' Smith said, 'I'm supposed to be looking for someone who's not here yet. Why don't we wait for him on the verandah?'

'Hey, good idea.'

Something prodded Smith in the back and he glanced round. Featherstone stood behind him. 'Calloway's here,' he said, 'time to get down to business. He's just come in through the private door.'

'Right,' said Smith. 'I'm sorry, Rhianna, but I've got to go. Duty calls.'

'Okay. Good luck, Isambard! Blessed be!'

'Bugger,' Smith muttered as he walked away. Once again the Empire had chosen a stupid time to need saving.

'Taste, my dear Smith, taste,' Featherstone opined. 'A spy must have good taste. All the splendid fillies here and you choose the answer that's been blowing in the wind. There must be a damned big cat round here to have dragged her in.'

'That's not on,' Smith said angrily. 'Just because Rhianna isn't dressed like a hussy with her arse stuck out—'

'Let's get to work, Smith. He's over there.'

Featherstone nodded and Smith realised who he meant: a tallish, neat young businessman was shaking hands and beaming at a table of wealthy, disreputable-looking types. Smith grimaced, surprised at how drunk he felt.

'What's the plan?' he asked.

Featherstone waggled his eyebrows. 'We wait 'til he's alone and snatch the beggar. I'll grab him, you hustle him out the back door and to my car. I've got some items of restraint in the boot.'

'Will that work?'

'Of course. You're a spy now, Smith. Confidence, remember.'

This sounded like a bad plan, even to Smith's addled brain. 'Might be a bit difficult getting him out,' Smith said. 'We could chuck him out of a window, I suppose. Maybe lower him on a rope.'

Calloway jerked his thumb over his shoulder and made an apologetic gesture. He turned from the table.

'He's going to the loo!' Featherstone exclaimed. 'Let's jump him in the bogs!'

A couple of passers-by took a small detour around them, and Smith said, 'Right!'

Featherstone stared at him. 'Well?'

'I was waiting for you to go first,' Smith said. 'I'll come along in a moment. We can't go together, can we? I mean, we're chaps.'

'Wait one minute, then come in,' Featherstone said, and he crossed to the wall and disappeared into the lavatory.

Smith looked around the room, trying to spot anyone he knew. Rhianna had disappeared completely, presumably unable to put up with the cigarette smoke and unfettered commercialism. Carveth had made herself scarce, although a small figure in the scrum around the bar might have been her. Suruk, Smith noticed, had acquired a visor from somewhere and was at a card table with a pile of chips in front of him. That looked very worrying.

Smith glanced at his watch. It was time to go. Feeling distinctly uneven, he headed for the lavatory.

The toilet was long and red, and looked like a cross between a science lab and a 1920's ocean liner. The tiles were scrupulously clean. As he entered, Smith saw a antique robot in a tuxedo sitting by the wall. It stood up.

'Good evening, sir,' it said and brushed his collar down. 'Might sir require assistance aiming the artillery?'

'Quite all right, thanks,' Smith replied. Quietly, the android left the room.

Further up the room, a suited figure stepped away from the urinal. It was the man that Featherstone had pointed out as Calloway. Calloway looked around and looked straight at Smith, and Smith at once knew that trouble was coming. Nobody made eye contact in the gents.

'Captain Smith,' Calloway said. He had a lean, thin smile. 'A little focus group tells me you're looking for me.'

'Maybe,' said Smith. 'What have you done with Featherstone?'

'Oh, he'll be joining us shortly, don't worry.' Calloway was several years younger than Smith and much better groomed. He looked annoyingly rich, Smith thought, but in a fight he would come off the worse – assuming that he also had a splitting headache and a strong urge to fall asleep.

'Let's talk outside the envelope, Smith,' Calloway said. 'Bounce some ideas around. My client, the Grand Hyrax, has gained pretty solid support across the board, owing to his charismatic speaking and the, uh, progressive crusade-based reform package he's planning to deliver. I'd say it's a no-brainer that in a timescale of, oh, one to three months he'll be looking to make good on the governorship. I'm being straight down the line with you, Smith.'

'Go on,' Smith said. He resented having to communicate with a lifeform that spoke like an estate agent.

'Okay. Let's try to take this forward, so we're both in the same ballpark. Maybe Brady here can help.'

Smith glanced around. The android had returned. It closed the door quietly and leaned against it, hands behind its back.

Calloway ran a tap and splashed a little water onto his expensive-looking hair. 'Brady, did Captain Smith come alone?'

'Apart from Mr Featherstone? I believe not, sir. He arrived with a young lady, who is otherwise absorbed for now. I believe he has also been seen with a greenskin, sir. A greenskin warrior.'

'I see. So, Smith, are you with me on this one? I'd suggest you get on board while there's still a window of opportunity. The Grand Hyrax is a reasonable man – he's not looking to reinvent the wheel, just to engage in a little religious genocide, maybe run with that idea a bit, but nothing I don't think we can't agree on. So, are you with the programme?'

Smith frowned. His head was swimming. 'What are you on about, man?'

The android Brady stepped forward. It took its hands from behind its back, revealing the hatchet it carried.

Calloway said: 'You're not with the programme, are you?'

Smith said, 'What?'

'Tackle this problem head-on,' Calloway said. He waved his fingers in front of the hand dryer and the sound of rushing air filled the room. 'Sunset him.'

Brady swiped with the axe: Smith leaped back, darted in, punched the android in the gut and then remembered that it was made of metal. Smith drew back, dropping into the Fighto first stance. Brady frowned and swung the axe at Smith's head and Smith sprang to one side, put his leg behind the android's knee and shoved it in the chest.

Brady was top-heavy: tiles shattered under its back as it hit the floor. The axe skittered out of its hand and struck the wall. Smith ran after it. Brady's eyes blinked frantically, and, like a zombie rising from the grave, it sat up and lurched upright.

'Regrettable,' Brady said, rubbing the back of its skull, and its free hand shot out and grabbed hold of Smith's jacket. Smith whirled around and buried the axe in Brady's head.

Smith let go of the axe and slowly Brady fell back and lay still. Its joints had locked solid, and the android looked like a broken doll. The dryers stopped. Smith looked at Calloway.

'Now then,' said Smith. He felt terrible. Calloway rocked in his vision: the Hyrax's PR man seemed to be on the deck of a floundering ship. 'I'm taking you in.'

A flushing sound came from the left and one of the

toilet doors opened. Featherstone emerged. 'Turned out nice again,' he announced.

'I've caught Calloway,' Smith said. 'The bugger set an android on me.'

'Oh dear,' Featherstone said. 'The stuff clearly hasn't worked on you yet.'

'What stuff?' Smith replied, then, 'Wait a minute! You poisoned m – urh – uh – oof.'

'My mistake,' said Featherstone, 'it has.'

3

The Fall of Didcot 4

Smith came to looking at a very blue sky with waves in it. Everything seemed pleasant and restive. Then he realised that it was not a sky but Featherstone's swimming pool and that not only was he the wrong way up and unable to move, but his trousers were down. It took very little nous to work out that the situation was bad.

His head and shoulders had been thrust through the bottom of a wicker chair, pinning his arms to his side. His hair brushed the carpet.

'Ah,' said a voice, 'so you're awake, Captain. Excellent.'

Featherstone stepped into view. He wore a black uniform with riding boots and very wide trousers. He was sipping a cocktail and smoking a cigarette through a long holder, and he looked absurd, Smith thought, before remembering that Featherstone was not the one wedged in a piece of furniture with his bare arse in the air.

'So, you see me in my true colours,' Featherstone remarked.

'You dirty chauffeur! Let me go at once!'

'I am not a chauffeur,' Featherstone replied, annoyed. 'I am a Ghastist.' He finished his cocktail and took a black officer's cap from the sideboard. He put it on. Two false antennae jutted from the brim.

'Traitor!' Smith cried, and thrashed. 'You filthy, scum-sucking, Gertie-loving traitor! By God, Featherstone, you'd better surrender now, or what I do to you with my fists will make the drop from the scaffold look like a jolly on Brighton pier!'

'Not so, my dear Smith. At least, not until we've had a chance to talk properly. You see, the Ghasts have made me an offer I couldn't refuse. Our empire stands for decency, civilisation, progress, equality – tiresome egalitarianism. The Ghasts have a far better idea of what constitutes fun. Once the Edenites have put the Grand Hyrax in power, this world will be as good as a colony of the Ghast Empire. And then, the Ghasts will want help from men like me – help in thrashing the living daylights out of the locals. How could I turn down a chance like that?'

Featherstone sighed. 'But enough talking. To business.' He opened a small cabinet and ran his finger along a row of things that Smith could not quite make out. 'Ah, that's it,' Featherstone said, and he drew out a long cane. 'You must understand, Smith, that I need information about the Secret Service from you. Later I shall get considerable entertainment beating your little pilot girl's backside until it turns blue, but this is business only. I'm not some kind of pervert, you know,' he added, flexing the cane.

'You're as good as dead,' said Smith. 'My men are close behind me.'

'But not as close as I am, old fellow,' Featherstone said.

The door burst open. Carveth and Suruk stood in the doorway. Carveth was holding a huge pistol – Smith's

Civiliser. 'Nobody move!' she cried. She blinked. 'Oh. . . shall I come back later?'

'No!' said Smith.

'How strange,' Suruk said. 'Which one is the female?'

The cigarette holder dropped out of Featherstone's mouth and landed on Smith's behind. 'Aargh!' Smith cried and it fell onto the floor. 'Bloody kill him, you idiots!'

Featherstone took a step towards the dressing table. 'Now look,' he said. 'There is a perfectly innocent explanation for all of this.'

'I'd like to see it!' Carveth said and she laughed.

'It's not funny!' Smith cried. 'He's a bastard traitor, and once he's done with me he means to beat your arse to death!'

'Oh, *right*,' Carveth said. '*Now* you tell me. Well, in that case – beat this!'

The Civiliser blasted into life and the recoil almost knocked Carveth flat. The bullet hit Featherstone smack in the chest and tossed him against the wall. He lay there, slumped and dead, at the end of a runway of blood.

Suruk strolled in, seemingly unbothered by the whole episode. He nudged Featherstone with the toe of his boot. 'Good riddance to him. Why is he dressed as a chauffeur?'

'This is the worst night of my entire life,' said Smith. 'Would someone mind getting me out of here?'

Suruk helped him out of the chair while Carveth looked away. Smith pulled his trousers up. 'Ow,' he said. 'Bloody cigarette burnt my arse.'

'I had a bad night too,' Suruk said. 'I played a game called poker. Nobody could read my expression because of my tusks, so I won a pile of little round biscuits and something called a yacht. The biscuits turned out to be plastic so I threw them all away. Most disappointing.'

'What a damned mess,' W said, forty-five minutes later. He sat on an angular chair, rolling a cigarette. He looked battered and shabby and, like all of them, out of place in Featherstone's modernist home. 'The worst of it is, I suspected him all along.'

'You could have told me that before he set light to my bum.' Smith stood at the far end of the room. At Carveth's request they had put a sheet over Featherstone's body. Suruk's request, that they punt him into the swimming pool, had been ignored.

'Well, not him specifically.' W licked the cigarette closed, took a little metal case from his pocket and dropped the cigarette in it for later. 'I thought someone here would be corrupt, but I didn't realise it reached this far.'

'Corrupt hardly covers it,' said Smith. 'My main regret is that it wasn't me who got to top the bugger. And that he pulled my trousers off.'

'This city seems to be riddled with Ghastists and potential traitors,' W said glumly as he stood up. 'I blame the so-called higher echelons of society, seeking to oppress the working man.'

'What this place needs is a proper British garrison,' Smith said.

'Very true. Most of the population certainly see themselves as citizens. But I doubt the army could spare the men to hold the place. Oh, did you see your lady friend?'

'Yes, thanks; that was decent of you. Although I don't think she is mine, as such. Think I missed my chance there.'

Carveth entered the room with a tray. 'Here's the tea,' she announced. 'When are we going to call the plods? That dead chauffeur creeps me out.'

'It strikes me that they must be pretty confident to try to take you out of the running,' W said.

'I suppose they know our plans as much as we do,' Smith said. 'Featherstone must have been telling them all along.'

'No doubt.' W took a cup from the tray and drained it. 'You wonder if this will force their hand. The police should have Calloway by now and without him –' His pocket made a ringing sound, and he took out his fob-phone. 'One moment. Sorry everyone. Hello?' he said into the receiver. 'That you, Wainscott? All well are we? Oh my God. . .'

He strode across the room and flicked on the television. A deep-voiced man stood on a rooftop, an armoured waistcoat over his shirt. Behind him, something in the city burned.

'– have stormed the missile defences in the name of the Grand Hyrax, proclaiming themselves the rightful rulers of Urn. The coup is being fiercely resisted by the local Citizen Guard, and the Edenite forces have been driven back to the missile compound and the spaceport on the West of the city, which they are currently holding despite being encircled. The Citizen Guard have released a statement claiming that they expect to completely defeat the coup within twelve hours.'

'So the Hyrax has played his hand,' W said. 'But not very well, it seems.'

'Quite,' said Smith. 'Now the cards are on the table, the odds are against him. To continue the poker metaphor, he'll soon "snap". That said, we ought to help out. I'd be happy to have a pop at Johnny Cultist.'

'I too,' Suruk said. 'There has been enough talk. Less jaw, more war, I say.'

The announcer continued, 'This is R. Trevor Humphries, reporting from – Good Lord, what the blazes was that?'

Lights in the sky – landing lights, hundreds of them. Ships were descending over the city, ray-shaped battleships.

Between his teeth Isambard Smith said, 'Gertie!'

'Oh, no,' Carveth said at his side. 'It's an invasion!'

'My God,' W rasped. 'That's what they grabbed the missile station for, so the Ghasts could land! There must be thousands of them!'

'Smashing!' said Suruk the Slayer. 'What are we waiting for? Let us kill everything!'

'Are you mad?' Carveth cried. 'Let's get the hell out of here!'

'That may not be so easy,' W said. 'Look.'

The picture swayed on the screen and faded out. In its place, a monster appeared: a mixture of ant and man in a high-backed, organic chair, its rough approximation of a face glaring into the screen. All Ghasts looked alike to Smith, but there was something about this one that disgusted him especially – something he recognised despite the facial scars and the glinting circle of its artificial eye.

'Ghast Empire calling!' it barked. 'I am 462, Assault Commander of the invading forces. As I speak, the space-craft of the mighty Ghast navy are deploying six divisions of elite praetorian shock troops to hold this world. You are now part of the greater Ghast Empire, Earth scum! Ahahaha!'

'462,' Smith whispered. 'My God. I thought I'd killed him.'

'Resistance will not be tolerated! All opposing us will be shot!' His face broke into a hideous smirk. 'Remember, people of Urn, anyone who co-operates and donates his more nutritious relatives to the new order will be spared. Anyone who resists us will die, for we are infallible, and the triumph of our legions shall be proof of our infallibilinessity! All glory to Number One!'

462 saluted with his pincers and antennae, and he faded from the screen. In his place the emblem of the praetorians filled the screen like a pirate flag: a stylised Ghast skull with antennae.

'Dirty aliens!' Smith exclaimed. 'This is British soil! Or it would have been in a couple of months.' He frowned. 'Six divisions, eh? There's a rifle in the car. Follow me, everyone – we're going to stop them dead in their tracks!'

The night sky was alive with lights. From the undersides of a dozen ray-shaped craft, searchlights swept the ground. Over the rush of thrusters, Ghast loudspeakers bellowed anything they could: ranting speeches from Number One; unfeasible promises of comfort under the Ghast Empire; crazy threats and jumbled insults.

All through the journey W sat in the back next to

Suruk, talking on the fob-phone to his colleague Wainscott. Suruk wound down the window and stuck his head out to get a better view, and the smell of burning rushed into the car with the warm night air.

'This is a terrible idea,' Carveth said. 'I mean, haven't you noticed that we're actually going *towards* the enemy? Four people can't defeat six divisions, especially if a quarter of them are hiding. It's like mooning people at light speed: it just won't work. At a guess.'

A jeep swung across the road in front of them. Smith braked hard, and a man jumped down and ran over. Smith pulled back his jacket and slid his hand onto the Civiliser. 'One moment,' W said, and he got out and paced across to the jeep.

The newcomer wore big shorts and a khaki shirt; At this distance he looked like a bearded, oversized boy scout. For a moment they exchanged words, then W turned back to Smith. 'The spaceport's taken!' he called. 'They've got the ships. We're trapped here.'

'Oh hell,' Carveth said.

W strode back to the car, coughing into his hand. 'They're unloading biotanks, Edenite battlesuits, the whole bloody lot. The place is overrun: the cultists are going crazy in the city. There's no way we can outfight this many. Even Wainscott thinks we're in trouble.'

The spy stood in the dark outside the car, fires and searchlights lighting the night behind him, the headlamps turning his face into a crumpled mess of lines. For a moment he seemed confused. 'Listen, Smith. We're trying to get everyone out of the city that we can. Forty miles east of here is a plantation called Chartham.

We'll meet at the bar there and plan our next move.'

'Wait,' said Smith. 'Where's Rhianna?'

'This is an emergency, Smith,' W said. 'I think—'

'It's an emergency for her, too. You know the Ghasts have always wanted her for her powers, and now they've got the chance. More than anyone, she's in danger right now. Gertie must be dribbling at the thought of getting hold of her. I would – if I were Gertie, of course. She needs a helping hand more than any of us right now, and I propose to give her one.'

W nodded. 'You're right. We can't have them taking her alive. Have you got a map?'

'Here.' Smith passed him the road map and W drew a cross on it.

'Here, at the edge of the city. St Carmilla the Tactile's school for Ladies of Unusual Talent. Once you've got her, meet us at Rick's Bar, Chartham plantation just as soon as you can. Understood?'

'Right,' said Smith. 'I'll be there.'

'Good luck.'

W strode over to the jeep. Smith spun the car in the road and they drove away from the flames into the night.

They took the back streets; the Ghast attack was swift and unexpected, but already people were pouring out of the city, fleeing to the great tea plantations and the townships that serviced them. Smith drove through the industrial district to avoid the traffic, past the hulking shadows of warehouses and packaging plants, beneath the smiling billboards. He glanced into the rear view mirror and saw a huge face holding up a cup beneath a moustache as wide as a bus. 'Tea – for vigour and regularity!' the slogan said. Far behind the picture, lasers flashed in the city.

'Bloody hell,' Smith said.

'Look on the bright side,' Carveth replied. 'At least we're driving away from the Ghasts.'

'And also from our own ship,' Smith said grimly. 'They'll have the *Pym* impounded by now.'

'We should return,' Suruk growled from the back. 'I hunger for blood, and this car is making me travel-sick.'

'You'd better not puke on the hamster,' Carveth said. 'If you hurt Gerald there'll be trouble. I empathise with him.'

'Because he stuffs himself with food and his cheeks grow wide?'

'Captain, I think he just called me fa—'

'Will you pipe down!' cried Smith. 'Just. . . be quiet, everyone.' He stared straight ahead, both hands on the wheel, sympathising with them too much to argue any more. She's afraid, he thought, and who wouldn't be? And Suruk: he must be frustrated to be going away from the fight. God knows I'd like a chance to bag Gertie Ghast right now, especially with that rotten bugger, 462, still dragging his big red arse around. He should be dead! I shot him in the eye!

'It's not easy for me either,' he said. 'I don't like running away like this. Part of me wants to be back in the city, giving those dirty aliens a prime consignment of lead – but there's a part of me that wants to be with Rhianna too.'

'I can guess which part that is,' Carveth muttered, and Smith pretended that he didn't hear. A dial rattled on the dashboard and a huge, gabled building loomed out of the night before them. The car rolled under gates wide enough for a castle and they pulled up to St Carmilla's.

Even this far from the General Government, the influence of Imperial London was strong. The school was a foreboding slab of Victorian High Gothic, riddled with carvings as if infested with artistic termites.

At the front of the school it was chaos: a swarm of young ladies was loading luggage onto buses, preparing to escape. Smith stopped the car and they stepped out into a sea of uniforms.

'That is a lot of fishnet, even by my standards,' Suruk said.

'Over a thousand eighteen-year-old girls, and they all need protection,' Carveth added. 'It's a hard old life, isn't it, Boss?'

'Follow me, men!' Smith said, and, brushing down his fleet jacket, he strode up the stairs to the front doors.

A thin, refined-looking woman stood side-on at the top of the stairs. She lifted her chin and looked over her nose as they approached. 'Good evening. Amelia Cleaver, Miss. How may I help you?'

'We're looking for Rhianna Mitchell,' Smith explained. 'It's an important matter.'

Miss Cleaver frowned. 'I see. Regrettably, Mr—'

'Smith, Captain Smith.'

'Regrettably, Mr Captain Smith, we have no-one of that name here.' Something in the distance exploded. Miss Cleaver looked around with distain. 'Really, some people,' she said.

'It's urgent,' Carveth said, her eyes flicking nervously in the direction of the sound. 'We have to rescue her before they blow this place up!'

'I very much doubt they shall, young lady,' Miss Cleaver replied. 'This is a respectable institution. We do *not* tolerate alien invasions at St Carmilla's.'

'Look,' said Smith, 'we were sent by an agent of the Parliament: we know him as W. He's a tall man who works on the *Daily Monolith*. He has a friend called Wainscott.'

'You had better come inside, then,' said Miss Cleaver.

She turned and led them into the hall: a cool, vaulted room of laser-etched red brick, lit by globes at its corners. Down the length of the hall ran a great skylight, and from it came ominous flickers of the city and the raiding ships.

Two girls hurried towards the exit.

'Ow!' Smith winced as they passed him. 'That girl pinched me!' He rubbed his bottom sadly. 'I wouldn't mind so much, if that swine Featherstone hadn't burned me earlier this evening.'

'You were lucky I was tooled up,' Carveth said. 'He wouldn't have stopped beating your arse if I hadn't pulled your piece on him.'

'What an interesting time you spacemen have,' Miss Cleaver said. 'Follow me, please. Now, at St Carmilla's we believe in turning out a better quality of psychically-trained young lady. Along with our more normal protégées, the Empire sends us its ladies of unusual talent and we try to instil some discipline in them before they turn their classmates into toast.'

'Do you actually believe any of that stuff?' Carveth said. 'People being psychic and all?'

'It depends how you define it,' Miss Cleaver explained. 'The ability to influence others is a subtle business.'

'Well,' said Carveth, 'I've seen no evidence to prove that psychic powers exist.' She blinked and scratched her head.

'I myself – wait,' Suruk said. His nasal holes twitched. 'Enemies.'

Carveth looked around. 'Where?' she said, but she drew her service revolver all the same.

Smith raised the Civiliser and stepped in front of the women. 'What is it?'

'Wait,' Suruk replied. He pulled out one of his larger knives, stepped back and threw it at the roof.

Half a second before the knife hit the glass, the skylight exploded. Smith spun and threw Carveth and Miss Cleaver to the ground as plastiglass rained around them. He looked up, cocking his pistol. Tendrils dropped through the roof, and there were forms on them: helmet-wearing, insectoid things, black coats flapping around them like wings as they slid down the ropes.

One of them did not slide. A Ghast thumped into the ground at Suruk's feet and he bent down and pulled his knife out of its body. The Civiliser roared in Smith's hand and the chamber spun, and a second Ghast shrieked and fell like a dead bat. 'Run!' he cried.

There were more Ghasts at the skylight, clustered on the roof. Carveth stared numbly at them, repulsed. Dimly, she realised that these were drones, not praetorians, and that the invaders considered them disposable.

Then one landed on its hooves beside her, and she spun around, her arm flicked up and she shot the thing four times.

Miss Cleaver was at a side door. 'Come along!' she called back to them. 'This way, everyone!' Suruk jumped up and sliced off the last eight feet of one of the ropes, and bounded through the door. Smith followed, and Carveth ran after him. 'Do get a move on, young lady!' Miss Cleaver called and, as Carveth ran inside, she slammed the door and bolted it.

Something heavy hit the door. Alien voices chattered and barked.

'You don't have long,' Miss Cleaver said.

Smith opened his gun and tipped out the empty shells. He fished one of the speedloaders from his pocket and dropped a new set of bullets into the Civiliser. 'We need to know where Rhianna is. Pass me your gun, Carveth.'

The scratching of claws on the door stopped. For a moment Carveth wondered if the Ghasts had gone away, and then they charged the door together. The door shook. Brick dust trickled from the edges of the lock.

Smith reloaded Carveth's gun and handed it back to her. 'Any thoughts, anyone?'

Miss Cleaver sniffed. 'Some of the girls – the more talented ones – were getting out the back way. I've told Rhianna to stay and wait for you there.'

'How?' Carveth said.

'It doesn't matter. Take the back way – careful on the stairs, don't run – and take the corridor on the left. She'll be waiting at the end.'

'Aren't you coming?' Carveth said.

'I can hold them,' Miss Cleaver said. 'I'll be fine, thank you.'

'I'll help you,' said Smith.

'Yes!' Suruk snarled. 'I will take their heads!'

TOBY FROST

'No you will *not*. I have invested far too much time and energy in Miss Mitchell's development to have it wasted in some galactic war. You will help her out of here. Well, Captain Smith?'

Smith paused. He looked at her and saw something like himself: a determination as great as his own, if not greater, and a strength of will that made him at once envy and pity her. 'As you wish,' he said grimly.

Thump. The door shook. A screw fell onto the carpet.

'Run along now,' Miss Cleaver said. 'Thank you for visiting our school, Captain Smith.'

'Thank you,' he said. 'Come on, both of you. We've got work to do.'

'Indeed.' Suruk drew two knives. He turned to Miss Cleaver. 'Good hunting, shaman,' he said, and jogged after the others.

'It cuts deep, leaving a woman behind like this,' Smith said between his teeth as they strode down the corridor. 'Very deep.'

The corridor was whitewashed and looked like the inside of a submarine. Pipes ran along the ceiling, lino squeaked underfoot and the smell of cabbage was thick in the air. It made him think of junior school, where he had been bottom of the class, and the memory made him afraid, which made him ready to fight.

The children had mocked him then, but there had been something prescient in their ridicule: they'd called him 'spaceman'. He couldn't remember why: he hadn't been listening at the time.

They were twenty yards further away when the Ghasts

74

broke down the door. The sound rang down the corridor and, like voices wafting up from hell, the barking of Ghastish followed it.

'What on Earth is the meaning of this?' Smith heard Miss Cleaver demand. 'Simply barging in here—'

'We seek two enemies of the Ghast Empire. You will—'

'I will do as I please, thank you!'

'Silence, human scum—'

'*Mind your language,*' she said, and the sheer force implicit in the words ran through them like an electric charge, like a tidal wave of polite indignation. 'How dare you speak to me like that? I am a British citizen. You will watch your mouth, young insect-man.'

'Very well. We seek—'

'Be quiet and stop making a fuss. What's all this nonsense about? Shouting and carrying on like this – it's an absolute disgrace. I've a good mind to report you to your senior officer. You at the back there – pay attention.'

'It is important that—'

'The people you are looking for are not here. They are far away, where you will never find them. It's time for you to go. Do you understand? Speaky English, do we?'

'Please—' said the Ghast. 'Underlings, I have orders that they are far away. We must leave at once.'

'My God,' Smith whispered, 'she has the Bearing.'

'The what?' Carveth said.

'I've heard it rumoured, but I've never seen it before – Shau-Teng, the ancient mystic art of the British. But it's been years since I saw anyone—'

'Right,' Carveth said, glancing back nervously. 'Tell me later, right?'

They hurried on, turned the corner, and suddenly they were at the heavy, soundproofed door that led outside. A row of raincoats hung along the wall, and a figure stepped out of them, from her hiding-place.

'Rhianna!' Smith cried.

'Blimey,' said Carveth. 'What the hell are you dressed like that for?'

Rhianna pulled her skirt down as best as she could. 'I told you it was a stupid uniform,' she said.

Smith looked her over. He had never seen Rhianna's legs before: they were very long. 'Nice boater,' he managed.

'Yeah, hi,' Carveth said. 'Now, can we get out of here?'

Rhianna moved to the doors, and stopped. 'Listen!'

The voices started again. Miss Cleaver said, 'You again? I thought I had sent you away. What nonsense is it this time?'

'The drones have left.' It was a Ghast that replied, but the voice was deeper, harsher, more like an animal's.

'Indeed. So will you, thank you.'

The thing let out a grunt of laughter. 'I think not. You see, we are praetorians. Your Bearing has no effect on our minds. You may, however, rest assured that the weaklings whom you corrupted will be shot. As will you.'

There was a burst of disruptor fire. A second's silence passed, and then Ghastish rang down the corridor: a snarling, cackling racket.

'Oh my gods,' Rhianna gasped, 'they shot her!'

Carveth swallowed. Her forehead was shiny with

sweat. She ducked down and worked one of the bolts back on the door. 'Just get the top bolt, would you?'

Smith peered around the corner. The Ghasts were creeping down the corridor with high, careful steps. He cocked the hammer of the Civiliser.

Rhianna ran to the door, stood up on tiptoe and slid back the bolt. She turned the handle, pulled it to her and let in the night air. In the doorway stood a praetorian sentry, its back to them, coat stirring slightly in the evening breeze. Rhianna froze, hand over mouth, eyes wide.

Suruk stepped forward, silently picked Carveth up and put her to one side. The Ghast rubbed its antennae together. Suruk raised his big knife, and it dropped with a low *whup* through the air. The Ghast crumpled and thumped against the tarmac; its head rolled away.

Smith looked back round the corner. One of the troopers was pulling a long-tailed biogrenade from its belt, and Smith flicked up the Civiliser and shot it in the arm. It dropped the grenade and the bomb landed upside-down, its legs and tail thrashing.

Smith looked back round. 'Come on!' he cried. The grenade went off with a massive flat *bang*; there were howls and snarls from the corridor. Rhianna scooped up her satchel and they fled.

'Who wants a beer?' Gilead strode into the spaceport with a cooler box under his metal arm.

The sides of spacecraft loomed up around him like cliffs, disappearing into the night thirty yards above his head. Most were transport shuttles, used to ferry tea up to the enormous container ships the Empire would send to collect the monthly supply. They weren't going anywhere now, Gilead noted with satisfaction. The planet was cut off.

His men stood about in their armoured battlesuits, talking and joking, guns in hand. They were the best fighting men in the universe, Gilead thought. 'Beer!' he shouted, and he shook one of the cans as he threw it to a lieutenant and laughed helplessly when the soldier opened it and beer sprayed across the man's visor.

On the opposite side of the spaceport a row of praetorians waited for the Ghast leader to arrive: grim, silent things that watched with disinterest and contempt. They stood in formation out of instinct.

Two chuckling Edenites in blue-grey battlesuits were supposed to be guarding the tarmac: they were currently studying an issue of *Horny Heretic Harlots*. One of the Ghasts stepped over and shoved them aside.

'Silence!' it barked. 'The high commander comes!'

With a wet sound like meat being pulled apart, a hatch slid open in the back of the command ship. A ramp folded down, smooth as a snake's tongue. Foetid smoke billowed from the rear vents and a figure appeared at the top of the ramp, as if coalescing from the smoke. Slowly, his helmet under one arm, 462 walked down the ramp as the praetorians jolted to attention.

462 wore a trenchcoat covered in insignia. His right eye was gone and, with graceless efficiency, his technicians had replaced it with a metal lens. The skin around the eye was dented and scarred, like the back of an ancient toad.

His scrawny body propelled him to the bottom of the

ramp and, as one, the Ghasts crossed their main arms over their chests, punched their pincer-arms into the air, banged their heels together and flicked their antennae, quiveringly erect. '*Ak nak!*'

'*Ak*,' 462 said casually, and one of his pincer-arms made a vague wave.

'Hey 462!' Gilead called, steering a slightly erratic path across the tarmac to the bottom of the ramp. Several beers had done him no good. He thought of putting his arm around 462's shoulders, but decided against it. 'Too bad you missed the fighting. How's it hanging?'

462 looked round at his stercorium, an organ shaped like an insect's abdomen that protruded from the back of his trenchcoat. 'Large and red,' he said.

'Uhuh. You want a beer?'

'No. I shall have an injured drone pulped for nutrition.' His eye flicked across the spaceport, taking in the decadent human control tower and its puny landing pads. 'I have orders for the Hyrax before he installs himself as Governor-Prophet-Emperor-God-King.'

Gilead's head nodded, and something unpleasant ignited behind his eyes. 'I've got some orders of my own, too. I'm going to have me some fun here.' He looked around, squinting. 'This place stinks. You give me the word, 462, and I'll smash these people up. Between you and me,' he added, leaning closer, 'I'm thinking of skipping out the sissy medieval stage and getting Ancient Greek on their asses instead.'

'And I would enjoy watching you tell them so,' 462 replied. 'Sadly, you must refrain from being Ancient Greek to any arse. This planet is under the control of the Ghast

Empire, and as yet I have no orders to permit you to conduct a reign of mindless terrorism. Never fear: they shall come through soon. And then, you will have your fun: the wretched citizens of this planet will enjoy no more *habeas corpus*.'

Gilead grinned. 'Reckon I might get me some of that, too. Dirty English women. Unbelievers are all sluts.'

At the edge of Gilead's vision, a Ghast reconnaissance skimmer darted onto the tarmac. It shot across the landing field, headlight weaving like a drunken firefly as it slipped between the legs of the spaceships and halted beside the command ship. The pilot, a drone, climbed down and ran to speak with one of the praetorians.

'What's that?' Gilead demanded.

'A messenger.' 462 beckoned to the pilot, and it ran over and saluted him.

'*Ak! Flak krak Britak ak-ak!*'

'What the hell?' Gilead said.

462 smiled as much as his scars would allow. 'Good news. Our heavy guns have defeated the human anti-aircraft batteries. Speak the rest so Captain Gilead can understand it, drone.'

'I obey!' The drone saluted again. 'Human Isambard Smith and the Vorl woman have escaped and their location is unknown!'

462 did nothing for a couple of seconds. 'Unknown,' he said.

The messenger nodded. 'Unknown! I am informed that our attack was swift and ruthless, intended to utterly crush all resistance. Drones like myself were used for their disposability, and the human scum were taken by surprise, but—'

462 nodded to one of the praetorians. It leaned forward, and, like a groundsman snipping away an unsightly branch, bit the pilot's head off.

'Dinner is served,' 462 said. 'This is unfortunate news, Gilead. Most unfortunate. I want them found!' He pulled his trenchcoat tight around him, turned and marched away. 'Found!'

Once they were out of the city, they stopped to allow Rhianna to get changed. Smith leaned against the car and looked back at the burning city. Great floodlights roved over the buildings, shining from the landing-ships. Capital City belonged to the Ghast Empire now, as did the whole of Urn.

Carveth stood next to him. The night air was warm. 'Guess we're not going home just yet,' she said.

'We will,' Smith replied. His voice was grim. 'I promise.'

'Gaze upon me!' a squeaky voice said behind them. They looked around: Suruk had put the praetorian's head on the roof of the car and was working its mouth like a puppeteer. 'I boasted of being a great warrior, and now I sit on the mantelpiece of Suruk the Slayer! Look upon me and despair, for once I was mighty and now I am a paperweight!'

'Do you have to do that?' Carveth said wearily. 'All that severed head stuff. Doesn't it strike you as kind of morbid?'

Suruk shrugged. 'No, it is fun. Besides, you are lucky it

is just heads I take. When I was a young brave I used to completely dismember my enemies. However Mazuran here disliked having all their members lying around.'

Smith watched the fires in the city, watched the wads of light on the alien ships that hovered over it. Very faintly, he could hear the sound of one of Number One's speeches blaring from one of the spacecraft. Somewhere in the darkness, a dog howled. Rhianna was pulling a kaftan over her gymslip. She dropped the kaftan and bent over to pick it up.

'You know, Carveth,' Smith said, 'I don't think I shall ever forget this moment.'

'Just because you can see Rhianna's pants,' she said.

'I meant the alien invasion, Carveth.'

'Oh, that,' she replied. She sighed. 'I'm trying not to think about that.'

4

The Rebellion Begins

Smith woke up at eight in a white, sunny room. Clear, clean light streamed in through the window. It was too nice a sky for anything evil to happen under it.

He washed at the sink in his room and dressed. He hid his rifle between the mattress and the frame of the bed and strapped the Civiliser to his side. This place was supposed to be safe, but there was no point taking chances.

On the landing he met Carveth. She was in her pyjamas, woolly slippers and dressing gown, and did not look like a key player in the struggle against alien tyranny. 'Ugh, Boss,' she muttered as she closed the bathroom door.

'Morning, Carveth. Bad night?'

'I had that nightmare about the electric sheep again. Hardly slept.'

'Well, best get ready. Today is the day we start the war against Gertie.'

'If I knew there was a war I'd've had a lie-in,' she said weakly, and she stomped off up the corridor, toothbrush in hand.

Smith went downstairs. The rear of the building was cramped and scruffy, cluttered with equipment for the bar at the front. At the bottom of the stairs he heard voices.

One was hard and a little wheezy and could only belong to W.

'Dammit, are you mad?' W rasped. 'You can't go back, man. It's insane.'

'I'll do what I want!' the second voice barked. 'You're mired in tradition. What we need is to bring it to the heat, right now!'

Smith opened the door. He was looking into the kitchen. 'Hello,' he said. 'Discussing battle plans?'

W glanced around. 'Smith, tell this damned fool that he's wrong. You take the pot to the kettle, not the kettle to the pot!'

'Rubbish,' said the other man. 'You may as well entrust the tea to a savage.'

Suruk strolled in. 'Greetings!'

'This hothead is Major Wainscott,' W said.

'Wainscott, Deepspace Operations Group,' said the man. 'Wasn't here, don't exist, pleased to meet you.' He put out a hand and Smith shook it. Wainscott was bearded, quick-eyed and quite small, and wore the largest pair of shorts Smith had ever seen. He was slightly dusty and made Smith think of a geography teacher and a tramp, things he did not usually connect with military prowess. 'Glad to meet you, Smith. *Dar urgai vashuk min*,' he added to Suruk, making a stabbing gesture.

Suruk laughed. '*Ungak mar shalad*,' he said running a finger across his throat.

'Likewise, sir,' Wainscott said, and bowed. 'I have great respect for your people. You are fierce fighters.' Still bowed over, he tapped a scar that ran through his hair, from the front to the back of his head. He straightened up.

'Major Wainscott is a master of unconventional warfare,' W added.

'Absolutely,' Wainscott said. 'Conventional military doctrine enables the opposition to predict one's plan of attack. Me, I pull 'em down, wave 'em round my head and go in with the old chap flapping in the breeze like the banner of Ghengis Khan. Scares the hell out of the enemy, every time.'

'I'm sure it does,' said Smith. He looked around the kitchen, uncertain how to follow this. Perhaps some of Wainscott's brain might have fallen out when he acquired that scar. 'Are those the tea fields out there?'

'Indeed,' W said. 'Pure, unpicked tea.'

Smith crossed to the window and looked out. Having arrived in the small hours, he had not realised the scale of the plantation outside. The deep green of the tea plants stretched on and on from the window to the horizon: pure life, pure tea.

'The blood of the Empire,' he said to himself.

'Which the Ghasts intend to stop,' W said. 'As we talk, the great plantations are harvesting as much tea as they can and hiding it. A second front has been formed, and we're trying to get as much tea as possible stashed away before the enemy can get to it.'

'Will the farms be destroyed?' Suruk asked.

W shook his head. 'Worse than that, I'm afraid. Rumour has it that Gertie means to put the plantations to some perverted use of his own. My contacts tell me that they intend to test out tea on their own shock divisions, in the hope of breeding moral fibre into their own men.'

Smith pounded his fist on the sideboard. 'Dirty swine!' he cried.

'So far, tea gives the Ghasts no strength,' W explained. 'In fact, it's mildly poisonous to them. But no doubt they'll try to harvest it for themselves. At any rate the Crusadists regard tea as sinful, and will probably ban the general population from drinking it in order to weaken their will to resist.'

'This is terrible,' said Smith. 'You're telling me that the Ghasts mean to use this entire world as a testing-ground to enhance their own legions?'

'Mankind's war may rest on this one world,' Suruk said. 'And from that, the whole human galaxy. *My* people, of course, are unconquerable warriors.'

Carveth came in, still in her dressing gown. 'Alright all. Got any cereal?' she asked, opening the cupboards.

'Quite,' W said. 'With tea in their veins, the Ghasts could become nigh-on unstoppable. What sort of cereal did you want?'

'Frosties would be nice.'

'There's some in the next one down. History shows us that the decline in tea-drinking was directly linked to the weakening of moral fibre between the two Empires. With prolonged absence of tea, there is an actual risk of permanent moral decline. There, next to the Rice Crispies.'

Smith shuddered. 'You're right,' he said. 'Without us to protect it, the sheer military force the Ghasts could muster would overwhelm Known Space in weeks.'

Wainscott had been listening quietly by the window. 'That's where we come in,' he said. 'The Deepspace

Operations Group, if I may say so, is the smartest, best-trained, best-equipped military unit in human history, excluding nobody. I would say that one member of the DOG is the equal of twenty elite Ghast praetorians.'

Smith turned to him. 'How many men do you have?'

'Five. Well, four if you don't count me. But by God we're good.'

Carveth poured out the Frosties. 'Well, as long as there's less than a hundred aliens in this interplanetary invasion force, it should be a walkover,' she said. 'We're stuffed.' She sat down.

'Not necessarily,' W said. 'We may well have an army of our own. I need to speak to my contacts to establish how many men are on our side, and what we'll be up against.'

'Good,' said Smith. 'The sooner we can hit back, the better.' He turned to the window again and saw a slim figure strolling between the tea plants, dark hair pulled back from her face by a multicoloured band. 'Well,' he said, 'why don't you talk to your chaps and we'll re-convene in, say, half an hour? It'll give us time to get ready, and we might have come to an agreement about bringing the pot to the kettle by then.'

It was only nine o'clock, but the sun was fierce. Worse than that was the humidity: it seemed to seep through Smith's shirt and into his flesh, leaching the energy out of him. He strode through the tea plants with his sleeves rolled up and waistcoat unbuttoned, hearing the leaves hiss as they brushed against his sides, wishing that he had brought his Panama hat.

Rhianna stood a little way further into the field,

motionless. She did not turn as he approached. He walked around to the front of her, keeping a proper distance, and saw that her eyes were closed. She was making a soft humming sound, like an aged fridge.

'Hey, Isambard,' she said. She wore a very long skirt, the usual sandals and an exceedingly small top, which seemed to have decided not to be a bra at the very last minute. Her dreadlocks looked like the offspring of an octopus and a rat, but in a good way. She was very beautiful, he thought, if slightly grubby.

'Hullo Rhianna. How'd you know it was me?'

'I recognised your footsteps. Beautiful here, isn't it? The colours are so bright. It reminds me of a picture Gauguin painted of Tahiti.'

Smith did not know much about art, but knew enough not to say that he knew what he liked. 'Well, I never knew that,' he said. 'I suppose he deserved a holiday, after all that cosmonaut business.'

Rhianna gave him an odd look. They walked through the tea together, talking.

'So,' he said, 'how's things? Still psychic?'

'I'm good, thank you. And yes, I have been working on improving my talents. I learned a lot at St Carmilla's. These days, I focus on my chakras, and I can feel. . . positive energy, flowing through me.'

Smith frowned, unsure what this meant. He had forgotten how difficult it could be to talk to Rhianna. A voice at the back of his mind told him that if he focused on Rhianna's chakras he too would feel positively energised. He decided that he had been spending too much time around Carveth.

'Well, that's jolly good. Don't suppose you can blow things up with your mind yet, by any chance?'

Rhianna frowned. Damn, he thought, I did it again. It could be very frustrating trying to date a pacifist while the galaxy crawled with creatures that needed a damn good kick. 'Sorry,' he said.

'I understand,' Rhianna said. 'It must be difficult to embrace peace when you come from a culture inherently steeped in latent violence.'

'What, England?'

'The British Empire, Isambard.' A gentle wind stirred the tea leaves, taking a little of the humidity out of the air. On the horizon, a sun dragon turned lazily, soaking the heat up on its wings, charging itself. It must be huge, Smith thought: perhaps eighty feet across the wings.

'Well, we're nowhere near as bad as the Ghasts,' Smith replied, annoyed. 'Or bloody Gilead's lot, imposing their gibberish on us all.'

'That's really heavy.' She sighed. 'Why can't we all be friends, and enjoy freedom of religion?'

'Damn right. This Eden cult should be banned. We need to resist these bastards until there's not one of them left. Passively, of course. Thing is, I could do with your help.'

She stopped walking and looked at him. 'Really?'

'Definitely. Alright, you can't blow up tanks yet, but you do have skills and, well, you know. I'd be worried about you otherwise.'

'That's very kind of you, Isambard. I'll think about it.'

She smiled, and he smiled back. For the first time in their conversation, he felt that he was reaching her.

'I worry about you,' he said. 'The enemy might come

here, looking for you. They're not like normal people: they have no concept of decency. I'd be afraid in case you did something dippy.'

Rhianna smiled slightly less. 'Like I said, I'll think about it,' she said. 'Just give me time to meditate on it. But don't hassle me, Isambard. That's what The Man does, remember.'

'I won't, I promise. We're having a meeting inside later. You'd be welcome to come and listen to us.'

Rhianna said, 'I think I'd better help out. With all those Imperialists in there, you could do with someone to help dialogue' – she made her weighing-out gesture – 'flow. I suppose there won't be anyone else to represent the voice of enlightened woman.'

'Well, we've got Carveth.'

'I'll be there.'

The television was on in the bar. A semicircle of big wicker chairs stood around it, and ten people were watching a long-bearded man on the screen, addressing the camera like a hermit explaining his avoidance of civilisation.

'This is showing every twenty minutes on every channel,' W said.

The Hyrax sat back in his throne and smoothed his beard.

'Citizens of Urn. Greetings in the name of the most gentle god, the bloody-handed Annihilator. I am the Grand Hyrax, or, as my passport now says, God-King-Prophet-Emperor of Urn. You may have noticed that last night a revolution occurred, putting me in power over all of you. Now that order has been restored, let me put you at ease regarding the situation.

'The British-sponsored democratic government is over and the governor beheaded. I am now supreme ruler, and you will worship me or die. This change took place for two reasons: one, to protect your liberty, and two, to halt the tide of godless heresy. I will address these points in order. First, though, let me thank the legions of the Republic of Eden, who have assisted me in this crusade.'

There was a commotion on the screen, and suddenly Gilead's big, blubbering face was thrust up against the camera. 'The best fighting men inna world,' he sobbed, and he took a swig from a bottle of weak beer. 'Bless you, in your powered armour, and your. . . hats. Bless you. Kill 'em all!' he yelled suddenly, as he either fell or was pulled off-screen.

The Hyrax smoothed his beard down and continued.

'Firstly, liberty. This coup took place to protect your liberty. Some of you may find this strange, as you currently have less liberty, owing to my regime being a vicious theocratic hell. Well, to use a phrase of a friend of mine, try thinking outside the box. It is well known that to have a large degree of liberty, it is necessary to surrender a small amount to allow for police, security services and the like. We have taken this concept a step forward: since you have surrendered *all* your liberty, you now have even more liberty to do exactly what I say or die like the filthy heretic scum you are. Feel free to agree with me on this point.

'Secondly, heresy. I don't think I have to explain this. The only people unfamiliar with the concept are the very heretics who invented it. As a result, only a heretic would fail to welcome the drastic and brutal actions I intend to take against suspected heretics across the globe. As soon as the situation calms down sufficiently for me to inflame it with a crusade, you will be able to watch heretics being dealt with on your very TV sets. And believe me, we know how to deal with heretics. On with the show trials!

'In the interim, the legal system has been simplified. You will now do exactly what I say. If in doubt, don't do it, especially if it makes you happy. In particular, tea is now banned. This evil drink has turned the pious into degenerates, and inflamed women with foul desires. It has turned their thoughts to disobedience, their once pious bodies to licentiousness, filled them with wanton lusts, the sweat glistening on their great, big, heaving—

'Anyway, tea production is to end from now on. Anyone drinking, growing or brewing tea is a heretic wallowing in the filth of their own depravity and will be subject to the full penalties of my new law! Heretics will be wiped aside! The nine-headed beast shall rise three times – three times – from the lake of fire, and crusade will envelop the galaxy! The unrighteous will burn in eighteen hells, and I – I alone – shall be crowned God-Prophet of the entirety of space, by me, the God-Prophet! You have been warned, you decadent, contemptible, hellbound, infidel scum!

'Thank you for listening.

'PS. This counts double for girls.'

The Hyrax shuddered, glanced off-camera, and the picture faded to the Crusadist flag. W glanced around the room and switched off the machine.

'Anyone want to say anything about that?'

Carveth put her hand up. 'Knob-end,' she said.

There was a murmur of agreement around the room.

'So,' Major Wainscott said, 'these are the puppets up which the Ghastist hand is thrust.'

'Bloody right,' someone said next to him. Three men and a girl sat by Wainscott, all wearing big shorts, long socks and heavy boots, like a football team sprayed up for desert combat. They were slight and wiry, like the major himself. These, Smith realised, had to be the Deepspace Operations Group.

'Well,' Wainscott added, 'I think they won't be up to much. It's the ones we don't see that promise to be trouble: these six divisions of praetorians and however many drones the Ghasts have landed.'

'So,' said Smith, 'both Gilead and 462 live. We need to work out how to hit back at these invaders, and quickly. Can we get an army together?'

'Exactly,' W said. 'I think there can be no victory without the help of the common people of Urn. No doubt even now committees are being set up to organise the fight back. My position on the *Daily Monolith* enables me to spread the truth and connect the people who will be leading the resistance against the Ghasts.'

'Quite,' Smith said.

Rhianna entered the room as quietly as her flip-flops would allow and sat down. Smith smiled at her and she smiled politely back.

'Miss Mitchell here is a citizen of the Free Colony of New Francisco,' W said. 'I can't tell you much more than that about her, although New Fran is technically allied to

Britain, and it is of paramount importance that she is kept away from the Ghasts.'

'Go over to them, will she?' Wainscott growled.

'No,' said W, and he coughed nastily into his hand and took a deep swig of tea. 'Quite the opposite, actually.'

Smith recalled the time when the Ghasts had captured Rhianna and had wired her to a machine designed to separate the alien and human parts of her. They had succeeded, in a way: the alien Vorl had appeared above her body like a vengeful ghost, proving that her pacifist instincts came from her human side by causing a dozen enemy troopers to burst like popcorn.

'Captain Smith and his crew,' W continued, gesturing with one big hand, 'know Miss Mitchell from before, and helped bring her to Imperial Space against serious odds. At the moment their ship is in the city, impounded by the enemy, who are enforcing a strict no-flying policy. However, we can rely on them all as men, women and things of pluck.' He sighed. 'Now, we need to establish a plan of attack.'

'It's simple,' Wainscott said. 'We need to kill Ghasts.'

There was a short pause, during which Wainscott realised that the room was looking at him. 'The details can be ironed out later,' he said.

'At the moment, Major, it would seem best if you worked on training up a force of commandos to disrupt the enemy,' W said. 'If you can train up the Caldathrians, you can train up anyone.'

'You trained the Caldathrians?' Carveth said. 'Bloody hell.'

The beetle people of Caldathro were a gentle, placid

race whose homeworld had been annexed by the Republic of Eden in the first week of the war. Their militias scattered and their king brutally gang-probed by whooping grunts, the beetle people fled to the hills and were presumed defeated. Here, with help from the Empire, they ate huge amounts of food and plotted their revenge: a month later, in a single night of squelchy, malodorous carnage, the beetle people flattened the Edenite camp with a gargantuan ball of their own dung. Their excretion-based fighting system had made them feared guerrillas, and they were now renowned as one of the most regular irregular units in Known Space.

'From what I've heard, the Colonial Guard is scattered but intact,' Wainscott said. 'We can try to gather them and train them for work in the countryside. No doubt many of the Teasmen will be glad to help, especially since the Hyrax is banning the crop they rely on to survive.'

'But will that be enough to retake the planet?' Smith asked.

'I don't know,' Wainscott replied. 'With nobody getting off-world, it's going to be difficult to warn the rest of the Empire until the next harvest – and that's three months away. This bloody coup has caught the whole planet by surprise, even my men – playing five-a-side, as it happens. And these are praetorians: the best fighters and the finest game that the Ghast Empire has to offer.'

'I know where you can find more men,' Suruk said.

The group turned to look at him. He crouched quietly on his chair in the shadows at the back of the room, his tusks rubbing together, sharpening.

'Well, not exactly men.' Quietly, with that odd grace

particular to his species, he stood up. 'I do not speak of this lightly. It is a matter of difficulty to me. Yet, the clan of which I am a part sits within this system of planets. Were I to speak to my kin and tell them of the great battle that awaited, a mighty army could gather and the sky would darken with our ships. Mankind could face the might of the Ghast divisions with the clans of the M'Lak beside them.'

'It's a good idea,' Smith said. 'All we'd need to do is talk to them. Provided we could get a ship through the enemy defences, it would work fine. I agree.'

'But how would you get off Urn?' Carveth said, turning to Suruk. 'They've got us trapped here. I mean, it couldn't be done, right? This is impractical, if not totally insane, right? Someone other than me thinks this is suicide, yes?'

Smith shook his head. 'It needn't be impossible at all. In fact, it's perfectly feasible. All you'd need to do would be to raid the airstrip where the Ghast ships are waiting, grab our ship, bypass the missile defences and evade the enemy navy. I wouldn't call that impossible, as such.'

Carveth made a huffing noise. 'Thanks, Boss. Operation Shot to Bits it is, then. I mean, only yesterday I was wondering how I could get round to dying in a fireball, and now I know.'

Wainscott rubbed his chin. 'Now that I think about it,' he said, 'that's just mad enough to work. And I'd know.'

'Well then,' said Smith, 'that's what we ought to do. In fact, this is looking like a better idea the more I think about it.' He stood. 'Gentlemen, my crew and I will accept this mission. Together we shall carry the message of hope deep into space, and return with victory. I,' he added, warming to his theme, 'shall represent the Empire. Suruk here, the various alien peoples whom the Empire is currently helping run their planets. Rhianna, if you'll come with us, you could represent your own people back on New Francisco. And Carveth, who's already agreed to join us—'

'That was irony!' She sat back and said, 'Look. I hate to interrupt this whole Fellowship of the Wrong thing we've got going here, but I'm really not cut out for it. I am a not-very-experienced sex-robot reprogrammed as a pilot. I'm sorry. This really isn't me.'

Smith thought. 'Hmm, maybe you've got a point there. This isn't a fellowship after all.'

'Good. I'm glad you're seeing sense.'

'I mean, I'm the only fellow in it, so I suppose it's more of an acquaintanceship. Yes, that's it! We'll all be flying together on the same ship, so that makes us: The Acquaintanceship of the Ship! Just like in that book I once read, *Lord of the Flies*.'

It was eleven. They stopped for tea.

Carveth was outside when a thought struck her. 'Oh my God, we're going to die,' she said.

A hand patted her on the elbow.

'Hey,' Rhianna said. 'Don't worry, Polly. You'll be fine. We'll get the ship back, and take off, and after that every-thing will be cool. Besides, even if it isn't, it doesn't matter. Death is only the prelude of the next cycle of the wheel of life, right?'

'Is it just me, or does the wheel of life go through quite a lot of cowpats?' Carveth said. 'You know, when I signed up I had this niggling feeling that something was wrong, but I couldn't put a finger on it. Now that we're about to go on a suicide mission worked out by a five-a-side football team, I'm beginning to suspect what it was.'

Rhianna folded her arms. 'Well, Polly, sometimes you just have to trust in things. Sometimes, life throws us obstacles, because, by overcoming those obstacles, we become in tune with the greater—'

Carveth snorted. 'For a vegetarian, you've got a lot of bull inside you.'

The front door opened. In the doorway stood a handsome, battered-looking man of about thirty-five in a white tuxedo, the remains of a cigarette hanging out of the corner of his mouth.

Carveth gasped. 'Rick Dreckitt,' she breathed.

He ran a hand over his unshaven chin, as if to check that his jaw was really there. 'Yep,' he said after a while, 'sure is, sister.'

'You see?' Rhianna said. 'It's karma!'

'Right then,' Smith said, leaning over the map. 'Plan of attack. I would suggest that Major Wainscott launches an attack on the missile defences to render them inoperable while we make a break for the ship. The trouble is, the missile silos are twenty miles from the spaceport. Even with the silos down, there's no guarantee that we'll be able to fight our way through the city to the spaceport.'

'If you try that, better call out the meat wagon first,' a voice said from the doorway. Smoke curled into the room. 'Crash that joint and you'll end up full of daylight.'

Wainscott glanced up. 'Who the devil are you?' he said.

Dreckitt stepped into the room. 'Just a bo looking to bang gums awhile,' he replied. He smiled.

Wainscott's eyes were hard and lethal. 'Not with me you don't,' he said.

W raised a hand. 'Easy there. This is Richard Dreckitt, former bounty hunter and now owner of Rick's Bar and Dinerama. He also happens to work for us from time to time.'

'Hmm.' Wainscott frowned. 'Why does he talk all wrong, though? Rum lingo like that makes a feller sound soft in the noggin.'

'It's because I used to stalk the mean streets of Carver's Rock,' Dreckitt said. 'I chopped out bounties for the company highbinders: most of my marks were crooks. I made some paper and gave up the grift to work out here. Hell of a lot easier running a bar than having some nut squirt you full of hot lead.'

'How absolutely disgusting,' Wainscott said.

W said, 'We need two passports, Mr Dreckitt.'

'Hot papers, eh?' Dreckitt took his cigarette out and looked around the bar meaningfully. His dark-rimmed eyes met the set faces of the men around the table, scanned Suruk's inhuman features, and stopped on Smith.

'They're for myself and Carveth, who's standing behind you.'

Dreckitt nodded and glanced over his shoulder. 'Hey,' he said, 'we've met before. You're that andy I was paid to put the hatchet on.'

'That's me!' Carveth said, and she gave him a big grin. 'Is this bar yours, then?'

Dreckitt nodded. 'It's a good gig: you have to learn how

to be nice to people, but less of them try to murder you.'

'Wow. Good that you didn't kill me, isn't it?'

'Kinda handy, sister,' Dreckitt said. He rested his elbow on the autopiano and looked back at the others. 'How soon do you need them?'

'For tonight,' Smith said. 'We need them by sundown.'

'I'll see what I can do. Access?'

'The port.'

'Alright. You people have a good time, or whatever.' He glanced at Carveth. 'Later, doll.'

'Can't say I trust that fellow,' Smith said when Dreckitt had gone. 'Dubious type, if you ask me.'

Still crouched on his seat, Suruk spoke. 'So we have learned three things. Firstly, in order to liberate this world we must strike with both my warrior brethren and with such forces as you gentlemen can make from the puny human population. Secondly, that once the enemy realise our aim, they will stop at nothing to prevent our escape. A weakened, captive population is of use to them, but if we fight like warriors, they will strive greatly to defeat us. And thirdly,' he added, glancing at Carveth, 'the gnome has no taste in spawning-partners.'

Inside the house Smith, W and Wainscott were studying a map. Suruk had retired to practise with his weapons. Rhianna was making the raiding-party a packed lunch and Carveth was on duty to handle the meat. Once she had put the ham in the sandwiches, there wasn't much for her to do but fret.

The television showed nothing except ranting speeches from the Crusadists. For reasons she couldn't understand, they had taken to destroying stereos, which offended their complex religious beliefs. One of the Hyrax's sermons blasted out of the television, while a horde of cultists danced around a scaffold, from which dangled a hi-fi in a noose. Carveth switched the television off, repulsed. Overnight Urn had turned from a slackly-run democracy to a playground for lunatics. Carveth was no fighter, but she felt that even she would enjoy planting her boot squarely in the God-Prophet's edicts.

There was nothing she felt like hearing on the panmelodium, so after checking Gerald's cage she stepped out to take the air.

It was very hot, as though some great cooker under the earth was trying to roast the land from within. A souped-up jeep stood at one side of the house a little way back from the road. The bonnet was up, and a figure in a vest worked on the engine, head down. As Carveth strolled over she saw that it was the woman from the Deepspace Operations Group.

'Hey there,' the woman said, straightening up. She was wiry and tough-looking, but her face was naturally attractive, and she smiled. Her uniform jacket hung from the jeep's wing mirror, and there were spots of oil on her vest. 'You're the android, right?'

Carveth nodded. 'Simulant. Polly Carveth.'

'Right. Susan.' She reached out, realised that her heavy glove was covered in grease and pulled it off. They shook hands. 'How's tricks?'

'Terrifying. How about you?'

'Not too bad. Just making sure we're all set to go.' She patted the jeep. 'It's quite a machine, this – fast and mean.

Runs on hydrocells, petrol, diesel at a push and even coal. Which means there's four times as much stuff to go wrong. Want to give me a hand? I know it's not a space-ship, but the same principles apply.'

'Well, I hardly know how a ship works either, so why not?' Carveth wandered round the bonnet. A self-calibrating Maxim cannon was mounted on a pintle on the front passenger door. It was slightly more advanced than the one gathering dust in the *John Pym*'s weapons locker. Carveth gave it a cautious prod, as if to check that it was dead.

'You ever use one of those?' Susan asked.

'Yes. The way I see it, if things get nasty, you're best off behind a big gun.'

Susan raised an eyebrow. 'Fighter, eh?'

'Coward, actually, big coward. I'd be the standard-bearer of the custard-coloured league if that didn't involve marching out in front. The bigger the weapon separating me and my preferably unarmed enemy, the better. Some of us aren't elite fighters, you know. When the firing starts, all I can do is try to keep my head down. And my dinner.'

Susan pulled her gloves back on. 'It's probably best you get offworld and fetch us some help, then. This planet isn't going to be much fun for a while.' She put her head back under the bonnet, and got back to work.

5

Checkpoint Gertie

The road back was almost deserted. The city squatted in the distance, quiet. No smoke rose from the tea refineries. It was a shocked, sullen silence, the silence of someone struck down whilst looking the other way.

Halfway back to the city a massive, armadillo-shaped vehicle rolled by on eight wheels, bristling with guns and stamped with the flame-and-angel insignia of Gilead's men. Speakers on the back blared out music, and a recorded voice repeated 'Welcome to the Empire of Eden! We are your friends!' As Smith passed it, he caught a glimpse of sunglasses and a filtermask behind an armoured windscreen, and a trooper yelled at them, 'How's it feel to lose, losers?' before the tank rumbled past.

From the boot Suruk snarled, 'Wait and see.'

'Shush,' said Smith. Carveth whistled and drove on, trying to look innocent.

Rhianna was under a rug in the back seat. Gerald's wheel rattled in his cage. 'Are we nearly there yet, guys?' Rhianna asked.

'Not far,' said Smith. 'Take us in via the Ghast checkpoint, Carveth. They're less likely to recognise us than the

Edenites. Without orders, they're less likely to blow us up for the hell of it, too.'

'Alright, Boss,' Carveth said.

Smith took the false passports out of the glove compartment. 'I hope this works,' he said, looking at the identification details. 'Your friend must have been in a hurry when he put these passports together. Or in the dark.'

'I guess he had to work quickly,' Carveth said. 'It can't be easy finding people whose identities we could take at short notice.'

'Bloody right. I'll be lucky if I can even remember my false name, let alone spell it. Head down, Rhianna,' Smith said. 'Here comes the checkpoint.'

There was a sentry chamber by the side of the road, a long, spine-like barrier sticking out of it to block the way. The thing had the unwholesome, biological look of Ghast technology.

As they approached, a pair of drones stepped into the road. One of them stuck its pincer up. 'Halt!'

Smith wound his window down.

'Attention, scum!' the nearer drone barked. 'Engine off!'

Carveth glanced at Smith. 'Off?' she whispered. He knew what she meant – *There goes our quick escape.*

'Off,' he said.

The car shook as she turned the key, then it was still.

The nearer of the Ghasts marched to the window and peered into the car, its antennae stroking the window-frame. 'Identification.'

Smith handed over the passports. A globule of drool fell from the Ghast's jaw, onto Smith's thigh.

The Ghast stared at Carveth for a second, then looked back at Smith. 'Is that a child?'

'No,' said Smith. 'Adult female.'

The second Ghast suddenly yanked its colleague away from the car. It spun it round, barked out a stream of orders into its face, turned and strode away, scowling. It walked to the back of the car and, in the universal language of tough masculine beings, started to kick the tyres. The car shuddered at each kick. Carveth's knuckles were white on the steering wheel.

The Ghast with the passports returned. It had stopped drooling. 'Your child is lucky. We have no orders to eat it yet.' It opened the top passport, peered at the picture, then at Smith. 'So. You are Arthur Fonzarelli?'

'Indeed so, my good man,' Smith replied.

'And the child is – how is this pronounced?'

'Parkins Mhambowte,' Carveth replied. 'Probably.'

The drone paused. 'Remain there.'

It joined its comrade at the back of the car, and they began a hushed conversation. For creatures usually unable to speak without shouting, they managed to whisper quite well.

'I knew this was a bad idea!' Carveth hissed, watching the Ghasts confer in the rear view mirror.

'Quite,' said Smith. He wore a battered civilian jacket supplied by W, and the Civiliser under it. He reached across his body and pulled the hammer down, ready to fire. 'I think your friend short-changed us. Anyone with an ounce of brain knows that Parkins Mhambowte isn't the name of a white female android.'

'I know,' Carveth said glumly. 'Android names all have an R in the middle.'

'Maybe we can reason our way out of this,' Rhianna said from under the rug.

One of the Ghasts cocked its disruptor with a hollow cracking sound. 'Everybody out!' it barked. 'Get out, scum! *Rak, rak!*'

'Balls,' said Smith, and he opened the door.

'And the woman under the rug in the back! Out, out, all of you!'

'Best do what they say,' Smith said, and he stepped out into the dusk. Behind him, Rhianna and Carveth followed suit. The boot stayed shut.

The first Ghast covered them while the checkpoint commander put all of its arms behind its back and puffed its chest up. 'Ah, so you thought to deceive us, did you?' it began. 'Puny earthmen thought to trick the Ghast Empire. Hah! We have found you out! We see right through you, Arthur Fonzarelli! You have attempted to illegally carry this woman into the spaceport!'

Very pleased with itself, it wiggled its antennae and gave them a toothy smirk. 'But there is more. We have orders – specific orders – to apprehend a M'Lak, a human male and two human females of your description! Yes, orders from number 462! Now, open the boot so we can get this over with and shoot you.'

Smith fixed the creature with a hard gaze. 'I don't think you ought to do that.'

'Silence! Open it!'

Carveth started to elbow Rhianna in the ribs. 'Psychic powers, psychic powers!' she whispered. 'Pop their heads!'

'Quiet!' the Ghast snapped. 'You, male. Open the boot or I strike a female!'

106

'Shoot them,' said the first Ghast, grinning. 'Shoot them both.'

'Silence!' the second said. 'Who is the secondary road-block commander here? *I* give the orders. You, human male – open the boot or I shoot one of the females!'

'I'll remember that,' said Smith. He walked to the back of the car, trying to work out how to warn Suruk. He bent down, reached to the boot catch with his left hand and slid the right across his chest, ready to draw. His fingers closed around the Civiliser, he pressed the button, the boot swung open – and there was nothing there.

Smith thought: *Suruk?*

'Nothing,' the Ghast said. 'These are not the humans we are looking for.' It glanced at its comrade. 'Ah well. Let's shoot them anyway.'

'Good plan!' the other barked.

'Do it,' Smith said, looking over the Ghast's shoulder.

'As you wish, human!' the Ghast replied.

'I didn't mean you,' Smith said, and Suruk's spear burst through its thorax and the Ghast screeched. The second trooper raised its gun and Smith leaped in, punched it in the jaw, threw it against the car as he drew the Civiliser and pressed the barrel into the Ghast's side. The alien looked down, saw the gun jutting into the folds of its trenchcoat and cried, 'Not the leather, Fonzarelli!' and Smith pulled the trigger and it fell down dead.

'I still think we could have reasoned our way out of that,' Rhianna said.

Smith put the gun away. 'Do you think anyone heard that?' he asked.

'That deafening gunshot?' Suruk said. He tugged his

spear from the dead Ghast and wiped it on the thing's coat. 'It is possible, yes.'

'Let's go,' Smith said. 'Carveth, you're driving.'

She nodded. 'Alright.' She climbed into the front seat and revved the engine. The others got in: Suruk and Rhianna in the back seats, Smith in the front, on the passenger side. Carveth passed Smith her service revolver and he wound down the window.

She glanced at him. 'Straight through, right?'

'Straight through,' Smith said.

Carveth looked over her shoulder. 'Hold on!' she said, and she took the handbrake off and kicked the accelerator.

Further down the road, praetorian 37012/B turned to its comrade, 264578/F. 'Which do you think is better,' it asked, 'backhanding them across the head, or kicking them when they're down?'

264578/F shrugged. 'I like both,' it said. 'They're equally vicious. However, what I really enjoy is—'

It never finished, because at that moment the reinforced bumper of a Crofton Imp smashed straight through the sentry box and mangled it. Its colleague spun around, raising its gun, and Smith put a Civiliser shell into its chest even as Suruk's spear cleaved off one of its pincers. The car ploughed through the barrier and suddenly they were no longer in the road: around them were the vast shapes of Ghast and Edenite troop ships, and the Imp raced between them, quick as a wasp between the flanks of cattle, as all hell broke loose.

A siren howled: Ghastish yelped over their heads from a loudspeaker. Four of Gilead's skytroopers leaped up and started shouting. Gunfire rattled out from behind and Carveth swerved around the landing gear of an Edenite ship.

Figures rushed in from the edges of the windscreen. Carveth swung the wheel and the Imp struck a power-suited Edenite with a clang, his armour sparking on the concrete before he rolled out of view. They plunged on, past the enemy ships, towards the *John Pym*.

Suruk hurled a knife, Rhianna ducked down, Carveth hunched over the wheel, teeth bared in desperation, a very small way from panic. On the loudspeaker, the Ghast voice was joined by a human one. Soldiers poured onto the airfield and the Imp raced past them. Sun dragons were massing in the sky. The Ghasts were bringing up a tripod-mounted disruptor gun: two of Gilead's men got confused and started shooting at them, and suddenly the spaceport was a cat's cradle of bullets and beams. Three cultists ran howling onto the field and blew themselves up, which helped nobody. The Imp shot through the flames and Smith saw that the ships before them were Imperial.

'That's our ship!' Smith cried, pointing, and at that moment a praetorian leaped onto the bonnet, smeared itself over the windscreen like a monstrous fly. It battered the glass with its claws, and Smith leaned out the window and the Civiliser clicked empty.

'I can't see a thing!' Carveth yelled, and Suruk hoisted himself out through the window, dropped onto the running-board and grabbed the praetorian by the neck. He tore it loose – it fell – the car bumped over it on wrecked suspension. 'Eat wheel, Gertie!' Smith yelled. 'Good work, Suruk!'

Carveth shifted onto one buttock and Smith helped steer as she fumbled in her back pocket for the key. 'Get the hold open!' she shouted, throwing it at Smith, who foraged on the floor for the dropped key as a Ghast hover-tank slid into view.

Smith grabbed the key as they came into range of the *Pym*. He glanced over his shoulder: Rhianna had closed her eyes and was making a humming sound and the tank was lining up its guns. He stuck his arm out the window and pressed the button on the key frantically. 'Work, dammit!'

The *John Pym* was fifty yards away – forty now. Smith's finger hammered the button, and – thank God – the lights on the ship flashed on, then off, and it was open. The hold door dropped like a drawbridge, Carveth turned the car right, tyres screeching, and behind they heard the low *Whumpf* of the tank gun. She swung further right: the disruptor shell could not compensate fast enough and flew past. Explosion to the left, far off.

She spun the wheel, and the rear of the *John Pym* was open to them. Carveth floored the accelerator. In the hold a drone, finding nothing worth looting, was drawing antennae on Smith's picture of the Queen. The car hit the ramp, left the ground, knocked the drone's head off, smashed into the back wall of the hold and was still.

Smith half-fell into the hold, stumbled to the back door and whacked the button. The door closed. He strode to the car. 'Everyone alright?'

Carveth gave him a cheery, vacant wave. He tossed her

the keys. 'Let's go,' he said, and Carveth ran to the cockpit.

Suruk stepped off the running-board. 'Rargh!' he said. 'Let's do it again!'

'Rhianna,' Smith said. She sat in the back of the car, eyes closed, humming to herself. Either she was meditating, or she had gone completely mad.

Something struck the side of the *John Pym*. It shook a little and dust fell from the roof. 'Go, Carveth!'

He looked into the car. 'Rhianna, we're taking off,' he said. 'You need to strap yourself in.'

'Not now,' she said, and she began humming again.

Suruk tapped his arm. 'Leave her, Mazuran. You must rule the ship.'

'Right.' He nodded, still uneven from the drive, and lurched into the cockpit.

The engines fired up.

'We're not going to do this,' Carveth called, wrapping her hands around the stick. 'Soon as we're up, they'll lock a missile onto us.' She switched the auxiliary power to the main thrusters as she spoke. Outside, gunfire. More tanks were pouring onto the strip. Someone was battering at the airlock.

'Just try.'

He strapped himself in; not that a seatbelt would do much against half a dozen heatseekers. The engines roared.

'Here goes!' Carveth said, and the ship tore from the ground. Bullets and lasers clattered against the hull. A railgun team ran out of cover, and Carveth swung the jets and sent them running, chased by flame. The *Pym* shot upwards, its oversized engines straining, and Smith gripped the armrests and prayed that they would not be shaken to bits.

As the ship rushed upwards, sun dragons whirled around it. Drawn by the chaos, they were attacking the landing site. Smith watched, awed. A dragon spat onto an Edenite tank and a bolt of static leaped from its mouth, frying the machine. Another was pulling the aerials off a transport ship. A dropping the size of a small oak fell onto and through the control tower like a tossed caber, partially collapsing it.

Great veined wings filled the screen for a second then disappeared. Smith came back to life. They had to move, fast. The sun dragons would fight anything smaller than a starship, W had said. He was surprised they hadn't already attacked.

Smith thumbed the radio, and chattering gibberish filled the cockpit. A human voice broke in. 'Great One, the unbelievers are attacking the missile array!'

Wainscott! Smith thought. 'They've hit the missile grid!' he said. 'We're safe! Apart from the A.A. guns, obviously.'

Carveth grinned. 'A.A? Pah! We're way out of range.' She leaned close to the window and made a rude sign. 'Try getting us now, tossers!'

'Don't get cocky,' Smith warned. 'Just key in the route and let's go.'

'Ah, we're fine at this altitude. They just look like big ants from up here.'

'They are big ants, Carveth.'

'Oh, yeah.' She typed on the computer. 'We're climbing. We'll be off Urn in two minutes.'

'Good. Let's check on Rhianna.'

Suruk was waiting in the hold. Rhianna still sat in the back of the car, meditating.

'Wainscott's attacked the missile silos,' Smith announced. 'We're safe to get away.'

'Thanks to my ace piloting,' Carveth said. 'And driving.'

'And my plan, if I may say so,' Smith replied, peeved by her stealing the credit.

'Ahem,' Suruk said. 'Actually, behold.'

He opened the door, and they looked in. Rhianna was indeed unharmed: eyes closed, humming, concentrating on something that Smith and Carveth could not see.

'So she hums,' Carveth said. 'So what? I can do that too, when I'm not flying the ship. Sometimes both at once.'

'No,' Suruk replied. 'You spoke of her powers, now you see them. Her thoughts protected us from harm.'

Carveth snorted. 'So it's her who stopped us getting shot?' she said. 'Prove it.'

Smith touched Rhianna's shoulder. 'Rhianna?' he said softly.

She opened her eyes. 'Hey, guys,' she said.

'I was wondering—' Smith said.

A laser hit the back of the ship. The hold controls exploded in a shower of sparks. The lights went off.

The lights came back on. Carveth got up from the floor and brushed herself down. 'Point made,' she said, and she ran to the cockpit.

'Well,' said Carveth, an hour later, 'I've checked the cameras best as I can. We're well out of orbit now, and there's nothing they could send up that could follow us. Missile-wise, we're safe.'

'Good-oh.' Smith lowered a digestive biscuit into his tea. 'So what's the damage?'

Carveth put her boots up on the dashboard. In his cage, Gerald's wheel squeaked. 'To be honest, Boss, it's hard to tell without going outside. But at that range, the laser wouldn't be strong enough to do much except mess up the electrics. I suppose we may have a slow puncture, but as it is, all I can be sure it's done is break the big door at the back of the hold. I can repair that as soon as we put down.'

Smith was impressed. Carveth's programming as a sexbot tended to intrude on her ability to describe the workings of the ship without resorting to crude innuendo. She was doing well so far.

'Which just goes to show,' she added, 'that if you're going to take a long beam without proper protection, you're best off getting it in the rear entrance.'

'Hmm,' said Smith. 'So what do you suggest we do?'

She shrugged and turned the page of her magazine. 'Land on the nearest standard-grav world and have a look. At worst I'll have to do a bit of welding.' She tapped the navigation console, causing the needles in several dials to spin wildly. 'We'll be passing Didcot 5 soon and I'll run a scan: if that's no good to land on we'll have a look once we get to Suruk's place, Didcot 6.'

'Righto. How long will the repairs take?'

Carveth sucked in air. 'Ooh, let's see . . . Give it, say, an hour to check the hull, two hours max to spray on new sealant, fifteen minutes to suck on my teeth and tell you it's tricky – about four hours ought to do it.'

'Four hours? Are you sure it'll take that long?'

'Call it five.'

Smith took a sip of tea. He tasted it, swallowed, and thought: this stuff is precious now. How long until our reserves run out? With Urn blockaded the army could not be kept in tea. Without the forces to liberate Urn the Empire would be slowly wrung dry – and then its moral fibre would break. The people of the Empire would be left helpless and, without spine, no more capable of defending themselves than foreigners. We have to work fast, he thought. The fate of the Empire rests on our skill.

Suruk strolled in, put his face close to the windscreen and looked out into space. 'Are we there yet?'

'Few hours yet,' Smith replied. 'We've got to do some repairs first. What's that you're reading, Carveth?'

She held up the magazine. 'This month's *Girl Android*,' she said. '"Ten Sexy Ways to Improve Your Processing Speed".'

'Why?'

'Oh, no reason.' She shrugged unconvincingly. 'Just thought I might. I mean, you never know, right?'

'She wishes to spawn with the other simulant,' Suruk said.

'What, Dreckitt?' Smith replied. 'Ugh. He struck me as a low sort of fellow. Not the type I'd want my crew dealing with. I take it you're giggling at the absurdity of the idea, Carveth?'

'Oh, of course,' she said, grinning behind her magazine. She frowned. 'On an unrelated topic, do I look fat?'

'Of course not.' They looked around: Rhianna stood in

the doorway. She entered in a swish of tie-dyed fabric. 'Body image is just a construct, Polly. You should be happy with yourself no matter what your size.'

Carveth checked the scanner and sighed. 'Which sounds very much like "Buck up podgy", if you ask me. I need to lose some weight.'

Rhianna picked up *Girl Android* and shook her head wisely. 'This is really terrible,' she said, flicking through the pages.

'Bloody right. Four pounds fifty and there's not even a photo story.'

'Polly, have you ever heard of Body Fascism?'

'Some disgusting alien practice, no doubt,' Smith remarked. 'Insult to nature, your Ghast.'

'No, not exactly. It's what happens when we adopt a restrictive concept of beauty and try to fit every type of person into one narrow stereotyped image. There are many different, diverse sorts of woman – one could be thin, or, um, larger, or—'

'Attractive?' Smith suggested. He felt that he was getting the hang of this.

'None of which stops me weighing far too much,' Carveth said.

Suruk turned from his study of the stars. 'You'd be lighter if I cut your head off,' he said. 'How about that?'

Smith looked over his shoulder. Rhianna was sleek and alluring. Her midriff was bare, which was something not often seen in the Empire. Somewhere or other she had discarded her shoes. 'You look nice,' he said.

She smiled; something inside him softened, and

something on the outside did the opposite. 'Thanks. You know, I'm glad to be back aboard.'

'I'm glad you're glad to be aboard,' he said.

'I'm glad that you're glad,' she said.

'Bleargh,' Carveth said.

Rhianna smiled over them all, like a saint. 'I'm going to have a little lie down, if nobody minds. I could do with a rest after this morning.'

'Of course,' Smith said. 'Do you need any help?'

'I'll be fine, thank you,' Rhianna said, and she pattered back down the hall.

Carveth watched her go. 'It's alright for her,' she said. 'Just look at her arse; it's not like some sort of horrible bus accident. Me, I only have to walk past a scone and I turn into a barrage balloon. You can stop looking at her arse now, Cap.'

'Sorry,' Smith said.

'Besides, you're forgetting that she's a scary freak.' Carveth peered into Gerald's cage. 'Leaving aside the fact that she once turned into a great big ghost, she's un-reliable. Whatever powers she may have, she can hardly control them.' She squeezed Gerald's water bottle thoughtfully. 'What we need is an army. Like Suruk's people.'

'Indeed,' Suruk said. 'Excuse me.'

He turned and left the cockpit. Carveth watched him go, heard the door to his room swing shut. She peered at Smith. 'What's up with him? He's run off as though I let one fly.'

'Strange,' said Smith. 'I'm not sure what's on his mind. Oh well, how long 'til we can land somewhere and sort out these repairs?'

'Didcot 5 should be alright to land on. We'll be coming into high orbit in about three hours. Ooh, what's that?' A light flickered on the dashboard. 'That's odd. There's a message coming through.'

She pulled down the communications monitor and watched as the message tapped its way across the screen. The printer chuffed and tapped the message out onto a roll of tape.

'Well,' she said, reading from the tape. 'Looks like there's an automated beacon down there. Let's see. . . *Please land on this planet.*' She glanced around. 'From the sounds of it, it's just a repeated signal, being given out by a machine. But it's nice of them to say that, isn't it?'

'It certainly is.' Smith nodded at the planet in the centre of the navigation screen, striped with intermingling gas layers. It looked like a ball of raspberry ripple ice cream. 'In that case, we ought to accept its offer.'

A science officer's goggled features appeared on the intercom, its antennae waving. 'Glorious commander, I request an audience!'

462 glanced up, irritated. On his desk was a bucket of water and a bag full of kittens, but now that would have to wait. He put the bag down and prodded the intercom. 'Enter.'

His guards showed the scientist in. Ghast scientists looked very much like drones, except that their coats were white instead of black. The scientist twitched and sniggered as it came in, a common habit among its caste. 'All hail Number One!'

'All hail,' 462 said, sourly. 'Sit.'

A bio-chair unfolded from the floor, engineered to take the special stresses of Ghast anatomy. The scientist flicked out its lab coat and stercorium and sat down.

462 said, 'You have interrupted my nutrition hour. This had better be good news, minion.' He pointed up at the picture above his head. Although the room was human in design, the motivational poster was newly added. It showed a sunset with Ghast characters underneath. 'Read it out.'

The scientist swallowed hard. '*Teamwork: what we do to avoid being shot.*'

'Quite. I hope you have been productive.'

'Yes, Glorious Leader, indeed. We have been most productive – but – but our results have been unsuccessful. We have compelled our praetorians to drink tea, to bathe in it – we have even sucked out their blood and replaced it with warm tea – but to no avail. We cannot give them moral fibre. It is impossible.'

'Rubbish! I was sent to this wretched world for a reason, not to hear you make feeble excuses about impossibility!' He paused, trying to remember. 'Maybe there is some other way. DNA splicing, selective heliostranding, perhaps? Can one mate with a teabag?'

The scientist shook its head. 'No, Mighty One. Even the humans cannot breed with tea.' It giggled involuntarily, and looked sheepish. 'Excuse me.'

'Go. Continue your work. I will send you more praetorians if you run out.'

462 watched it leave. Idiots, he thought. Perhaps the research would become a little less impossible if he had a few technicians shot.

Grinning at the idea, 462 picked up the bag, only to find that it was empty. In the confusion, the kittens had got loose.

A drone slipped in, and passed him a message and scurried out. 462 read the message, screwed it into a ball and spat out a long, complex curse as he strode to the door.

Two praetorians stood guard outside. 'Follow,' he said.

They took a staff hover-car from the Ghast compound to the old Senate house, now the Hyrax's palace. The new regime had started as it meant to continue: there were bloodstains on the street outside the palace, and armed thugs muttered slogans as they watched the road.

The praetorians shoved aside a pair of robed Crusadist guards. 'Get me Gilead,' 462 barked, and he turned up the collar of his trenchcoat against the sun. A cultist led them inside, and at the top of the stairs 462 pushed him out the way and strode into what had been the office of the governor two days before.

He interrupted an argument. Calloway and the Grand Hyrax were yelling at one another across a mahogany desk. Calloway looked round and cried, 'Thank God, someone sane! Tell this madman that he can't have his way!'

462 was not greatly interested. 'What does he want?'

'He wants to abolish talking,' Calloway said. 'Talking!'

'Not talking!' Spit had gathered in the Hyrax's beard. 'Only speech! Listen, idolator, and learn the truth!' He jabbed a grimy finger at Gilead, who sat by the wall, sullen and brutish. 'He is not a true Edenist! He rejects my sacred laws! Oh Holy Annihilator,' he cried, gazing at the

GOD EMPEROR OF DIDCOT

ceiling, 'thank you for making your humble servant such a genius! All praises to the Annhilator, through me!'

'He wants to ban talking!' Calloway cried.

The Hyrax nodded and tugged a wad of hair from his beard. 'Aye! Banning speech will cause misery, and misery is piety! For everyone else. Words are engines of sin, and thus I shall reduce sin by banning all words, except for "The Hyrax is great". How can people sin then, if every time they speak they must sing my praises? How will women call me a grubby little sleaze *then*?'

462 looked at Gilead. 'Well, well, Gilead. I allow you to run this planet and yet already I find you humans squabbling like. . . little squabblers. What is wrong now?'

Gilead stood up. His bullish head on his robot body made him look like a lump of corned beef on the end of a fork. 'Nothing's wrong,' he said. 'We just need to iron out a few. . . er. . . creases.'

'Creases?' 462 shuddered with fury. 'Creases? You should be crushing this planet, and you argue about puny human speech?'

He paused and his vicious eyes moved to the window. All four upper limbs behind his back, he gazed across the city and his voice became distant. 'I have just been informed of two disturbing developments. Firstly, the human ship which escaped during the raid on the space-port was the *John Pym*, the vessel of Isambard Smith. I am disappointed that you did not tell me, Gilead.' He turned, and the bright sun caught on his metal eye. 'I wonder: did you fail to tell me because you did not consider it important enough, or because you feared my response?'

121

'Now look,' Gilead began. 'I hate that hellbound denier as much as anyone—'

'And secondly, your men fired on mine! How dare you!' he shrieked, and the room froze around him. Even the Hyrax was still, staring at the Ghast with wide, frightened, angry eyes. 'Your morons shot at my troops! The praetorian legions are under *my* control! Nobody may throw their lives away but me!'

'They got confused!' Gilead protested. 'You unbelievers all look the same!'

'The same? How – *how* – do I look like a pink moron with two limbs too few and a moustache?'

'Maybe we can come away with some positive action points from this,' Calloway suggested. 'These issues would seem to impact on—'

462 drew his disruptor pistol and pointed it at Calloway's nose. 'Shut up.'

Calloway made a small, terrified noise. 'Oh my God,' he squeaked. 'I just touched base.'

462 shot him. The spin doctor spun on the spot, fell against the wall and 462 shot him three times more.

'Consider yourself downsized, Mr Calloway.' 462 holstered the pistol. He looked around the room. 'Things must change, gentlemen. Until now there has been too much. . . how do you say it in English. . . pratting about like a great big fanny. No more. I myself will deal with the *John Pym*. In the meantime, let this corpse be a lesson, Grand Hyrax. There will be no other incidents like this.' 462 turned to the door. His praetorians waited for him there, ready for violence.

At the doorway he looked back. His eyes had narrowed

into cunning, venomous slits. 'I have read your new laws. Pathetic. Pointless edicts about women. A waste of time.'

'Don't forget fairy-sin,' Gilead put in. 'We need to get tough with fairies.'

'I am not interested in semantics, Gilead.'

'Them too. Big-nosed heathens.'

462 clenched his fists and mouthed a short prayer to Number One. 'Fine. Have your little religious tyranny, but remember, both of you: I put you here, and soon you will pay me back. The Ghast Empire let you take this world. We made you – you in particular, Hyrax. We made you. Don't forget it!'

The ship cut through the lower layers of cloud into a savage storm. 'Bit bumpy!' Carveth said, and the *Pym* rattled, sending the dashboard ornaments into a frenzy of nodding.

'Hold it steady,' Smith said. 'Got somewhere to land yet?'

'Thought I'd try somewhere flat,' Carveth replied. The scan was distorted by the storm but, even so, it looked like strange, untrustworthy ground. The land undulated into weird, wind-blown shapes: hills, crevices and thin, curving pillars that could pierce the underside of the ship like a spike.

One of the legs touched down. A sensor bleeped, the ship creaked and rocked and as Carveth cut the thrusters they felt the undercarriage settle onto the springs. The engines stopped and suddenly they had landed.

'What a craphole,' Carveth said. 'Let's have some tea.'

Five minutes later they met in the sitting room. Carveth

printed off the screen of the diagnostic computer and spread the sheets across the table. Suruk crouched in an armchair in the corner, sharpening a knife while Rhianna searched through the galley cupboards for anything pleasant to eat.

'Right, everyone.' Carveth brushed her small hands together, making her look unexpectedly competent. 'I've had the computer analyse air samples, and it's good news, sort of. This is a type sixteen unclaimed world in semi-primeval state. Solid ground, light atmosphere, no native life. Rock structures are probably silicate with a high sodium content.'

'In practical terms?' Smith said.

'I have no idea. I just read that off a printout. But it's breathable.'

Smith sat down at the table and glanced over the print-outs. They reminded him of the last maths exam he had taken when he was fourteen and, incredibly, they made even less sense. He studied the map warily, in case he was called upon to find its hypotenuse. 'So a human could live out there?'

'Yes.'

'Or a Ghast,' Suruk said. His whetstone slowly scraped down his knife.

Carveth shrugged. 'It's a very primitive place. You'll love it, Suruk. No sentient life forms for you to kill, though.'

The M'Lak peered at the map. 'Small, windy and without intelligent life. We have found your homeworld, little woman.'

Carveth frowned. 'It bothers me, though. The odds are

124

all wrong. Naturally breathable worlds are about as common as an Amish striptease.'

'Well,' said Smith, 'what about the signal you mentioned? Might someone be planetscaping it?'

Carveth nodded. 'It's possible, although they've got a long way to go before it reaches Basic Kent Standard. Someone's been here, but – well, if it wasn't for the signal and the building, I'd have thought they were long gone.'

Smith said, 'Building?'

'Yes, the one with the shuttle next to it.'

'Shuttle?'

'So what would everyone like for dinner?' Rhianna asked.

'Dinner?' cried Smith, and, feeling that he was getting stuck in a rut, he added, 'What's the choice?'

Rhianna held up two cardboard packets in a manner that struck him as oddly erotic. 'Well, we've got synthetic ham, or synthetic lentil curry.'

Smith looked at the boxes. Both had pictures on the front: the two meals looked like different forms of toddler sick. 'I'll skip the synthetic ham, if you don't mind. I've gone off the stuff ever since they started abbreviating it to Sham. Synthetic lentil curry, please.'

'Slurry for me too,' said Carveth. 'So, what should we do?'

'Check for our enemies,' Suruk said. 'If we have to slay anything – which would of course be a dreadful shame – it is better that we should go hunting for it, and not it for us. We should at least scout the area.'

'Building and shuttle are next to each other,' Carveth

said. 'It wouldn't take more than ten minutes if we took the car, even in this storm.'

'We'll drive over there,' Smith said, 'all four of us. Will the car still work?'

Carveth shrugged. 'I can't see why not.'

'Right,' Smith said. 'We'll finish dinner, then drive over. It's going to be nasty out, so wrap up warm. Can someone find Rhianna a pair of boots?'

In the cockpit, the tape was spooling out of the printer. Carveth had seen the first part of the message, the part that said, 'Please land on this world'. Now, unnoticed, the ticker was clicking again. More paper rolled out of the slot. It read: *and save us from this hellish place.*

6

Damned Children!

The car picked its way through the storm. Great pillars of rock loomed over them like giants emerging from the mist.

Muffled against the cold, Carveth pointed with a mittened finger. 'Just over this hill,' she said. A huge column formed out of the storm and she peered at it. 'Don't like the looks of this, Boss.'

Smith's pistol was at his side. The shotgun was in the boot, along with his rifle. He wore goggles and a hat. 'No?'

She shook her head and turned the heater up to full. 'I don't know. These columns look way too phallic to be natural. It gives me the willies.' Carveth leaned in and studied the dials on the dashboard. 'We should be there by now. Almost on top of it—'

A shape burst into view like the prow of a ship cutting through a bank of fog. It looked like a green metal cliff. The car bumped past the battered flank of a military shuttle, its green sides pitted and scratched. The cockpit was dirty and there were no lights on. Beside the cockpit, ten feet above the car, the chipped cartoon of an eagle winked and gave them a cheery salute. Letters around the drawing said: UFSAAF.

'Free States,' Smith said. 'It's allied territory, at least.'

A buggy stood beside the shuttle, a tarpaulin whipping around its wheels. It was solid and heavy, built for this kind of terrain.

Carveth looked up at the shuttle. The wind had scrubbed the paint away from the sides, leaving streaks of bare metal. 'Must have been here ages.'

'They wouldn't have just left it here,' Smith said. 'They must have abandoned it for a reason.'

'I don't like this,' Rhianna said. 'It just feels. . . wrong.'

Smith pointed straight ahead, squinting into the storm. 'Bloody hell,' he said, 'what is *that*?'

It looked like the carcass of a gigantic beetle, minus the legs. It lay flat on the ground, sixty feet long, engineered to weather the storm.

Smith stopped the car. 'Ghasts. Everyone out.'

They opened doors and hurried, heads down, to the back of the car. Carveth opened the boot and took the shotgun. Smith took the rifle. They said nothing as they loaded up. The wind set the bobble flapping on Carveth's woolly hat.

'I suppose you're going to say that we have to look inside,' she said. Her gloves made heavy work of the gun.

'The very fact it seems to have been made by Ghasts is reason enough,' Smith replied. 'Who knows what evil Gertie has been plotting in there? Ladies, stay here,' Smith said. He looked at Suruk. 'Fancy something new for the mantelpiece?'

The alien lowered his mandibles and gripped his spear in both hands. 'Let us begin.'

'Can I help?' Rhianna asked.

Suruk shook his head. 'It may be booby-trapped. Let us who have no boobies go first.'

Smith jogged out, bent low, rifle ready. Suruk paced beside him. The wind battered them and howled at their ears. Smith glanced left and right, at the high towers around them, and wondered if these too were the work of Ghasts. The dark, sloping side of the building rose up ahead.

Rhianna watched them disappear into the wind. 'What's going on?' she asked.

Carveth fumbled out a pair of binoculars. 'Hang on. They're going in. . . up the back.'

Suruk was first. At the rear of the structure, a high, spherical iris lock stood open, its edges puckered and frozen from disuse. He stopped at one side, waited for Smith to catch up, and nodded at the inside. Smith nodded back, and together they lunged around the doorway.

It was a hall, high-ceilinged and dark, lit only by a few half-dead florescent roof-lights. The floor was ridged, the walls also. Smith had the nasty feeling that he had climbed into something's ribcage via its fundament.

The remnants of Ghast propaganda posters hung on the wall: Number One shook his claws and fists at Earth; a praetorian gazed towards the future, head titled up in a kind of arrogant rapture; a grinning Ghast, in what might have been conceived as a relaxing setting, was doing something baffling yet vigorous with a set of Indian clubs. They all looked meaningless, like empty threats.

Time comes for us all, Smith thought. Even the Ghasts, with their dreams of conquest, become nothing: just dust and bone. Space swallows us all, turns us to dust. That hole in the wall looks like a doodah. Yuck.

In the centre of the room stood a short, barrel-sized plinth. On top of it was a starfish-shaped control panel, which allowed five operators to work at once. The operators lay around the base of the machine, very dead.

They were Ghast scientists, their white coats spattered with their own blood. Smith beckoned Suruk over and pointed. 'Shot,' he said. 'Bullet wounds.'

The M'Lak nodded. 'Here,' he said.

Pipes ran from the base of the plinth to the walls: thick, veined tubes fixed to the floor. There were half a dozen recesses in the walls, big enough for a man to stand in, like sentry boxes.

'Strange,' Smith said. The words *dirty alien stuff* sprang into his mind, but there was something uncomfortably familiar about those recesses in the walls.

'Look,' Suruk said.

There were humans on the ground. A dozen armoured men and women lay against the far wall in the shadows, as if they had all travelled there to die. They wore camouflage. Smith did not need to see the stripes on their uniforms to know that they were the crew of the shuttle outside.

'They are all dead,' Suruk said. 'Bullet wounds. They shot themselves.'

Smith nodded. 'You may as well get the others. Whatever happened here is long finished. For once it's us who've turned up late to the fighting.'

*

'So,' said Smith, 'I suppose they must have come in, killed the Ghasts, and then committed suicide. That would seem to be the only course of events that makes sense.'

'But why kill themselves?' Rhianna stood a little way back, looking nervous. The wind howled around the building as if lamenting the dead creatures inside.

'Well,' said Smith, looking at the bodies, 'foreigners are known to be excitable.'

'Oh, come on,' Carveth said from near the doors. 'You mean they killed the guards and had a massacre to celebrate? Most people settle for a couple of beers, not a rifle under the chin. They must have meant to do themselves. Maybe they despaired of being inside a building made from a beetle's bottom.'

Smith bent down and came up with a piece of paper in his hand. 'This chap's holding a note. . . Let's see. He's given it a title: *The Thing in the Building*, by Captain Howard Poe. I wonder if this will help.'

He paused, scanned through the words, and began to read.

'*As these, my final moments, draw to a close, I can only theorise that the most merciful aspect of the human psyche is its inability to correlate the horrors it views into a totality of blackest nightmare, from which it must needs retreat into merciful oblivion.*'

'Keen Scrabble player, from the sounds of it,' Carveth said.

'*My story begins last May, when my squad and I carried out a raid on this post on storm-haunted Didcot 5. We were informed that the garrison was minute, valuing secrecy over numerical fortitude, and we overcame the*

Ghasts easily, then paused to celebrate our success. Oh, Irony! If only I had known of the depths of squamous terror and cthonian hell to which we would descend!

'Now, *where was I? Cthonian hell. Right. As we explored the vault of the Ghasts, we perceived tanks on the wall, monitored by a barrel-shaped control panel. My men and I drew closer, and I recalled fragments of the forbidden, night-swathed book I had once read—*'

'How do you read a night-swathed book?' Carveth said. 'Wouldn't it be a bit dark?'

Smith shrugged. 'Probably a metaphor. Now, pay attention. It may be going somewhere. This man was obviously suffering from something serious.'

'Terminal verbal diarrhoea?'

'Shush! Listen.'

'*My men spread out, and I approached the strange, liquid-filled tanks, my trembling hands gripping my cock—*'

Smith turned the page.

'*–ed rifle. It was a scene worthy of Goya or the wildest Cubists, for in the tank, so far removed from the sane world of mankind or the comfort of rational law, I saw that which sent me over the abyss of horror, into the Stygian night of madness. It was – A MAN!!!*

'*Well, a boy.*'

'What?' said Carveth. 'That was rubbish! Doesn't he say anything else?'

Smith frowned. 'It becomes rather incomprehensible now. *Batrachian foulness . . . Ia! . . . it cannot be . . . All-consuming horror . . . Pencil getting blunt . . .* And that's it.'

Carveth snorted. 'Well! It could at least have been a fish-monster or something. And to think that all this time I've been damn near weeing myself for nothing.' She looked at the pile of bodies. 'Well, they're all dead. Can I go now?'

'What a totally horrible story,' Rhianna said. 'They all killed themselves. . . that's really bad.' She shuddered. 'Still, I suppose it just goes to show that militarism is ultimately self-destructive,' she added, brightening a little.

Smith looked around the room. It was a mausoleum for the Ghast scientists and the soldiers who had come to fight them. Whatever had killed them, be it madness or some physical enemy, was gone. Smith had expected a battle, and then had hoped for an explanation, but had received neither.

Smith turned to Carveth. 'They sent that signal you picked up from their ship. If you head back now, I'll get to work on the transmitter. I should be able to record a new message. Maybe that way we can warn the Empire about Urn.' He sighed. 'It's worth a try anyway, though I doubt it'll have sufficient range. You may as well head back, Carveth,' he said. 'The sooner you can start on the repairs, the sooner we can be on our way. You could take that buggy outside – those things are virtually in-destructible – and we'll see you back at the ship.'

'Good,' she said with evident relief. 'Typical, isn't it? I find twelve men and they're all the wrong kind of stiff.'

'On second thoughts, that's an order. Leave.'

'Righto, Boss.'

He looked around at Rhianna. 'Do you want to go back

with Carveth? I'm sure there'd be plenty of room in that buggy. It looked like it would still work.'

She shook her head. 'I'm alright. I feel safer here with you.'

'Really?'

'Really.' She took a step closer to him.

'Well,' he said, 'erm, good. I mean, there's nothing alive here – although I can keep you safe, should anything happen.'

She smiled at him; he smiled back. A few seconds passed.

Some emergency sensor inside Smith noticed a dangerously high level of sexual tension and made him step away from it. 'Well, crikey,' he said. 'Suppose this transmitter won't fix itself, eh? Since Suruk's from another planet and you're a girl, I suppose I'd better get on with it.'

'I'm sure I could do something,' Rhianna replied, smiling slightly less. 'Not all women are useless, Isambard.'

'True. In that case, come and hold the torch.'

Suruk took a long, thoughtful look around the cavernous room. 'Nobody to fight at all,' he said glumly. 'We are warriors, not tourists!'

'Damn strange,' Smith said. 'And a nuisance. It bothers me too, Suruk – these men shooting themselves, that note – it's just not right. Some evil is at work here.'

It did not take long to reprogram the transmitter. Smith typed in a new message – 'Gertie has Urn, send dread-noughts' – and sent it into the ether. Then he fetched blankets from the UFS ship and laid them over the dead soldiers. It seemed the best thing to do: hardly a burial, but it was better than leaving them exposed.

As the car reached the *John Pym*, Smith realised that something was wrong. The light was on in the cab of the buggy and Carveth still sat in it. Lights were on in the *Pym*, too – and as Smith approached a figure moved across the cockpit, too short for anyone who should be there.

'Trouble,' he said. He stopped the car behind a low hill, out of sight of the ship. 'Stay here, everyone,' he said, and he got out, taking the rifle with him, and ran quick and low over to the buggy, the wind pushing him on.

He reached the far side of the buggy and climbed up to the cab. He knocked on the door, Carveth opened it and he scrambled inside. Smith slammed the door and the storm was gone.

She sat at the driver's seat. She looked at him a little blankly, as if not quite certain where they'd met before. 'Hi again,' she said.

'Hello,' he replied. The cab was big and warm. 'Why aren't you in the ship?'

She blinked. 'Ship? Oh, *that* ship. Kids've locked me out.'

'What? What kids?'

'Kids who've got it.'

'What? What the devil are you on about?'

'Kids came along. They wanted it, and it's theirs now.'

A sense of horror was building up in Smith's gut. Suddenly, he had stepped into a world that was not just dangerous but inexplicable.

'So,' he began, wrestling with the words, 'so let me get this straight. . . Some children showed up and you sold them our ship. Are you mad?'

Carveth raised her mittens. 'No, no,' she said placatingly. 'You've got it wrong.'

'Thank God!'

'I gave it to them.'

He was not sure if he had just screamed. 'You did *what*? You *gave* our ship away! You idiot! You stupid, stupid woman!'

Carveth wriggled on her seat. 'There is a reasonable explanation for this, you know.'

'I'd bloody like to hear it!'

'It seemed a good idea at the time,' she said feebly. 'Honestly. I had no choice.'

'No choice? What kind of reason is that? You gave our ship to children! Right, that's it,' he declared. 'I'm going to get it back.'

'You can't,' she said. 'They've locked the doors.'

'What? You didn't even take our stuff out first? I bloody well hope they can't fly it. What in hell's name possessed you?' She started to say something, but he wasn't listening. The fist of his mind was thumping the pieces of the jigsaw puzzle into place. Suddenly it all made sense. 'Possessed you,' he said numbly. 'Possessed you. Carveth, this is what those Americans saw. This is what made them kill themselves. Psychics.'

She nodded slowly, pained, and he felt guilty for shouting at her. He drew back. 'So we're locked out,' he said.

'Yes.'

Smith took a deep breath and ran a hand through his hair. 'Well,' he said grimly, 'they're just going to have to let us back in again, aren't they? Stay here.' He opened the door, climbed out and slammed it behind him. He strode across to the car and looked inside.

'Right then. What works with children?'

'Cranberry sauce!' Suruk said.

'I think you may have misunderstood the question. Rhianna?'

'I – I guess I can deal with children. Why?'

'Right. A bunch of sprogs have conned Carveth into giving them the keys. They seem to have used some sort of psychic power on her. We're bloody lucky they don't know how to fly it, but they've got the Haynes manual and it's only a matter of time before they figure it out. We have to get back inside.'

'Boss,' Carveth said from behind. He glanced round. The sheer amount of clothing she wore gave her the outline of an oversized toddler. 'I was thinking: you remember those recesses in the walls of that Ghast place? I reckon they were growth tanks. For simulants.'

Smith said, 'You mean these children are androids? Don't you lot come out fully grown?'

She nodded. 'We do, but who knows? It's just. . . well, they have powers. I don't remember giving them the ship. I remember them coming to the door, and I remember sitting in the cab of that truck thing, but I don't recall anything in between. It's like I was missing a load of hours. I've never known that to happen before.' She frowned. 'Without a hangover.'

Rhianna said, 'You mean they *made* you do that? With

137

psychic powers?' To Smith she said, 'I'm coming with you. I may be able to counter them.'

Smith thought about it. 'Alright then,' he said. 'But be careful.'

She got out of the car and closed the door. Smith gave the rifle to Suruk and together they walked through the wind towards the ship. The storm had eased a little, but it threw Rhianna's skirt around like a tie-dyed rag. Smith's coat flapped out behind him.

As they approached, the airlock opened. In the doorway stood a boy of about nine, in long socks, shorts and a well-pressed tank top. He did not lower the steps.

'You, boy!' Smith called.

'Stop right there,' the boy replied. 'This ship belongs to us now. You may not enter. Go away.'

'Righto,' Smith said. He turned, stopped, turned back again and called out 'No, *not* righto! This ship is ours, and you stole it. Come down from there at once and bugger off.'

'Go away, you rotter,' the boy said. 'Who do you think you are, coming here and making a big stink? You'd better scarper, or there'll be trouble.'

A girl joined the boy on the steps. She had a pleated skirt and pigtails but otherwise looked identical to the boy. 'Beetle off!' she shouted.

'I'm coming in,' Smith declared. 'If you don't naff off on the count of three, I'll thrash you senseless, you little brat!'

The boy and girl looked at each other, as synchronised as the figures on an old Swiss clock emerging to strike the hours. 'I think we should show him what for,' said the girl. 'I think his girlie should be made to stop him.'

'I agree,' the boy said. 'This spaceship is wizard, and it's ours now.'

Softly, Rhianna said, 'I don't like this, Isambard.'

Smith took a step forward and the girl stuck out her hand. Rhianna grabbed her head and folded as if struck. 'Resist him!' cried the boy.

'Rhianna!' Smith cried.

She darted out and sat down in front of him.

'Resist!' the girl yelled.

Smith took a step towards Rhianna. She closed her eyes. He sidestepped, hoping to get round her: she shuffled quickly aside and blocked his way. 'Rhianna!' he said. 'Rhianna!'

'She belongs to us now!' the boy called.

'Just like your ship!' said the girl.

'You little bastards!' Smith yelled. 'This woman is under British protection! Give her back!'

'Boo to you, you old codger!' the boy replied. Smith felt something bore into his skull like a searchlight: a beam of thought, raw and powerful. *Kill her*, it said, *kill her now*, and he summoned up his moral fibre, met the beam full-on and thought, *Stick it, moon-sprog*.

Mittens tugged his sleeve. He whipped around and saw Carveth. 'Come on, Boss,' she said. 'Let's go.'

'Dammit, they've got Rhianna!'

The android glanced at Rhianna, who still sat in their way. 'Just be glad she only does passive resistance,' she said. 'Otherwise she'd probably – Boss. . . uh-oh.'

Carveth leaped at Smith's neck. She was startlingly

quick, her hands unexpectedly strong. She grabbed his throat, frothing. 'Wiwiwiwi,' she garbled.

A piece of rock hit Carveth in the back of the head and she fell. Smith grabbed her, threw her over his shoulder and ran back to the buggy, where Suruk waited with another, larger, rock ready in his hand in case she awoke.

'Well,' Smith said, 'I think we know what happened to the Americans.'

Suruk nodded. 'A bad death.'

They sat in the cab of the buggy. The heater was on. Carveth slowly rubbed her head. 'What I don't get is why they hit me with a rock,' she said.

'Who can say?' Suruk said.

'My head feels terrible.' She leaned over and continued scribbling in the notebook on her lap.

'They must be some sort of Ghast experiment,' Smith said. 'That's what this place is for – research. The soldiers must have stumbled upon it and the Ghast technicians set those children-things on them. Then they must have turned on the soldiers. Or vice versa.'

'Children of the Ghasts,' Suruk said.

'Quite. The Ghasts must have engineered them in those tanks. It makes sense, I suppose. The Ghasts were fascinated by Rhianna. They've been trying to make something like her out here – I suppose they succeeded, in a way. Dammit! We've got to get our ship back, before they work out how to fly it!' He looked at Carveth. 'How about you?' Smith said. 'Any ideas?'

Carveth had been scribbling something on her notepad

for the past half hour. She shook her head. 'Polly's still collating.'

'Carveth, you've been collating for ages. You must have come up with something. Let's have a look.'

He took the notebook from her and peered at it. 'What is all this?'

Carveth said warily, 'A plan.'

'Hmm,' said Smith. 'It doesn't look like a plan. It looks more like a picture of some ponies.'

'That's just a doodle. Look, this is us, up here.'

'Riding the ponies.'

'Well, yes.'

Smith's eyes hardened. 'Carveth, this is not good enough. I asked you to figure out how to get back the ship – which *you* gave away – and you've spent the past half-hour drawing a picture of little horses. What the devil are you playing at, woman?'

'Right!' she yelled, and she snatched the notebook back. 'Right! No more ponies!', and she started to tear out the pages with reckless fury. 'No more ponies! No – more!' She threw the pages at the dashboard and they fell at her feet. She burst into tears.

'It's all my fault!' she wailed. 'I didn't mean to! They made me give them the ship, and now they'll leave us here and no-one will rescue Urn and the Empire won't get any tea and we'll lose the war and the Ghasts will invade Earth and exterminate the human race and I'm fa-a-at!'

Shocked, Smith said, 'No, Carveth! There's always hope!'

'Just look at me! I'm like a balloon!'

'I meant getting the ship back, and the whole saving Earth thing.'

'So I'm still fat?'

Patiently, Smith said, 'No, you're not fat. And as the person who knows the most about the ship, could you tell us if there's another way in? Before I wring your chubby neck,' he added under his breath.

'I locked the bay doors too,' Carveth said. She sniffed loudly. 'You can't get in at all unless you climb up the broken leg and open the floorboards, and—' She looked up. 'Hey, yeah. You could do that. I mean, if they were looking the other way. . .'

Ten minutes later, Suruk crouched behind a particularly unwholesome-looking rock, ready to wield the sacred spear of his ancestors. He leaned over and said, 'What do you see?'

Carveth drew back from the edge and looked back at him. 'Can't see much. Rhianna's still sitting there – she's out of it. We ought to get her back soon; her coat's open, and she's not got enough on underneath. No sign of the Cap.' She pulled back her coat and mitten and looked at her watch. 'He's got five minutes.'

'I see. This is not how I would have chosen to spend my time, little woman.'

'Really? You mean you didn't *want* to get brainwashed and have the ship stolen?'

'Do not mock me. This is not warrior's work, creeping up on a pack of infants. I should be fighting, up to my arms in blood – not distracting creatures a tenth of my size.'

'Well, got any better plans? These alien children are no pushover, you know. They have incredible powers; they managed to take over my brain.'

'Clearly they are mighty. Locating it through your skull would be no easy task. Frankly I am surprised they did not think it was just a spare piece of breakfast and look elsewhere. Personally, I would rather creep inside the ship and slay these beings with a blade.'

Carveth was shocked. 'They're children, Suruk.'

The M'Lak shrugged. 'So? When I was young, I would have been grateful to have been killed swiftly with a knife. Children these days don't know they've been spawned.'

Carveth's radio went off. 'Boss?'

'I'm in place,' Smith said.

'Is Rhianna alright?'

'She's unconscious, but she looks pretty good. I've got it in hand.'

'I feared as much. Alright, let's go.'

'Righto. Good luck.'

Smith closed the radio, pulled on his hat and goggles and ran from cover to the rear of the ship. The wind howled around him. Rhianna was motionless. He wanted to put his coat around her to keep her warm, but it would be visible from the ship and would alert the children. Instead he jogged into the shadow of the ship, towards the landing legs.

Now, which one was it? Left back, she'd said. He flexed his fingers in his gloves, trying to recall the best way to climb a pole. Smith realised he had not climbed anything since he had been eight, and all he could remember of it was rope-burn and the smell of socks. Well, he'd just have to try.

As he reached the leg, shouts came from the front of the ship. Smith peered into the storm and saw two figures approach, waving their arms.

'Hey, kids!' Carveth called. 'We've got some stuff here for you!'

Smith looked at the leg and wondered whether the loose cabling would help him to climb up or fry him to a cinder. Oh well. He tensed his muscles, jumped up, and caught hold of one of the struts used to raise the leg.

There was a scrape of metal on metal and the airlock door opened. Above Smith, a child's voice called, 'We told you to go away!'

'We have food, brain-spawn,' Suruk said.

'What sort of food?'

Smith pulled himself up, teeth gritted. He sat on the strut, bracing himself for the next stage of the climb, listening to the wind as Carveth and Suruk made up their response.

'Beer?' Suruk said hopefully.

'Beer tastes of wee and sick,' said the child. 'We don't want your—'

'Ginger ale!' Carveth called. 'And pies!'

'Hmm. . .' said the child. 'How much ginger ale?'

'Lashings, of course. Enough for a super picnic.'

'Wait there.'

Smith heard the door close. He drew upright and climbed into the cavity where the leg retracted during flight. The noise of the storm lessened. It was a dark, bad-smelling hole, the sort of place popular with rats and hitchhiking aliens. He took his penknife out and opened the screwdriver, then got to work on the panel above his head.

Negotiations over the ginger ale had started again. Carveth clearly knew how to talk to children on their own terms – probably, he reflected, because she was not unlike a child herself.

The panel came away in his hands and he dropped it. The sound of it striking the ground was muffled by the wind. Smith was not worried about the children hearing him – it was them sensing him that he feared.

There were some more cables above him. He stuck his head through them, feeling like a meatball being pushed through spaghetti. His scalp impacted with the inner plating, and he readied the penknife again, this time using the Phillips head.

Smith worked quickly: not even a nine-year-old could talk about party food forever – although Carveth probably could. He took out one screw, then the second, then the third, and finally, the fourth dropped into his palm. He pocketed it and prepared his secret weapon.

There had been some emergency rations in the American buggy, and they had come in foil packages. Smith removed his goggles and leather hat, unfolded two empty packages and put them on his head. He put the hat back on over them. He smelt of barbecue sauce, but if it stopped the children taking control of his brain, it was a small price to pay.

Smith pushed the plate up a fraction and peeked through the gap. He was looking into the hold. He glanced left and right, then listened: nobody. Quickly, he pushed the panel aside and climbed up. He was in.

He stood up and put the panel back. Smith knew how to move quietly. Legs bent, he advanced across the hold, towards the lounge.

He stopped, his breath loud in his ears, listening. Very carefully, he leaned around the door.

The lounge was empty. Smith stepped onto the rug and hurried across the room. The lounge led into a corridor, which in turn ran straight to the cockpit. The cabins branched off the corridor.

There were voices in the corridor. Small feet pattered on the metal floor.

'Corks, that's an awful lot of ginger beer,' a child said. 'Think of the picnic we could have with that!'

'Huh,' said a second. 'I don't believe a word of it. They're trying to swiz us. That stinker captain probably wants his ship back. Besides, think of all the ginger beer we can have when we're running Earth.'

Devil children, thought Smith. They needed a damn good talking to.

'I just felt something,' said a girl.

'Maybe we should demand more ginger beer,' said another.

'Something nearby. . .'

Smith felt a mind turn on him like a spotlight, a sudden, penetrating beam of intellect tearing at his brain. He closed his eyes, tried to block it, and then they had him.

A child stood in the doorway, pointing. 'Look, there he is! He's got in!'

'The blighter! Make him scram!'

'No,' said another child. 'Make him die.'

And suddenly the beam was no longer a searchlight but a burning ray, a laser, cutting into Smith's brain, slicing away the links between body and mind—

'Make him shoot himself!'

Shoot myself, thought Smith. Now there's an idea. Why didn't I think of that earlier?

He looked down: he was surrounded by staring clones, hands on hips, glaring into his soul. His right hand came up and the Civiliser was in it. It rose in front of him like a cobra rearing to strike.

'Do it! Shoot yourself!'

Smith put the cold barrel under his chin. No, that would make a terrible mess. He frowned, trying to remember the socially acceptable way of blowing out his brains. How would a gentleman do it? From the side, or barrel in the mouth?

From the side. His thumb cocked the hammer. Somewhere, deep inside him, a little part of his mind said: Is this what I really want?

It wasn't. Suddenly Smith realised that killing himself was a bad idea. But the gun would not go away. Under his hat and improvised brain shield he felt sweat crawl through his hair. The best he could do was not to fire; to put the Civiliser down was like moving a mountain. It seemed a cruel irony that he was about to Civilise himself.

From outside, he heard Carveth's voice, as if through water. 'Do you want this ginger beer or not? Because if you don't, I'm taking it back to Smugglers' Cove!'

'An adventure with smugglers!' a boy cried, and the beam weakened. Smith saw one of the children turn from him, shook his head and ran straight into the opposite wall. That woke him up a lot. Their grip was still strong, but he knew what he must do. He lurched across the room, into the kitchen area. His shaking hands dropped the gun, threw open the nearest cupboard, found the jar and tore off the lid.

They knew what he was doing now, and they were fighting him. He grabbed his wrist as if choking a snake, gritted his teeth and hauled his fist towards his mouth. He strained – hardly able to breathe – and rammed half a dozen teabags into his mouth. He bit down and pure, unstrained tea rushed into his system. Grabbing a carton from the counter, he gulped heavily on the milk. Moral fibre shot through his body. As if shaking a demon from his back, he roared and threw off their mental control, grabbed the Civiliser, pointed it at them and cried 'Hunf ub!'

They stared at him, baffled.

Smith swallowed a wad of tea. 'Hands up,' he said. 'That's better.'

They put their hands up, slowly. 'Are you a smuggler?' said the nearest child.

Liquid trickled down Smith's scalp. For a horrible moment he thought that his brain had actually melted, but then he realised that the foil tins on his head had not been quite as clean as he had thought. 'Men!' he called. 'Get Rhianna in!'

Suruk and Carveth helped her through the door. 'Golly!' cried one of the children, spotting the alien. 'It's a real-live colonial!'

Smith coughed. His mouth was still packed with

tea-grit, and the remnants of the teabags were proving quite hard to swallow. 'Children!' he declared. 'I am very disappointed with you. Not only have you tried to steal my spacecraft and murdered a dozen allied soldiers, but you've been very disobedient when I asked you to give it back. *This will not do.*'

There was awkward shuffling among the children. One said, 'Sorry, sir.'

'That's better.'

Rhianna sat down on the sofa, rubbing her head. A child peered at her. 'Are you my mummy?' it asked.

'I don't think so,' she said.

Carveth looked around the room. 'Are they going to use their powers again?'

Smith shook his head. 'I doubt it. Have some tea. It seems to block them out.'

He paused. His head ached, and he glanced around the room to make sure that none of the children were trying their psychic tricks.

He blinked the thought away. 'Well done, men,' he said. 'It was only you distracting them that saved me. They nearly escaped with our ship.'

She shrugged. 'Well, ships don't just repair themselves. I'd best get out there and sort us out. Don't let Suruk eat anyone.'

Smith looked into the kitchen area. Suruk was surrounded by small figures. He looked puzzled. 'Is it true that you eat people?' a child demanded, intrigued by him.

'No.'

'Are you good at dancing?'

'Only on the skulls of irritating children.'

'Gosh, can we see? Do you have a big tail in your trousers? Steve Hyrax says that all greenies have great big tails.'

Suruk leaned over and picked the boy up by his jumper. 'Say that again,' he said.

The boy swallowed and looked into Suruk's maw. 'You have big tails, and you run round stark naked, chopping each other's heads off—'

'Who told you this?'

'Steve Hyrax. He's one of us, but Gertie came and took him away a year ago, and we've not seen him since—'

'Mazuran,' Suruk said. 'Come here, now!'

'So the Hyrax was one of them,' Rhianna said half an hour later. 'No wonder he could mesmerise the crowds like that.'

They sat in the lounge, drinking tea. Carveth was somewhere outside, checking her repairs. Smith leaned over and took a biscuit.

'Quite,' he said. 'The Ghasts must have engineered those children, and once they got one that would do what they needed, they artificially aged him and sent him to Urn. A devilish plan.'

Rhianna nodded. 'That's. . . that's really nasty,' she said, and Smith felt the familiar urge to put his arm around her. '. . . Whoa.'

'Against an enemy without moral fibre, it would be devastating,' Smith said. 'Their concerted mental energy almost had me. As it was, I was lucky that they were distracted long enough for me to eat raw tea.' He picked a bit of grit out of his teeth. 'Of course, I suppose the

Ghasts didn't expect the people of Urn to be such regular tea drinkers. Nor, I suppose, did they reckon on a UFS ship interrupting them.'

Suruk said, 'So what of these spawn? Will they be destroyed?'

'We'll alter the transmission and warn Fleet Control to have this place quarantined.' Smith nodded at the cupboards. 'We can spare some food to tide them over. Perhaps, with the help of the Imperial code and regular tea, they can learn to lead normal lives.'

The airlock door opened, and Carveth returned, slamming it behind her. 'Hello,' she announced, stepping into the sitting room and pulling off her coat. 'I've sent the kids back to the Ghast place. We're done outside.'

'Much damage?' Smith asked.

She shook her head. 'I had a lot of helpers. They're good workers, those children. Little Julian looked out for Titty while she checked the hole in the *John Pym*, while I used a digital screwdriver to help Roger, Dick and Fanny. What'll happen to them when we're gone?'

'Apparently, they will be given provisions,' Suruk said. 'It is no wonder humans are so weak. On my world, the young are left to fight among themselves, ensuring that the strong survive. It never did me any harm. Now, if you will excuse me, I must go and polish my skull collection.'

7

The Sauceress

It was great to be back in space. Smith swigged from his
bottle of beer and crossed the sitting room to the drinks
cabinet. The doors parted with a hydraulic whine, and he
squatted down to see what was left inside. He peered at
the bottles: gin from the Indian Empire, navy rum capable
of standing in for bleach, a bottle of tequila from which
Suruk had already removed the worm, some sort of self-
mixing snowball canisters that Carveth had bought – ah,
there it was. At the rear was the ship's bottle of sherry. He
fished it out and poured a double measure into an unfolding wine glass.

Suruk was in the hold, whirling his spear in what he
called the Corrosive Panda style. Rhianna had retired to
her room to meditate and Carveth was piloting the ship,
or at least in the control room. The door was ajar and
Smith could hear her singing along merrily to The
Specials. He strolled down the corridor and joined her in
the cockpit.

Carveth's feet were up on the console, where the less
important controls were, and she was reading a pastel-
coloured book with a cartoon of a bride and a
squid-headed monster on the front.

'Hullo,' said Smith. 'What's the book?'

'It's called *Love Craft*,' she said. She turned it over and read from the back: ' "Sophie thought that Ben was the one – but was he an alien star god hell-bent on destroying Earth?" '

'Girl's stuff, eh?' Smith said. 'Thought I'd bring you a drink.'

He passed it to her. 'Cheers, Cap,' she said, beaming. Carveth took a deep swig of sherry. 'That's good.'

'It's bad form to drink alone,' Smith said, taking a sip of beer. 'How's the ship doing?'

'Well, we're still inside it, so we've not sprung any leaks. Journey time estimated at thirty-six hours standard. Provided they don't eat us when we get there, we'll be fine.'

'Good.' Smith looked over the control panel, past a row of polished dials, some brass switches that did something or other, and over to the map on the main monitor, where a dotted red line crawled across the screen, showing their progress through the system. 'Been feeling a bit bad, actually,' he said to the monitor. 'Shouldn't have sounded off at you earlier. You did a good job getting the ship back, you know.'

Carveth shrugged. 'I probably shouldn't have given it away. You know, if there's one thing worse than fighting aliens, it's not fighting aliens but bloody kids instead. One of Oscar Wilde's, that.'

'Really?'

'No.' She belched. 'That was, though.'

The door opened and Rhianna came in. Because she tended not to wear shoes on the ship, she was able to move silently between rooms. Smith found it unnerving that he never knew where she was: once he had dreamed that he had run out of paper whilst using the lavatory, and that she had popped out the cistern and handed him a new roll. 'Hi everyone,' she said.

Rhianna adjusted the band that held her dreadlocks in place. She had shed her heavy coat, and now looked very much as before. 'Now, there's something I want us to all do.'

Carveth gave Smith a sour look.

'Oh yes?' said Smith.

'Okay,' Rhianna said. Her voice had a patient, slightly weary sound, like a primary teacher trying to halt a classroom riot. 'Now, I understand earlier that there were some. . . negative feelings expressed. Some bad energy was created, and what does bad energy produce?'

'Farts,' Carveth said.

'Disempowerment. So, both of you, I think we should renew our. . . our oneness as a group by expressing our real feelings, in a sort of—'

'Don't say it,' Carveth muttered.

'A workshop.'

'Ugh.'

'So come along: I'd like both of you to open up to one another, to try to move beyond the stigma you must feel. I know it's difficult, being British, but try to – to put into words the emotions you truly feel. Let your positive feelings flow.'

Carveth looked at Smith and scowled. *Sorry*, he mouthed.

'You're alright, Captain,' Carveth said.

There was a pause. 'Anything more, maybe?' Rhianna prompted.

'You're quite alright, Captain.'

Smith nodded. 'Likewise, Carveth. Carry on.'

'Oh, come on, guys,' Rhianna said. 'Make up properly, and you can both forget that you ever argued.'

'We *had* forgotten,' Carveth said.

Rhianna turned to Smith. 'Now then. Isambard, you can lead. Big hug.'

Smith got up. 'Righto!'

'Hug Polly, not me, Isambard.'

'Oh, right.' He approached Carveth warily, as if about to dance with a porcupine. She stuck her arms out like a tin robot. They hugged, disdainfully. 'Aw,' said Rhianna, and embraced them both.

Carveth's eyes suddenly widened and she pulled away quickly. Smith sat down. Rhianna said, 'Now we're all friends again!' and she left the room.

Carveth swallowed hard. 'I feel violated,' she said.

'Yes,' said Smith, choosing his words carefully. 'Much as I like Rhianna, all this positive energy stuff leaves one feeling rather deflated.'

'You sure as hell weren't deflated when she put her arms round us. You could have someone's eye out with that.'

Smith spent the next couple of hours fighting with Suruk in the hold. It was not easy to move around their battered car, but that gave Smith an advantage, for Suruk had a longer reach than him.

The M'Lak whipped the spear around his head; Smith sidestepped and came in with a sword-cut that Suruk

TOBY FROST

knocked away with the flat of his hand. Suruk flicked the butt of the spear up at Smith's head, and the captain ducked and rolled back and came up panting.

Suruk grinned. 'You use the Spherical Panther style,' he observed. 'You have got better with a blade.'

Smith puffed. 'It reminds me of when we first met.'

'The Spherical Panther?'

'You trying to stick a spear in me.'

'Ah, yes. Happy days.' The alien paused, weapon readied. 'I am glad that you fight well, friend. And not just with guns, but properly.'

'I need a sit-down,' said Smith. 'I wish I hadn't had all that beer.'

'I am serious, Mazuran. My homeworld is a place of honour, but honour must be won. You should watch your harem well on my clan's world, in case someone decides to chop off their heads.'

'They're not my harem, Suruk. Rhianna doesn't seem to regard me as a man at all, and as for Carveth – well, I may be a space captain, but there are some places even I wouldn't boldly go.'

'True. But the weak females may be better left locked on the ship. My people are fierce, and all are martial artists of great skill. My father, for instance, once spent eight moons in the wilderness, seeking the way of the Hidden Masters of Gorong. Wise and fast is my father, but he never found them. They are not called the Hidden Masters for nothing.'

'Thanks for the advice.' Smith slid his sword back into the scabbard on his hip. 'It's always best to tread carefully when dealing with other cultures,' he agreed, reminding himself of the time when he had coughed up tea when some idiot foreigner had tried to make him drink it without milk. Bloody trade talks. Bloody Japanese ambassador. Bloody swordfight.

Carveth appeared at the door with a tray. 'Tea's up,' she said. 'We've made good time. In a few hours we should be able to start landing. I've put that bottle of wine we got at the service spacestation in your bag. May as well bring them a gift.'

'Great,' said Smith, taking a mug. 'Although I doubt they even know what wine is.'

'We're on autopilot, if you're wondering,' Carveth said.

Although fine in the darkness of space, the autopilot had developed a tendency to initiate landing procedure when confronted by bright lights, which was useful near landing strips and less useful near the sun. 'Did you take Rhianna some tea?'

'I asked, but she didn't want any.'

Smith frowned. 'She certainly is strange sometimes. I wish I knew what makes her tick.'

'Freeing the Disabled Lesbian Whales,' Carveth said. She sipped her tea and sat down on a packing crate. 'You know what your problem is? You're too nice. That's why someone like Gilead would get women, if he had a body. He's got a dark streak. Women find that exciting. You would just seem safe.'

'Safe? I've killed over a dozen people, Carveth. God knows how many aliens. Several with my hands. One with my nose alone. Admittedly he had an unusually weak immune system and I sneezed on him, but you see the point.'

'Yeah, but you still *seem* safe,' Carveth said. 'Women want a challenge, someone they can work on, change. To women, dangerous and bad are often sexy things.'

Suruk said, 'So bad deeds are good in the eyes of women?'

'Well, it depends, but yeah, sometimes.'

'Interesting.' Suruk picked up the tea-tray and bopped Carveth on the head with it. She fell backward off the packing crate. 'Was that good for you?' he said. 'Because I thought it felt splendid.'

'You bastard!' Carveth said, rubbing her head. 'Ow!'

'Suruk, stop that at once!' Smith barked. 'I'll have no woman struck with a tea-tray on my ship. If you carry on like that, there'll be no shore leave for you. And remember: no shore leave means no frenzied violence.' He wagged his finger, unsure how he could enforce this rule.

'Sod this, I'm off before you split my skull,' Carveth said. 'Better check our flight path. Don't want to nudge a planet or anything.'

Smith finished his tea. 'I think that's enough sword practice for today.' He turned to Carveth. 'I'll head up to the cockpit in a moment.' He gathered up the cups. 'Coming, Suruk?'

The M'Lak shook his head. 'I shall be in my room. I wish to rest before we land.'

Smith paused and said, 'Alright, then. See you in a bit, old chap.'

A small car rolled into the drive of the farm, towards the big barns and the plantation shop, past a sign that read *Brian and Shula Welcome You*. A woman hidden in the undergrowth followed it with her rifle.

The car stopped, the door opened and W climbed out piece by piece, unfolding his long body like a concertina. He looked around slowly, as if surprised to find himself here, and coughed into his handkerchief. The woman in the hedge checked his profile against a database.

The door to the farm shop opened and Major Wainscott ambled out, eating a piece of toast. His sleeves were rolled up and there was a Stanford machine-gun slung over his shoulder. 'Hullo,' he said, rubbing at his beard. 'How's tricks? They do good jam here.'

They shook hands. 'Not too bad,' W said. 'Well done on the raid.'

Wainscott smiled. 'Yes, we had some luck there. It'll be a week before they get the missile grid working again. My techie knows her stuff. We lost one chap from the Citizen Guard and four injured for about forty cultists and a dozen Ghasts. Not too bad. We were able to smash up a good deal of equipment before a load of praetorians showed up and we had to withdraw. We took what we could, dumped a fake codebook on the chap who bought it and headed for the hills. All in all, pretty good.'

A lone bird chirped in one of the tea-fields. The crop was yellowing, turning sickly. 'Bastard Gertie sprayed it,' Wainscott explained. 'They're doing a sweep of the plantations, starting from the city. They did this farm two days ago. They used Black Smoke on the stuff they didn't burn. We'll be safe here for a while: they've no need to come back.'

'That's a low trick.' W scowled.

'There's worse,' Wainscott said. 'Yesterday some of my people caught one of these cultists creeping through the tea with a radiation bomb strapped to his back. I'm pleased to say that they did the bugger before he could let it off. No doubt planning to poison the tea. They can't use helicopters: the sun dragons'll short out anything that flies, so they're trying to sneak under the radar instead.'

W stared out across the fields of dying tea. 'This isn't just an attempt to stop the tea, it's an attempt to wipe out Urn. There'll be a famine if there's no tea.' He coughed and glanced around. 'They'll pay for this, Wainscott.'

Wainscott said, 'We took a captive.'

'Really?' They turned from the field and walked towards the barns. 'I hope you've not duffed him up,' W said. 'We're fighting this war like civilised people.'

'Oh, don't worry. He spilled the beans easier than a can of beans with a big hole in it. We set up the recording equipment, and the fellow told us he'd got a better stereo in his tank. We asked him what else he'd got, and he told us. Natural braggart, your invader. Just through here.'

Susan stood at the barn door. She saw them coming and hauled the door aside.

There was a tank in the barn. It was a Republic of Eden machine and, even now, two men W didn't recognise were washing the slogans off the side. Gun barrels and missile racks jutted from the shadows above their heads.

'It's quite a bit of kit,' Wainscott said. Susan tugged the door closed and neon strip lights flickered into life. 'We've got some chaps in the Guard who could work it, and they're training up others. Already there're factories on the far side of Urn trying to improve on the design. Now, listen to this.' He crossed to a table, where a small stereo stood. 'This is the man whose tank it was,' he said and, after a moment's fumbling, a voice came from the speakers.

'. . . and we've got robot suits that fly, with armour all over them, and they have like ray guns, except they're super ray guns that'll fry anything, and there's missiles on them too, and – and this one thing that you target some bug or greenskin and it'll tell you his blood type and eye colour even before it goes straight through him, which is so cool 'cos blood goes everywhere, and you people are so dead because we have the best weapons ever, ever.'

Another voice said: 'Keep your hands on the table, son.'

'And God hates you.'

Wainscott switched the machine off. 'Wallies,' he observed. 'Bloody wallies, but they have technology up to their ears. If we mean to beat these cultists we need to fight them on equal terms. As it stands, we've got rifles against gun emplacements, jeeps against tanks.'

W stared glumly at the tape recorder. 'And even if we do, we've got the praetorian divisions to fight our way past. We're seriously outgunned.'

Wainscott peered at him. 'I hope you're not getting cold feet, old man. It wouldn't be on if you decided we shouldn't fight.'

W shook his head. 'Oh no, we'll fight alright. It's just whether we'll all die in the process that's the issue.'

'Oh, I see.' Wainscott brightened suddenly. 'Well, that's all right then, isn't it?'

The small side door burst open, and a woman in robes strode in. She was an eagle: tall and straight-backed with sharp eyes and a sharper nose. She threw her arms open and cried, 'Beware, for a terrible doom is coming!'

'What? Who're you? How did you get in here?' Wainscott said. His gun was in his hands.

'I walked between the rows. The land hid me, for I have come to help you free it.'

Wainscott did not lower the gun. 'Born in a barn, were we?'

'No, but this *is* a barn.' She closed the door behind her. 'Sorry. Now then – beware, for death comes to Urn!'

W sighed. 'Who are you?'

'I am the Tassomancer, the Sauceress, the seer of the Teasmen! I am the Prophetess O'Varr, and I saw something nasty in the future!'

The two men exchanged a look. 'Bonkers,' Wainscott said. 'Definitely bonkers. And how did you see the future, Prophetess O'Varr?'

'I read it in the tea-leaves. And it's Samantha, please.'

Wainscott put his finger in his ear and wiggled it. Susan quietly drew a knife. 'Well, super,' he said. 'Now, I really have to get on—'

'And I know what with, Wainscott! You seek the liberation of Urn. I come from the conclave of the Teasmen. Last night, the representatives of the great collective plantations met in secret. The Teasmen have voted, and they will support your cause. For there can be no justice while the crop dies and the Teasmen starve. In the name of He who Picks and Brews, let us join you!'

W thought for a moment. 'Well, the Empire's never turned down help just because it's being provided by a loony. I say yes. What about you, Wainscott?'

'I am *not* a loony!' Wainscott retorted. 'How dare you? The doctors said I. . . Oh, what about *her*? Oh, I *see*. Well, she's got the chaps, so why not?'

W smiled slightly. 'Excellent. Welcome, Sam O'Varr.'

Back in the cockpit, Carveth watched Didcot 6 grow larger in the windscreen, spreading across the screen like mould. She prodded the sensor array, and a spool of paper clattered out of a slot on the dashboard. Carveth tore the paper off and read from it.

'Earth gravity, 22 hour day cycle, silicated carbon base, fully breathable, no serious native diseases, radiation tolerable, expansive duty free. I can see why Suruk's clan moved here.'

'Yes.' Smith stood behind her, watching the yellow-green ball spin before them. He was only half listening. 'It's been a long while since I saw his family,' he said. 'I first met them back on Avalon Prime on the other side of the Empire, while I was on holiday.'

'Oh yeah? Nice bunch, are they?'

Smith recalled his first glimpse of House Agshad, as they hurdled the parapet and charged bellowing into the fort. 'Not exactly, no.'

'So what happened?' Carveth asked, and she immediately started rooting round under the main console. 'Oh look, there's some chocolate down here.'

Smith had been travelling the Empire before training as a space captain. Part of the Grand Astrotour had involved a trip to Avalon Prime see how the colonials lived.

Shortly after Smith arrived, everything went wrong. It

had all started when a M'Lak called Ergar the Eviscerator took a stroll along the cliffs overlooking the Beach of Dalgath, a noted beauty spot. On the way, he met a family of British tourists, who asked him to show them the quickest way down to the beach. Being a logical and helpful sort, Ergar pushed them off the cliff.

Three days later, a dreadnought shelled Avalon Prime from orbit, and the M'Lak declared open season on mankind. The British drew back to their regional garrisons and prepared to resist the alien horde, but they were badly outnumbered. The aliens were thrown back as they tried to storm the fort, but Imperial soldiers fell too. As losses rose, every able-bodied man was pressed into service.

'And before I knew what was going on, I was in the armoured trousers of an Imperial marine,' Smith explained.

Carveth shrugged. 'People need companionship at a time like that. Don't blame yourself.'

'No, the marine was out of the trousers when I put them on. He'd been killed earlier. You're not listening, are you?'

'Of course I am. Go on.' She came up from behind the console with half a chocolate bar.

'Well, the Morlocks were savage enemies: fierce and determined. Though they only carried spears and knives – they don't much like fighting at range – they swarmed up the walls faster than we could manage. Eventually, we ran out of ammunition, and it was our swords against theirs. I must have bagged three or four of them like that, and then I came up against Suruk. He was a terrible foe to face.'

'I thought he was supposed to be hard.'

'Terrible from my point of view.'

'Gotcha.'

'Anyhow, I did what I could while the others primed the base reactor. We were overrun before we could blow ourselves up – which was for the best, I suppose. The Morlocks said they hadn't had such fun for ages, and they let us go.' Smith blinked, as if waking from a dream.

'And you were best of friends ever since?'

He shook his head. 'No. We parted company as warriors of different tribes, enemies by circumstance, but comrades in battle. I became a space captain, and Suruk's people moved here, to Didcot 6. It was three years before fate threw Suruk and I together again, in Debenhams. But that's a different story.' Smith moved away and shrugged. 'Well, bring us in to land, Carveth.'

'Right away,' she said.

In his room, surrounded by trophies, Suruk crouched on his stool. He needed to save his strength for meeting his family.

The skulls stared at him with sightless eyes. Ghasts, Humans, Yull, Croatoan, Procturan Ripperspawn – all worthy enemies. But Suruk had promised to return to his people at the head of a mighty army, and these humans did not count as such. Smith was a bold fighter, but Carveth was a coward, and the only time Suruk had seen Rhianna wield a pair of blades was when she had cut up tofu with scissors. They were not the warlords he had promised to bring back to his family.

And besides, there were only three of them.

And when his family knew that he had broken his word, and returned in failure, things were likely to get serious. There would be violence, which was fine, but also disgrace. For what good was a warrior who went back on his word?

Suruk's eyes narrowed as he looked at Gan Uteki, sacred spear of his forefathers. If he was called out, the sacred spear would slay its own kin. That was bad, very bad indeed.

8

The Prodigal Spawn

The landing pad was wide, empty and surprisingly neat. A skinny figure waited at one side, its outline wavering in the hot air. It was a hundred and nine degrees.

'Most of the buildings are underground,' Suruk said as the ship touched down. 'It keeps the atmosphere moist and makes them easier to defend if we are raided by the scumbag Yull.'

'The Yull?' Carveth said. 'The human sacrifice Yull?'

Suruk's fingers tightened around his spear. He was dressed for the occasion, festooned with trophies and knives. 'Indeed. They claim we blaspheme against their gods. The Yull are shameful and vicious – worthy enemies for a warrior. A tiny pixie like you would stand no chance.' Suruk flexed his mandibles. 'Now, come. I shall speak for you, lest you are found wanting.'

Carveth stood up. 'Of course,' she said, smiling sweetly. The four of them walked out to the airlock and Carveth spun the wheel and pulled the door open. Heat and sunshine flooded the ship.

'Follow,' Suruk said, and he stepped out the door and dropped out of sight. There was a soft thud below.

'That's for the tea-tray,' Carveth said, throwing the switch to extend the steps.

They walked into the sun, shoes clanging on the metal steps as they entered M'Lak territory. Suruk waited at the bottom of the steps, dusty and slightly more angry-looking than before.

Rhianna wore a big floppy hat. Shading her eyes, she said, 'He's coming over here.'

The alien approached with the characteristic gait of the M'Lak: light and elegant, loping slightly. As it came closer, Smith saw that it wore a shirt and dark trousers. A jacket was draped over its arm. The alien's boots reached only to its ankles, without the armour plating Suruk wore. It looked strangely dapper.

Suruk stepped forward. '*Jaizeh!*' he cried, raising his spear in salute. '*Uth Suruk, Agshad moshak, Urgar sushar!*'

'Hello, Suruk,' the M'Lak said brightly. 'Nice of you to drop by.'

Suruk turned. 'He speaks English to honour you,' he hissed. 'You are favoured.'

'Oh, we speak English all the time,' the M'Lak said. 'It saves bother. I'm Suruk's father, by the way. Agshad.'

'Agshad Nine-Swords, who took sixty heads at the Battle of Arthak Gorge,' Suruk explained. 'A king among warriors and a credit to the line of my ancestors.'

'Oh, go on,' Agshad said. 'You'll make me embarrassed. Now, Suruk, aren't you going to introduce me to your friends?'

Suruk stepped to one side and pointed to them in turn. 'This is Isambard Smith, who I named Mazuran, a travelling warrior who I am proud to call friend. This here is Rhianna Mitchell, a seer much favoured of Smith, with whom he craves to spawn. And this is Carveth, an item of little importance. Yet it is she who steers the iron beast in which we came, which in the human tongue is called: "Space Ship".'

'Sheffield class, isn't it?' Agshad said.

'Yes,' Carveth said, pleased.

'Nippy, but bad on corners, I'm told,' Agshad said. He smiled behind his tusks, which were shiny and white. 'Well, it's a pleasure to meet you all.'

'Father, I bring you a gift,' Suruk declared. 'This skull I cut from a praetorian, an elite soldier of the Ghast Empire. With no respect for the rules of war this monster assaulted us not four days ago, and with my blade I cleaved its head from its shoulders in honourable combat. This gift I make as proof of my prowess and to honour our ancestors.'

He bowed and passed the skull to Agshad. 'Thank you,' Agshad said. 'Here. I got you a gift too.' He passed Suruk a plastic bag.

Suruk lifted something out of the bag.

'Hey,' Rhianna said. 'He's got you a jersey.'

'The receipt's in the bag, just in case,' Agshad said.

'So from whom did you acquire this thing?' Suruk asked.

'John Lewis,' Agshad said.

Suruk peered into the jumper, found the label and said, 'It says "Pringle". I have never fought one of those.'

'It's for golf,' Agshad explained.

Suruk smiled. 'Ah, golf. It has been many years

since I swung a club. Perhaps this visit I may try again.'

'Indeed?' Agshad said. 'You do know it's a non-contact sport now, don't you?' He turned to the humans. 'Well, welcome to Didcot 6. I hope you'll have a pleasant stay. The ground-car's that way.'

The car smelt of newness and M'Lak. Suruk's room had always had a faint scent of ammonia; now the smell was unmistakable. Smith sat in the back beside the window and watched the town open up around them.

The buildings were underground, and the shops were advertised by signs; Smith was surprised how many estate agents and cafes there seemed to be. Perhaps the M'Lak had become a little more refined: it depended how you interpreted the delicatessen signs that read "Fresh meat here – proud to serve the community".

Low domes protruded from the ground: air filters for the houses below. The M'Lak were not very gregarious, and their homes tended to be fortified to protect them from raiders, not just from space, but from neighbours using any pretence to start a fight. Imperial Beverages had once run a successful advertising campaign aimed at the M'Lak in which a new tenant sought to borrow a cup of sugar from the flat above, and began a twenty-year feud in doing so.

Carveth nudged Smith. He leaned over. 'Suruk's dad seems alright, doesn't he?'

'Yes, not too bad. But be careful, Carveth.'

The car rolled off the road and down a slope. Shadow enveloped it, and they slid into a garage. Agshad halted the vehicle and helped them out. He stepped over to a door and typed a number into the keypad. The door swung open and they walked into the ancestral home of the line of Urgar the Miffed.

The hall was large, white and empty. The walls were smooth, and the sparse furniture was chrome and glass. The only colour came from the subtle glow of soft lights and an abstract painting on the far wall. Slightly awed, they stopped just inside the door and looked around. It was at once poised and casual, artless and carefully designed.

'Where are we?' Suruk said.

'The old hall,' Agshad replied. 'We did a bit of decorating. Your brother worked out the design. He's ever so clever.'

'But – the trophies,' Suruk said.

'Trophies?' Agshad frowned. 'Oh, those? In the attic. They don't really fit with the concept your brother was going for. Besides, all those skulls everywhere. . . it's a bit morbid, isn't it?'

'Morbid? Father, those are symbols of our honour!'

'Of course. And they're still here, don't worry. Ah, here's Morgar.'

Another M'Lak entered the room from a side door, shutting it neatly behind him. He wore a black roll-neck jumper, dark trousers and glasses, and his mane was drawn into a neat pony-tail.

'Suruk!' he exclaimed. 'Good to see you, little guy!'

'Morgar. I greet you with honour, sibling.'

'Yes, of course. Honour to you too, right?'

'These are my comrades,' Suruk said, indicating the others.

Morgar nodded. 'In partnership, eh? Well, take seats, everyone. Make yourselves at home.' He dropped onto the sofa with a swoosh of leather, sitting on it rather than crouching, and yawned. 'All the cut and thrust gets tiring, you know.'

'True,' Suruk replied, 'but battle is its own reward.'

'Battle?' Morgar opened his mandibles and laughed. His laugh was lighter than Suruk's. 'Oh, I didn't mean literally. I mean at the office. The pen is mightier than the sword, and all that.'

'That depends very much where you ram it,' Suruk observed sourly. He sat down in the human fashion, to which he was not accustomed. Not having buttocks, he grimaced.

'Morgar has made a killing in the city,' Agshad said. 'I'm very proud of him.'

'Blood feud?' Suruk asked, hopefully.

'Architect,' Morgar replied. 'Ursath, Morgar and Brown, although Brown's very much a silent partner. Dad here's gone into accountancy.'

'Accountancy?'

'Absolutely,' Agshad said. 'There'll always be books to balance. It's interesting stuff. So, what do you do these days, Son?'

'I quest for honour!' Suruk declared. 'I hunt the deadliest prey in the galaxy and do battle with them in the name of Suruk the Slayer and the glory of our tribe!'

'Oh,' Agshad said. He exchanged a look with Morgar. 'So, you haven't enrolled for law school, then.'

Suruk stared at them. Smith, Carveth and Rhianna looked at Suruk. Everyone looked blank.

'We were hoping you'd become a doctor, or a lawyer,' Agshad explained. 'This family hasn't had a doctor yet.'

'But I am a warrior!' Suruk retorted. 'My trade is war!' He paused, and a new emotion crept into his remorseless eyes. 'This hall. . . the trophies. . . You're. . . not warriors any more, are you?'

'Well, times change,' Morgar said. 'Now, can I offer your friends a G&T?'

Suruk and Morgar left to prepare the drinks while Agshad went off to find some photographs of his holiday to Nigellus Prime. Carveth glanced at Smith. 'So much for getting our limbs pulled off,' she said.

Smith said, 'This is a little worrying.'

'I think it's terrible,' Rhianna said. 'These poor indigenous people have been forced to accept Western values. Our cultural imperialism has burdened them with comfort and sanitation. Their standard of living must actually be similar to our own. Terrible.'

Carveth scowled. 'Well, there goes the mighty army – less battle-scarred than battle-scared. Unless we decide to smash the Ghast Empire with a massive VAT fraud, I'd say we're stuffed.'

In the chrome kitchen, Suruk watched as Morgar took things out of the fridge. 'So what of my old comrades?' he asked. 'Are they all. . . architects like you?'

Morgar shook his head. 'Oh, heavens no.'

'Ancestors be praised.'

'Some went into underwriting.'

'Underwriting? What is that?' Suruk growled. 'Surely

some still remember the old ways. What about Hunar Blackblade, Margath the Despoiler, Azman the Vile?'

'Despoiler Blackblade Vile? Solicitors.'

'Orgak the Bone-Cruncher?'

'You mean Orgak the Number-Cruncher. Accountant. He works with Dad.'

'Azranash the Pain-bringer?'

'Dentistry.'

'That is something, I suppose. Things certainly have changed. I remember when this room was decorated in wall-to-wall gore.'

Morgar began to mix the gin and tonic. Suruk watched him pour out the gin, then the tonic, into not three glasses, but six.

'What are you doing!' Suruk cried.

Morgar glanced around. He blinked. 'Just making the drinks. Why?'

'Morgar! You should know better than that!' Suruk strode over and snatched the bottle from his hand. 'This is human drink, not for the M'Lak! Mankind brought this with him to ruin braves. Surely you know that!'

Morgar stood there, confused, watching Suruk with a mixture of surprise and concern. 'Suruk, it's good. You should try some.'

'No! Morgar, you have hidden your trophies, turned from the way of the warrior and dressed like a human, but no more shall you drink the pink man's fizz-water! This I will not allow!'

He hurled the bottle of tonic at the ground. It bounced.

Suruk picked up the bottle. 'I said, "This I will not allow!"' he cried, and threw it at the floor again.

'It's a plastic bottle,' Morgar said.

Suruk looked at the bottle for a moment, huffed, picked it up and passed it to Morgar. 'Carbonated drink is the ruin of warriors,' he said. 'Remember that.'

'I'm not a warrior,' Morgar said, and he shrugged and took in the drinks.

'So, what brings you here?' Agshad asked. 'Have you persuaded Suruk to take up a profession?'

Smith shook his head. 'No, sir. We have come to seek your help.'

Morgar set the tray down and passed the glasses around. They sat round a long, highly-polished table. Suruk sat between the humans and his family, scowling more than usual. As Smith watched, the alien's mandibles swung down into their fighting position, then back up again.

Agshad sipped his gin and tonic. 'Of course. How can I assist?'

'We need an army,' Smith said.

Morgar and Agshad exchanged a glance.

'The Ghast Empire has annexed Didcot 4, also known as Urn,' Smith said. 'They have cut off the British Empire's supply of tea in a bid to weaken our armed forces. We were able to break out of their blockade, and came here on Suruk's advice. He told us that we would be able to recruit an army here to liberate Urn.'

'Oh,' Morgar said. '. . . A fighting army?'

'No, a ballroom dancing army,' Suruk said. 'Twit.'

Agshad raised a hand. '*Spawn, behave.* Captain Smith, you ask much. Were it a mere quarterly statement, or even the settling of some dubious petty cash, I would oblige you as a friend of my son. But this. . . our war-host has not gathered for many a fiscal year.'

'Sir, it is vital,' Smith replied. 'The people of Urn are brave and tough, but they are too widely-scattered to face the Ghasts properly. But with the help of an army such as yours, they would stand a fighting chance.'

'And should Urn fall,' Suruk added, 'The British Empire will be without tea. Without tea, they will have no moral fibre, which will leave them greatly weakened. And should the British fall, no doubt the Ghasts would turn to us next. Join our quest, Father. It will be fun.'

'This is madness!' Morgar exclaimed. 'We are civilised people, not savages. It's all very well for you, running around saving the galaxy, but some of us have responsibilities. What do you think will happen if I don't sort out the Gathrags' summer house by the end of the week? Trouble, that's what! Sorry to raise my voice, but *really*.'

Aghad took a deep sip of gin and tonic. 'As the head of our household, it falls to me to balance these arguments, like entries in the same ledger. I understand the seriousness of what you say, but mindless violence is no longer our way.

'Captain, I cannot promise you anything. But if you wish, I will call a meeting of the elders. Tomorrow we will gather at the Henge of Judgement, the traditional place where the elders would meet to discuss war. Perhaps fate will favour us if we gather at such a place, where once our ancestors stood.' He brightened suddenly and a smile creased his scarred, aged face. 'But enough of that. Who'd like risotto?'

*

It was night. The household slept. In slippers and pyjamas, Polly Carveth made her way through the darkness of the living room. Her shin hit a sharp-edged, modernistic coffee table and she stumbled and hopped about, cursing the stupid lust that had made her transfer the batteries from the torch to her Mark 9 Industrial Pulsatatron. Carveth took a step backwards, bumped against a doorway and fell into the kitchen.

Light opened above her and a wave of cold struck her body. Suruk stood beside the fridge, the door open. 'Is that any help?' he said.

'Whoa!' She got up and brushed her thighs down. 'Just came in for a glass of water.'

'Of course,' the M'Lak said. 'We have running water, now that we are proper people.'

He took a glass from the sideboard, filled it and passed it to her. She took a grateful swig. 'Think I overdid it on the risotto.'

'Ah.' He slid out of the darkness, the light catching on his tusks, throwing the furrows of his face into hard relief.

It had never occurred to her that Suruk might be menacing. On the ship, she had always regarded him as an amusing piece of scenery: strange, naïve and dangerous, but ultimately a friend. Now, confronted with the knife-wielding monster close up, and wearing nothing more than loose trousers and a T-shirt that said 'Little Princess' across the front, she felt a flicker of uncertainty.

'Couldn't sleep?' she said.

'Indeed. I had a curious dream, perhaps a prophesy. I dreamt that there was a meadow full of little people like you outside my house. I stood in my home and let off a siren, and all of you little people came inside for dinner.'

'You gave us dinner? That's nice of you.'

'Something like that.' Suruk licked his lips and rummaged in the fridge. 'So,' he said, 'you have met my kin.'

'Yes,' she said. 'They seem. . . nice. I suppose that's not a good thing though, is it?'

Suruk shook his heavy head. 'I doubt you would understand.'

'I don't have any relatives,' she said, pouring another glass of water. Her voice grew thoughtful. 'I suppose my closest family are the ship's autopilot and my electric toothbrush: one's a computer and I've slept with the other.' She sighed. 'You know, Suruk, if I'd have known your homecoming was going to be like this, I'd have put the stairs down for you when we landed.'

Suruk said, 'If I had known my people had such little respect for random violence, I would not have used it upon you.'

Carveth thought for a moment. 'That's comparatively good of you,' she said.

Suruk resumed his perusal of the fridge. 'Balsamic vinegar, goat's cheese – feeble. Even the lady's fingers are fake. Have some olives,' he said, holding out a plastic box. 'They are green and oily – no wonder my brother likes them.'

Suruk put the olives back and closed the fridge door. Suddenly the room was dim, and he was another grey shadow among the furniture. 'You should rest,' he said.

'Yeah.' In the dark she was a maroon blur of warmth. Conventional vision was impossible, but his atrophied night-sight watched the blur step closer and reach out. Carveth's small hand took hold of his.

'I'm sorry how it's all worked out,' she said, and she squeezed his hand.

'Go to bed,' he replied, not squeezing back.

She took her hand away and stepped back. 'You don't do touching, do you?'

'No.' He watched the blur wander to the door. 'But thank you, anyway.'

The Henge of Judgement rose around Smith like a circle of grim-faced, disapproving guards, twenty feet high. The monoliths had been carved to represent great chieftains and victories of the past. Wind and ages had rubbed symbols and features smooth, wiping them clean.

As they walked towards the centre of the henge, Suruk pointed to the stones. 'This one shows Azranath the Wise, who walked the land when death was but a dream. This, on the left, is King Lacrovan, who could throw his spear so far that it travelled all the way around the world and returned to his hand with six enemies impaled on it, like a kebab of scum.'

Rhianna said, 'What an amazing culture.'

Carveth shuddered, feeling the eyes of the ancients on her.

'This here is Tathrax, the warlord who led us against the British. Great ones, all of them. Now, speak only noble words, for we approach the Great Table.'

In the centre of the henge stood a mighty stone, flat on top but tapering below, like an inverted pyramid. On the flat surface, a picture had been cut into the rock: a M'Lak in stickman form, holding a spear and running through a landscape of skulls, waving a severed head and grinning insanely. Characters ran down the sides of the picture: one side in red, the other in blue, as was traditional. The other stones were old, but this was ancient beyond imagining – and as sacred as it was aged.

Suruk raised his spear so that its shadow fell across the picture. He saluted the image, drove the butt of the spear into the ground and stood at the edge of the table in silent reverence: head lowered, eyes closed.

'Excuse me!' a voice called. 'Excuse me, gentlemen! Yes, you! Can't you read?'

Suruk's head flicked up. A M'Lak paced through the henge towards them, hands on hips, a cap on his head. He strode up to them, looked them up and down, and said, 'Come on, back behind the fence.'

Suruk's mandibles opened. 'What?'

'You heard, mate. Back behind the fence with the others.'

'Foul one, you dare to interrupt my communion with the spirits, to tell *me* to leave this sacred place?'

The official nodded once, firmly. 'Yes, sir, indeed I do. There's a fence up, and it's for a good purpose: to stop weirdos coming in and doing their funny stuff in the henge. Yes, sir, weirdos.'

His brutal head slowly turned to look at Rhianna.

'Excuse me,' Smith said, 'but are you trying to insinuate something? That is a guest on my ship that you're talking about, and I can tell you that she is not a "weirdo".'

'Then might I ask, sir, why she is embracing a rock?'

'She's not embracing it. She's listening to it.'

'Quite, sir. This is a site of archaeological significance, not some drop-in centre for people who smell of joss. Back behind the fence, or I shall have to order you to leave.'

Smith glanced at Suruk, who was beginning to froth.

'Come along, I've not got all day,' the official said. 'Loonies,' he added, quietly.

'Excuse me.' Morgar had appeared beside them. Smith had not seen him approach. The ability to creep up on the unsuspecting clearly ran in the family. 'These people are with me. Morgar the Architect, pleased to meet you.' He stuck out a hand and the official shook it. Morgar withdrew his hand rather slowly. 'Perhaps we can come to an arrangement here.'

'Go right ahead,' the official said. He glanced at Rhianna. 'But don't make a mess, understand?'

'Of course,' Morgar said. 'This way, all.'

They returned to the Great Table. As they walked, Carveth leaned over and whispered, 'That ticket bloke was the toughest thing we've seen on this planet so far.'

Smith observed sourly, 'I must say, I can hardly believe how decadent these people have got. Not only has Agshad's mighty warhost gentrified itself, but I do believe I've just seen an officer of the National Trust taking a bribe. It's like–' he struggled for a word that would express his distaste sufficiently – 'France.'

Figures approached the far end of the table, striding across the ground from the gift shop: aged M'Lak, no smaller than Suruk but with more pronounced, inhuman features. Among them was Agshad. Flanked by Morgar and Suruk, Smith stepped up to the Great Table. He stood there, uncertain whether he should introduce himself and begin.

Clearly the surroundings reminded the elders of their glory days. 'So I cut off its head and dragged the monster's body for eight miles, despite it biting off my hand,' an elder with one tusk was saying.

'Eight miles?' another demanded. 'Eight miles? You were lucky. I would get up, fight for honour all day, then stagger twenty miles home with both my arms in a plastic bag.'

'Luxury!' said an elder with one eye. Agshad cleared his throat sacs, noisily.

'Gentlemen!' he growled. 'Honoured business associates, pillars of the community, this is Captain Isambard Smith of the British Space Empire. He has come here to seek your help regarding a matter of great importance to his people. With him is my son Suruk, an antiquarian and friend of Captain Smith, who will vouch for him if needed. Gentlemen, I give you Captain Smith. There,' he added quietly, as if to say, *I have fulfilled my obligations.*

'Let me make this clear, gentlemen. I do not come here seeking help in a war that has nothing to do with you. I come here to offer you assistance in fighting our common foe. Number One intends to conquer the galaxy, and to do so he has engineered an army far larger than anything you or I could produce on our own. Even together we will have a tough fight on our hands – but a fight we can win, and a fight that will bring us victory instead of certain death.'

Smith looked them over.

'The Ghasts have no scruples. Their sole aim is to conquer the universe, and the only reason they would spare your lives is to use you all as slaves. The Empire offers you the chance to meet them head-on, with my people as your allies, and to stop their evil plan in its tracks. Because believe me, sirs, once we are defeated the Ghasts will turn on you.'

An ancient, scarred M'Lak fixed his eyes on Smith. 'The Ghasts have offered us incentives to stay out of the fighting. They tell us that this war is between Earth and Selenia, and that we need not concern ourselves with it. In return, they have promised us distribution rights on a vast amount of canned food. What can the British offer us to match that?'

'Freedom,' said Smith. 'And dignity.'

'They gave me a crate of red wine,' another elder said. 'And some balsamic vinegar.'

'Gentlemen, please listen!' cried Smith. 'This is not about tinned goods, or stocking your cellars. This is about life and death! What good will *Cotes de Rhône* be to you when Ghast stormtroopers march through your cities, killing all before them?'

'We could break the bottles on their heads,' the elder said. 'It would really hurt, especially if we only used the cheap stuff.'

'That would sting something awful,' said the elder with one tusk.

'Please try to understand.' Smith looked away, his head aching with frustration. 'I know our history together may not be too good. I know we've disagreed at times—'

'Oh, water under the bridge,' said the elder with one eye.

'– but our Empire cannot defeat the Ghasts on its own. With your help, we can liberate Urn, keep our army strong, and keep all of our worlds safe from tyranny. But without your help, we are too few. There are some odds that even British people cannot overcome.'

The elder with one eye opened his hands helplessly. 'Two alien races, far away. I'm sorry, Captain Smith, but I really don't see the relevance of this. We have business to look after, work to do. This isn't the Dark Ages, you know.'

Around the henge, the elders murmured their agreement.

Smith opened his mouth, but he was drowned out by a bellow of rage. Throat sacs inflated, jaws wide open, head thrown back, Suruk roared at the sky. As they recoiled in shock he sprang onto the Great Table, onto the sacred inscription.

'Shame on you!' he cried. 'Shame on you, cowards and fools! You will fall, this land will fall, and you will cry to the ancestors to save you, and they will spurn you just as you spurn them! As your houses burn, as the tribes are driven forth as slaves instead of warriors, you will remember this day and curse your mealy words a thousand times! These humans, these little pink things, have more honour than you! This—' he jabbed a finger at Carveth, '*this* stunted jester has more honour than all of you put together!'

He stopped, panting. There was an awkward pause, and the group noticed a familiar figure standing beside the Great Table, looking up at Suruk.

'Right, you,' said the official. 'That's quite enough. Hop it.'

'Well,' said Morgar, 'it's been nice seeing you again.'

'Huh,' Suruk said. 'I suppose the same. What can I do but wish you well? Apart from hacking you into pieces, of course. But even that would hardly seem worth the bother.'

They stood on the landing pad in front of the *John Pym*. It was hot, and the satellite dishes of the clan-houses seemed to waver in the haze.

'Here,' said Carveth, and she passed Morgar the bottle of wine from her bag. 'Cheers for putting us up.'

'Thank you,' Morgar said. He peered at the label disapprovingly. 'Hmm. French, eh? I wonder what region it is?'

'Europe, stupid,' Suruk said.

Morgar looked at his brother and sighed. 'Look, I feel pretty bad about the way this has turned out—'

'Perhaps the Ghast legions will perk you up,' Suruk said coldly.

Smith elbowed Suruk in the side.

Suruk said, 'Goodbye, brother. Goodbye, father. I thank you for the jumper.'

'Thank you for the skull, Suruk,' Agshad said. They bowed to one another. 'Goodbye to all of you. Good luck, Captain Smith. I hope the ancestors look well on you. And Suruk, if ever you do think about going to law school, I can always send you a prospectus.'

*

Above Didcot 5, the *Systematic Destruction* slid into orbit. On the bridge, 462 watched plasma torpedoes corkscrew through the peach-coloured cloud, into the storms. There was a brief flash of light, then another, and, a second later, a third. Only then did he turn from the window.

An orderly stood beside him. 'Supreme Ship's Commander!'

'Minion.'

'Report on planet surface follows! All life should have been destroyed. Threat almost certainly neutralised.'

462's eye narrowed. ' "Should be?" '

'Um. . . is.'

462 put his hands behind his back and walked to his seat. 'So, Project Midwife is finished. Good.' He sat down, thinking. No doubt the Edenite buffoons on Urn would be making a mess of things. Still, it did not matter. Tea was useless to the Ghast Empire and, once he returned, he would give the order to strip Urn of everything the Ghasts could use before destroying it.

'Sir!' another orderly called. 'A message has come from our entirely neutral allies the Yull. They state that a craft similar to the human ship *John Pym* has landed on the M'Lak world of Didcot 6. I am pleased to inform you that we have sufficient torpedoes remaining to—'

462 lurched upright and cuffed the minion across the jaw. 'Silence!' He sank back into his chair slowly, as if deflating. His mechanical eye ached. 'No. To attack their world would violate M'Lak airspace. The enemy could paint us as aggressors and invaders – which is, of course, totally untrue. No, there are other ways. I think we can

find someone altogether more disposable to do our work for us.'

He rubbed his hands, claws and antennae together, and began to laugh. The orderly, not wishing to be shot, joined in.

Carveth turned from the monitors and said, 'Course set for Urn, boss.'

'Thank you, Carveth.'

Things were subdued on the *John Pym*. Rhianna had retreated to her room, leaving Smith and Carveth in the cockpit. They sat quietly, depressed and a little embarrassed, as if at a wake for someone they hardly knew.

'It's going to be bad news when we get back,' Smith said. 'For everyone.' He sipped a glass of gin and tonic. Given the lack of allies, he had decided to ration the ship's tea for emergency situations. He was already itching to brew up, despite having only enforced the new rule for half an hour. 'Bloody aliens. All of them. Bloody stupid, unreliable bunch!'

'On which subject,' said Carveth, 'where's Suruk gone?'

'In his room. Trying on his new jumper, apparently, which probably means ripping it into bits. I'd leave him to it.'

'Perhaps I ought to see how he's doing. After all, he did say that I had more honour than all his tribal elders put together.'

'He also called you a stunted jester. Don't push your luck. I'll do it.'

Smith brushed his jacket down and strolled along the corridor. He felt empty and tired. Suruk's door was closed;

the next door down, Rhianna's, was open. He raised his hand to knock on Suruk's door and paused, uncertain of what to do. Things seemed pretty quiet in there. Perhaps it was best to leave the alien to it: like Smith, the last thing that would cheer him up would be people urging him to 'let it all out', 'have a good cry' or some new-age rubbish like that. What was a 'good cry' anyway? A happy grieve? A merry mourn?

'Hey there.'

He glanced around: Rhianna lounged against the door-frame of her room, arms folded, watching him. 'Hello,' he said warily.

'Coming in?'

'Er, alright then,' he said.

She stepped away gracefully and he walked into her room. It was alien territory, even less familiar to him than Suruk's weapons racks and skull collection. The first impression was of an explosion in a sari factory: drapey things hung from the walls and ceiling. An item like a poorly-constructed wheel dangled above the bed, trailing feathers as though it had been used to bludgeon a thrush. Trinkets jostled with suspicious-looking plants on the shelves. It was all extremely exotic, and hence made him think of Fry's Turkish Delight.

'Came to see Suruk really,' he said. 'Must be a bit of a shock for him. Maybe he's best off on his own. Can't hear anything smashing in there, so he's probably alright.'

Rhianna said, 'It must be really hard for him,' and sat down on the mass of pillows, tassels, rugs, throws and ethnic litter that made up her bed. 'You know, I really. . . *feel* for those poor indigenous people, deprived of their way of life by colonialist imperialism.'

'*We* didn't deprive them,' Smith retorted, stung. 'It was their choice to chuck in their traditions for accounting and risotto. I tell you, they were a damned lot easier to rule when they were demented savages. The only crazy thing down there now is the paving on their bloody driveway.'

'I know.' Her voice was softer. 'It's so sad.'

She leaned back, and it occurred to Smith that he would like to kiss every inch of her body. Well, most of it: some bits needed a clean. Maybe if she had a wash and asked nicely. There'd have to be something in it for him, like getting her to put on an English accent. Yes, an English accent and some sort of smalls – big smalls. . . Noticing the beginnings of what his old friend Carstairs referred to as 'Trouser-prong', he turned to the bookshelf and read the titles of some of her books. His eye skimmed over a grisly selection of volumes about lentil-rearing and Beat poetry, and stopped on some hippy diatribe entitled *Rage Against the Washing Machine*. He felt considerably less excited now.

He turned round and nearly yelped: ghost-like, she had slid across the room in a soft waft of joss and was now quite close to him. 'I never thanked you,' she said.

Smith swallowed hard. Somehow Rhianna frightened him in a way that the shock divisions of the Ghast Empire did not. 'What for?' he managed.

'For rescuing me from those children.'

'They were just children,' he said, glancing at the door. 'Nothing much.'

'They were psychics, Isambard. They could have killed me.'

'Oh, well, all in a day's work, eh? Nothing to worry about.' Dammit, she had shifted between him and his escape.

'I owe you.'

'Oh, nonsense, nonsense.'

'I think—'

'Oh my God, did you hear that? Bloody Carveth no doubt, haha, probably done something I need to go and look at. . . so. . . so, I'd best go and look at it, hadn't I? Yes!' he added, in case she disagreed and, so saying, he bolted to the door, yanked the handle, sprang into the corridor, slammed it behind him and fell against the opposite wall, panting with relief.

Bloody hell, he thought, thank goodness I escaped that! She could have been all over me there! Damn foreign women, forward as anything and depraved with it, no doubt. Blimey, one moment longer in there and she probably would have pinned me to the wall and stuck her hands on my—

'Balls!' he said bitterly, and he walked back to the cockpit, cursing himself, the Morlocks, the Ghasts and everything else. The gin and tonic was calling to him.

Morgar wrapped the praetorian skull in a plastic bag. He took it down to the family hangar that afternoon. He opened the hangar door with the remote control and stood in the doorway, looking at the clan spacecraft. It was a tough, battered, powerful thing, its prow a patchwork of spikes and soldered armour plates. Some of the trophies still lingered on the front: Morgar had thrown most of them away.

He sighed, took out the praetorian skull and drove it onto one of the spikes. It jutted from the front of the ship, aggressive and empty-eyed. There was a noise behind him, and he spun around.

'Dad?'

'Hello,' Agshad said. He was carrying a tin of paint.

Morgar nodded at the ship. 'I just came down here to put that skull away that Suruk brought us. By the ancestors, he does come back from his holidays with some right old tat. Thought I'd stick it here. . . it just seemed sort of appropriate.'

Agshad chuckled. 'Nostalgia, eh?' He stepped into the garage and patted the ship with his free hand. 'Ah, we used to have some laughs in this old thing. When I look back at it all. . .'

'What's that you've got?'

'This? Oh, just some old red paint and a brush. I just thought I'd store it here, just in case I ever feel like paint- ing the business end of anything red. . . you know, go faster stripes or something.'

They stood there together for a while, looking at the ship.

'We're being hailed!' Carveth cried. 'Someone's calling us!'

Smith jolted awake, spilling the remains of his drink over his lap. 'Where?'

Carveth folded down a console and her fingers clattered over the keys. 'On the left. Four ships. Dart-shaped.'

'Ghasts!' Suddenly Smith was very awake indeed. 'They must have followed us here. Put them on loudspeaker.'

Carveth reached out, and high-pitched noises came from the speakers: squeaky, breathless, angry sounds.

'Well, it's not Ghasts,' Smith said. 'It could be worse.'

'British offworlder scum! You are in sacred Yull space, offworlder cowards! Today you die, British! *Hup-hup!* Yes, cut out hearts for the war-god! *Hwup!*'

'Good God,' Smith said. 'The lemming-men of Yull!'

'Kill you slow, offworlder!' the speaker screeched. '*Hephuphephuphup!*'

'Tell them we mean no harm!' Carveth cried. 'Calm them down or something!'

The door flew open and Suruk stormed in. He leaned across Carveth, toggled the speakers and roared, 'Scum of Yull! Pirates and murderers! I will slay you all!'

'Dirty M'Lak!' the Yull shouted back. Carveth had the nasty feeling that she was trapped between two broken amplifiers. 'So M'Lak are now cowards too! Polite after-dinner chat no match for frenzied assault of Yull! Prepare to die! *Hup-hup!*'

'We will wade in your blood, filth!' Suruk snarled. 'Today you will know that one of the M'Lak has not embraced cowardice!' He flicked off the intercom. 'Woman, turn this ship and prepare to fight.'

'Bugger right off!'

'The lemming-men will try to ram us,' Smith said. 'Do you think we can outpace them?'

'I can bloody well try,' Carveth said. She turned the ship, and in the edge of the windscreen Smith saw four specs of light, the engines of the Yull dart-ships. Carveth pushed the throttle forward. A sudden rushing, scraping sound came from the rear of the ship, and the floor began to shudder.

'Full ahead,' said Smith.

'This *is* full.' The *Pym* was fast, but it had more mass to move than the darts. Flashing dots appeared on the radar, slowly drawing closer. It would take only one Yull ship to destroy them, Smith knew. Looking at the faces of the others, they knew as well. 'Stay here,' he said, and he leaped up and ran into the corridor.

He banged on Rhianna's door. 'Rhianna?'

She looked out, saw his face and said, 'What is it?'

'We're under attack. I need you to do your psychic thing.'

For once there was no discussion. 'Okay,' she said, and she hurried inside and hopped onto the bed. Pressing her fingertips to her temples, she closed her eyes and said, 'Um-umumum,' like an instrument tuning up.

Smith hurried back to the cockpit. 'What's the state of play?'

'Not good,' Carveth said. She was wearing the sighting goggles: always a bad sign. She tapped the navcom. The dots were a third closer.

'Turn left,' Suruk said. 'Local debris field.'

'Alright,' Carveth said. The ship swung. Metal glinted at the edge of the screen: ragged, whirling junk. It'll tear us apart, thought Smith, and then: better that than dying at the hands of the Yull.

'Take us in,' he commanded.

The specs grew alarmingly. Smith could see individual lumps of debris now, pieces of ships and broken satellites, the rough edges gleaming like saw-blades as they spun.

'You'll have to slow down to manoeuvre in there,' he said.

'The Yull think that too,' Carveth said. 'How close are they?'

'Close. Leading ship has forty seconds to impact at this speed.'

She nodded. Under the goggles, she was biting her lip. Carveth reached up and toggled the brake controls. 'Here we go,' she said.

The *John Pym* met the debris field. Part of a solar array shot past them on the left, its ruined panels glistening like fish. The *Pym* sped into the field at top sublight speed, and at once they were surrounded by a host of wrecks. Carveth opened the radio.

The speakers burst into frantic jabbering. Ahead, the remains of a troop transport dwarfed the *John Pym*. They darted past its empty hull like a barracuda past the flank of a whale.

'Now you die, mangy offworlders!' screamed the lead lemming. '*Yullai!*'

Smith looked up from the scanner – 'Carveth, he's bloody close! Collision in four, three—'

She tapped the accelerator, and then at once braked and pulled the nose up. Fire blasted from the back of the *Pym*: the Yull saw it, threw his ship forward and overshot as the *Pym* swerved and pulled away. The lemming-ship shot past them into the debris. For a second it slipped between the wrecks – then, almost lazily, a dented rocket rolled onto its side, one of its stabilising fins swung down and batted the Yull out of existence.

Being a vacuum, no sound carried to the *Pym*. But it did

not matter. 'Blam!' Carveth yelled into the intercom. 'How's that, wankers? Haha!'

'We kill you, kill you slow!' the Yull warbled over the intercom. 'Pull out your whiskers, British!'

'Three more incoming,' Smith said.

'Can they see us from here?'

'No.'

Carveth flicked off the radio and cut the engines. Suddenly the room was completely quiet. A few buttons glowed on the controls. Otherwise, the only light came from space itself.

They lay among the debris, camouflaged by broken metal. The Yull had wanted to run them down; now the initiative lay with the Empire. The *John Pym* looked as much like dead metal as it could.

Silence. Smith could hear Carveth breathing, hard and fast. He leaned across to her and whispered, 'Tea?' It was, after all, an emergency.

She nodded. He crept to the kitchen, made the tea and checked on Rhianna. She was still meditating. He did not risk breaking her concentration.

As Smith brought the tea to the cockpit, Suruk passed him the binoculars. 'Look,' he hissed.

The broken ships reminded Smith of dead sharks, of scaffolding and ferris wheels. Between the wreckage, a needle-shaped craft picked its way through the debris, hunting them. Searchlights flicked from its nose across the broken metal. It looked like a missile with wings.

Smith looked at Carveth. 'Plan?'

Carveth looked at Suruk. 'Delegate?'

'We must move fast,' Suruk said. 'I suggest we lose

weight by jettisoning the mascot out the airlock. Or better still, I eat the mascot.'

Carveth grabbed the hamster cage. 'No way. Gerald is as much a part of the crew as you are, Suruk. He stays.'

'Gerald?' Suruk said, giving her one of his special smiles.

Carveth clicked her fingers. 'Wait! That gives me an idea!'

Half an hour later, Smith finished strapping the cargo webbing across the hold. 'How're you doing?' he asked, looking up.

'Well,' Suruk said. He had pushed their battered car to the very back of the hold, next to the rear doors. It was the only thing in the hold not tied down.

Smith looked around the hold. 'That'll do,' he said. 'Let's go.'

They stepped into the living room and closed the door behind them. Suruk spun the wheel until the airlock was sealed.

In the cockpit, Carveth was watching the scanners.

'Anything?' Smith asked.

She looked up. 'No. They're circling, looking for us. That's about it.'

'Good.' Smith sat down in the captain's chair. 'How fast can you get the hold open?'

'Pretty quick,' she said. 'There's an emergency option for ejecting hostile life forms. It'll blow the door open in half a second.' She looked back at the scanner. 'Look, Boss, even if this works we'll have them on our tail straight away.'

'Of course. But this should prove a distraction. Get ready to power up.'

She wrapped her hands around the stick. 'Right.'

'Prepare the hatches. Ready to blow?'

'I was *born* ready to blow, Captain.'

'Power up.'

Carveth threw the switches: around them lights flickered on, the floor trembled, machinery began to hum. The ship came alive. Smith opened the radio and shouted 'Let's get out of here!' He jabbed a finger at Carveth and she flicked a switch.

The hold doors blew open. It depressurised in an instant, and the car was flung from the back in a rush of air. Smith glanced at the rear monitor. Spinning in the vacuum, the Crofton Imp made its final journey.

From nowhere a light dived towards the car. '*Yullai!*' the speaker screeched. 'Die, filthy offworl – oh, wait a min—'

The light hit the car and exploded. 'Go!' cried Smith, and the android threw the throttle forward and the ship roared around them.

The *John Pym* blasted free of the debris field. Suruk laughed. 'Two Yull dead!'

'And two behind us,' Smith said. Two more points of light had appeared on the scanner. 'Full speed ahead, Carveth!'

Her eyes were huge behind the goggles. 'Right.'

Smith watched the scanner, then the monitor. The dots were closing – closing fast. A dial on the scanner whirled. 'Twenty seconds to impact!' he called.

'Brace yourselves!' Carveth cried.

Smith stood up. 'I'll tell Rhianna.'

'No time!' she called. 'Strap yourself – what the hell is that?'

She swung the ship left, and Smith staggered across the cockpit as the *Pym* turned. He stumbled back to his seat. 'What is it?'

'Big ship coming up planetside!' Carveth said.

Something huge rose into the rear monitor. At first sight Smith thought it was a bulldozer, for the whole front was hidden by metal armour – part bulldozer blade, part ram.

The first Yull ship died in a flash of light on the blade. The second tried to dodge but it was too slow, and the massive prow clipped the dart-ship, spun it and smashed into its side, and it was destroyed.

'Hello Suruk!' said the radio. 'Hello Suruk's friends!'

Suruk was on his feet, staring at the speaker. 'Father?'

'It's me,' Agshad said. 'Everyone alright there?'

'Better now that you're here,' Smith said. 'Good flying, sir!'

'And pleased that you have decided to follow the path of honourable combat,' Suruk added.

'Well,' said Agshad, 'we've never really liked the Yull, have we? Vicious buggers – fluffy, too.'

Smith said, 'Sir, I would ask you once again to join us. Urn, and the whole Empire, needs skilled fighters like yourself in its battle against tyranny. Join with us, and you need never worry about lack of honour, or enemies.'

'Hmm.' Agshad fell silent. 'I've got a golf lesson next Tuesday, but I can't see why I can't put that back a few days. Yes, alright. Count me in. It might be fun. Let me see what the others think. How about the rest of you fellows?'

The speakers rattled with a roar of approval. Carveth turned in her seat and stared at Smith, wide-eyed and grinning.

'They fight with us!' Suruk cried. 'The House of Agshad goes to war!'

'Well,' said Isambard Smith, 'that is good news. Time for tea, I think.'

PART TWO

So you can see that the making of tea is in essence a revolutionary act, because it lends support to the common man in his struggle to civilise the galaxy and establish a fair deal for its inhabitants. Yet at the same time it links us with the past. Think of the many people who have drunk tea before you, perhaps from the same pot, and you will have some idea of the connexion that tea gives you with your ancestors, like a row of carriages drawn forward by the same engine.

It is this very link between the revolutionary and the traditional, the progressive and the established, that stands at the heart of the philosophy of tea. And it is this idea that fills our enemies and their hired arse-kissers with fear . . .

Why Tea Matters, underground publication of Urnian resistance, author unknown.

1

Return to Urn

They docked with Agshad's ship before they got within range of Urn. They sealed the *Pym*, headed through the airlock and met Morgar on the other side. 'Sorry about the décor,' Morgar said. 'It's all a bit, you know, dead.'

The clan spaceship was really a troop carrier. It had little in the way of missiles, guns and what Suruk tended to call 'pansy stuff', but was well-equipped for ploughing into things and initiating boarding actions. Best of all, though, it contained over six hundred M'Lak and enough armoured ground-skimmers to transport them all.

Morgar led them through the central chamber, a huge, drum-shaped room. There were niches in the walls, and each niche was now the home to a warrior. Clearly the arrival of Suruk on their world had thrown M'Lak society into something of a cultural crisis: Smith saw one fighter looking at a bare patch of wall, trying to decide between a skull and a picture of some people dancing on a beach.

The control room was dark and confusing, crowded with trophies and big levers, and looked like a cross between a castle dungeon and a signal box. A lantern had been attached to a chain that hung from the ceiling, and under it Agshad was eating a cheese sandwich.

'I would offer you seats, but it's all a bit spiky in here,' he said. 'My commendations to your pilot, by the way. Shooting that car out the back of your ship was wily indeed.'

'Oh, well, it was nothing,' Carveth replied.

'You surprised me, Father,' Suruk said.

'Sometimes I surprise myself. Your brother and I happened to be talking about the old days, and just then we got a call from Xanath the Fell-Handed at flight control, and he bet me three flagons of balsamic vinegar that we couldn't fight off the Yull. . . and three flagons is a lot, especially if you like salad as much as I do.'

'Will the Yull retaliate?' Smith asked.

Agshad shook his head. 'I doubt it. They don't own that space really; nobody does. If it gets nasty we can always claim the Voidani space-whales ate their ships for minerals. Nobody messes with them, not since they ate the Japanese fleet and passed it off as research.'

'Father, we must speak of war,' Suruk said.

'Yes, indeed. Morg, what's the word among the others?'

Morgar's tusks opened. He wore a steak knife on either hip and an apple corer in his belt. 'They're pretty keen, Dad. It was when I told them there would be no croquet under the Ghast Empire. That made their minds up.'

'Your ship won't stand a chance against Urn's missile array,' Smith said. 'But maybe we could put down on the opposite side of the planet, out of immediate range, then make our way cross-country to join up with the others. That might work.'

'Then we shall make ready to disembark,' Agshad declared. 'I shall have our friends sharpen up their blades. We shall be ready to leave in an hour's time.'

On the way back to the ship, Suruk smiled. 'My people are remembering the old ways,' he declared.

'Yes,' Rhianna said. 'Amazing.'

'Indeed. Soon the rivers of Urn shall run red, and the tea-fields shall echo with the rumbling of a thousand rolling heads. Ahaha!'

'I'm really happy for you,' Rhianna said, but Smith couldn't help noticing that for someone in flip-flops she got back to their ship pretty quickly.

Landing was difficult. The *John Pym* went first, to scout out the territory, while the M'Lak waited in orbit.

They landed on the far side of Urn, where the tea grew thick and dense, and where opposition to the new rulers was strongest. There was no problem finding people to help: no sooner had the *Pym* touched down than a skinny farmer ran out of the fields to greet them. She was called Jasmine Potts, and was a Lieutenant in the Colonial Guard. She had been training a squad of Teasmen how to fight, and her husband worked for the railway.

Within an hour the *John Pym* had been loaded onto a huge freight car, guarded by railmen and disguised with farm machinery. Major Wainscott was waiting to meet them at the other end, and as Smith opened the door the Major came forward to shake his hand.

Lieutenant Potts saluted. 'I've brought Captain Smith, sir.'

Wainscott responded with the Urnian greeting: left hand on hip, right hand held out to the side. 'Good work,

Jasmine.' He turned to his guards. 'Let's get this unloaded. Come with me, please, Smith.'

They were at a branch depot, one of the many stations that had carried tea from the great plantations to the spaceport, ready for export to the Empire. A water-tower loomed over the station like an Aresian walking-machine: next to it, a tea-tower just as big. It was a beautiful day, although a little humid for Smith's tastes. The sky was clear and startlingly blue; the tea-fields rippled in a gentle breeze. They were brilliant green, the colour of a young lizard. They seemed to radiate health.

Waincott noticed Smith's interest. 'The crop here's good, but not for much longer. Bloody Ghasts are poisoning the tea,' he said. 'Of course, there's plenty stashed away, but we need to think about the future too. Given enough time the bastards will have ruined the entire planet's harvest. And that's not the worst of it.'

'No?'

'No,' Wainscott said grimly. 'Come on. We'll talk more inside.'

They left the siding and headed towards a row of railway sheds big enough to hide the *John Pym*. Wainscott led the way, the others following, and Smith took up the rear. He tugged his collar, uncertain whether his sweating was due to the heat or Rhianna's beautiful arse. Under some insubstantial skirt-thing like a scaled-up hanky, her trim bottom wiggled with every step, beckoning him to join her in a short, intimate conga line.

He shoved the thought aside, angrily. His chances of getting anywhere with her were minimal now. She had spent most of the flight back in her room. Whatever unguessable thing he had been supposed to do, he hadn't done it, and he knew that she wouldn't do anything in response to whatever it had been meant to be. Smith suspected that she now saw him as a contemptible, worthless eunuch, or, in the parlance of women, a friend. He wondered if you got the same bad deal if you played for the other team, but he knew that he could never get used to the facial hair.

They stepped into the cool of the warehouse. There were tables here, maps and radios and plans. Smith looked over the nearest table and saw a pair of machine-guns, Ensign laser rifles and a tube of explosive like an anaemic sausage.

'I'm looking forward to handing Gertie a bit of no good,' he said.

'Damned right,' Wainscott said, halting in front of a large map pinned to the wall. 'Gather round, Smith and Co.'

He jabbed a finger at the map of Urn. 'Now, here's the situation. Capital City's where Gertie and his chums are based for now. They still creep out to poison the tea, but their patrols are getting less frequent. It's as though they're waiting for something. The Edenites still come around, and we've done well there, capturing tanks and such, but we wouldn't risk going into the city.'

'No?'

'Not without one hell of a lot of chaps. It's there that the Edenites keep all their stuff – and there that the praetorians and their tanks are based.'

'I see.' Smith peered at the map. 'Well, we have also had some success. Suruk's people have agreed to help us.'

'Excellent!' Wainscott barked.

Quickly, Smith told him of their adventures, and as he listened to the story Wainscott scowled, laughed, rubbed his beard and smoothed down his shorts in all the right places. Finally, Smith praised his crew and said, 'And that's about the sum of it.'

'Good lord. The Hyrax a creation of the Ghasts, eh? It doesn't surprise me. Those children must have been the devil to overcome. And we have the help of this chappie's colonial friends?'

'Yes, several hundred,' Smith said.

'That's excellent news. Just wait till I tell W.' Wainscott turned to Suruk. 'These comrades of yours – what's their agenda?'

'Neuter,' Suruk said. 'I thought everyone knew that.'

'Well, we'll need everyone we can get. We're going in.'

'In?' said Smith. 'To give the Ghasts a pasting?'

'And get our knackers shot off?' Carveth added quietly.

'Indeed. We've got no choice.' Wainscott's voice was heavy and cold. 'Two days ago we raided a warehouse the Ghasts have been using. We thought they were printing propaganda leaflets there, and we planned to change some of the words around, draw a funny tash on Number One, that sort of thing. Instead, we found this. Piles and piles of them.'

He reached beside the table and lifted up a board.

It was clearly some kind of advertisement, and depicted a Ghast sporting a ferocious grin, raising one of its hands in a thumbs-up gesture. Around the picture were Ghast characters, at once ugly and ornate.

'Good God,' Smith whispered.

'Quite,' Wainscott said.

'Uh?' Carveth put in. 'For those of us who don't talk funny talk?'

Smith translated, following the words with his finger. '*I love people –*'

'Makes a change,' Carveth said.

'*– for all my meals. New People: available in regular, family pack and fun-sized child. The free-range choice of the new galactic order.*'

'Christ, that's terrible!'

'Indeed,' Smith replied. 'The Ghasts have come to this planet to steal its resources for themselves. Now that they have found out that they cannot benefit from tea, they intend to poison the land and devour its inhabitants. You're right, Wainscott: it's time we got a big rocket and shoved it up Gertie's junta. What about the Hyrax and the Edenites? Do they know about the Ghast plan?'

Wainscott snorted. 'Even if they do, I doubt they care. It'd serve us heretics right.'

'Still, there may be some defections.'

One of Wainscott's men brought them tea. 'There'd better be,' said the Major. 'They may be buffoons, but the sheer amount of materiel the Edenites have will make them very difficult to defeat. It's one thing to charge into a horde of praetorians wearing only a grenade-belt and your boots, but let me tell you: it's a different thing to run naked at a tank.' He shuddered and Smith, realising that he was listening to the voice of experience, shuddered too. 'So far, we've been lucky and smart. But any attack on the city would mean open battle with the Edenite military –

and at the moment, even with your alien friends, that would be suicide.'

Smith looked around the room: at the map, the racks of weaponry, and the sign that Wainscott held. 'Well, there must be something we can use,' he said.

Carveth raised a hand. 'How's about an EMP bomb? Electro-magnetic pulse. That'd knock out the Edenite tanks and battle-suits – probably most of their guns as well.'

Wainscott shook his head. 'No can do. You'd need a nuclear explosion to generate that, and that's about the only law of warfare that the Ghasts can be relied upon to obey. We don't zap them, and they don't zap us.'

'I should think so too,' Rhianna said.

'Knockers.' Carveth took a sip of tea. 'Well, what about an explosively-pumped flux compression generator? To enhance the frequency characteristics for optimum target coupling, you could try running it through a high-quality vircator – that's a virtual cathode oscillitator, if you're wondering.' She glanced from face to face and added, 'Why are you all looking at me like that?'

'You said words,' Suruk said.

'Quite,' said Smith. 'Assuming any of that makes any sense at all, how come *you* know about it?'

Carveth shrugged. 'Well, I just happen to read a lot. To be honest, I saw the words "large pulsing vircator" in a magazine, misread, and finished the article. It had a rubbish story, but interesting props.'

Wainscott said, 'Well, if the girlie wants to try it, I can spare a couple of men to help.'

'Sounds good to me,' Carveth said. 'Nice men?'

Smith turned to the map. Thoughtfully, he followed the railway with his finger. 'In the meantime,' he said, 'we need to bring Agshad's people down to join us.'

'No problem there,' Wainscott said.

'Good. We need to keep up the pressure and mobilise as many Teasmen as we can.'

'Our commando units grow by the day,'

Smith tapped the centre of the map. 'I'd like to scout out the city,' he said. 'Maybe I could meet with W, too. And then this,' he added, pointing to the sign, 'will be consigned to the dustbin of history. Everyone agreed?'

Suruk raised a hand. 'About this evil Ghast plan to devour humans.'

'Yes?'

'Will there be a value pack?'

Gilead knocked on 462's door. When he did not get a response, he opened it anyway. Nobody could hide from the Great Annihilator, and therefore nobody had a right to hide from Gilead, his agent on Earth.

462 had retreated to his quarters as soon as his ship had landed. The Ghasts seemed very stand-offish, Gilead thought: the praetorians openly despised their holy allies and even the drones were reluctant to help keep the peace. It was as though the situation did not matter to them, as if once the Edenites pulled back they would come in and wipe the slate clean.

Perhaps they would. They were, after all, the agents of apocalypse. With apocalypse would come the Great Scouring of the Galaxy, and the ultimate victory of the Republic of Eden. Then the doubters, reds, weirdos and

British would be whisked away to simmer in Hell while Gilead and his sensibly-dressed comrades would rise to take their place with the pure of heart and get down and dirty with some hot seraphim.

462's chambers were thoroughly Ghastified. Ribs and orifices had appeared on the walls and something like a huge vertebrae ran across the roof. Gilead entered, a little nervously. A portrait of Number One glowered at him. Framed on the far wall was a picture of a soaring bird, and under it the words: 'Let nothing get in the way of your dreams, especially unarmed civilians.'

Gilead advanced into the room. On a wall screen, propaganda was playing. Music blared. Ghasts were doing aerobics in lines, picking up balls and holding them above their heads. Without their trench coats and helmets, they were nude.

462 sat in an armchair with his back to Gilead, focused on the screen. As Gilead approached, he noticed that 462 was kind of twitching—

'Oh my Lord!' Gilead cried. 'You dirty weasel!'

462 leaped to his feet, pulling his coat around him. 'Get out, get out!' He whipped around and barked, 'How dare you interrupt me, human scum! You will leave now or be shot!'

'I don't have to take orders from a dirty worm-burper! I saw you! You were – you were stony-grounding!' Gilead drew himself up straight. 'That's a sin. I spend all day beating confessions out of these liberal-democracy sickos and I come back to find you poisoning your soul!'

462 lunged forward, hissing, and Gilead flinched away from the long head. The Ghast's mouth was open, and he

could see rows of sharp teeth inside. Gilead's metal back met with the wall and he stopped. 462 slid closer, a real, physical threat.

'Oh,' he said softly, and his voice was a malignant hiss, 'do you think you are dealing with one of your underlings that you can bully into obedience? Do you think that this is puny human pornography? Do you think that I would even have anything as inefficient as an Earth-groin? Pathetic fool! This is *The Unstoppable Victorious Triumph of the All-Conquering Glorious Will of Our Master Number One, not Gertie Does The Galaxy!* Do not judge me by your weakling human standards!'

Gilead did not know what to do. He stood there, aware that his mechanical body could probably hurt 462 quite badly, but uncertain as to the consequences. What happened if you hit an angel of the apocalypse?

'While we discuss sin,' 462 said, 'how has your operation to rid Urn of "heresy" been going, while I have been away? From what I'm told it is not going very well. How will you encourage your men, I wonder? The Yull I used failed me, and, were they not dead already, I would have had them shot. How about you? Are your minions dead who have failed to conquer Urn?'

He pulled back from Gilead, who breathed again. 462 turned and took a step away from him. 'The Hyrax has been useful, but he is running out of time. When open battle begins, it will be you and I who will count, not our figurehead. And that time will come soon.'

Rick Dreckitt knew that the back room of the Black Kettle was trouble as soon as he walked in. It was what they had called a Tea Bar. Dance hall music played softly and the names of specialist teas were written on the walls, served by dispensing machines in the shape of butlers. In the shadows of the room sat tea fiends, brewing up. The air was heavy with the smell of the leaf.

A sallow youth at the far wall noticed Dreckitt and raised a china cup in a mocking salute and nodded at an empty table. Dreckitt sat down, unsettled by the unfamiliarity of the place. He was used to smoking cigarettes under a blinking neon sign, and the lack of a pall of smoke in the centre of the room made him uneasy.

The boy swaggered over and put his walking stick on the table. He sat down quickly, leaned over and said, 'Looking to get brewed?'

'No,' said Dreckitt. 'I'm just here for the music, kid.'

The boy laughed. 'Only one reason people come to the Black Kettle. I know your type. You're looking for a hit from the pot.'

'What if I am?'

The dealer chuckled. Ever since the Grand Hyrax had banned tea, there had been good money in selling it on the side. He opened his jacket and took out a plastic bag. 'So, what'cha want? I've got some Earl, some Assam, some Darjeeling. . .'

Dreckitt looked at the bag. Cut with nutmeg, no doubt. 'Huh. That's small beer to a gunsel like me. Friend, I want the Tea of Death.'

'The Tea of Death? You're crazy.'

'Yeah.'

The dealer sighed. 'Your choice. Hell, the only reason

I'd want a thing like this is to poison somebody. . . You're not out to poison someone, are you?'

'That offend your moral sense?'

The young man scowled and took a sealed bag from his pocket. 'There you go. One cup from that and you'll never come down. Pure, uncut moral fibre.'

Dreckitt's left hand was on the gun strapped to his thigh. With people like this, there was always a risk of violence. That was the trouble with the underworld: two bit punks, always on the lookout to snuff a private dick. A dirty business.

There was tea in the bag, about enough to make a cup and a half. It looked like grit, he saw - and then, as he held it up to the light, he noticed that it had a violet tint. This was it, alright: the purple tea of Urn, the death-juice. One sip could boil the brain of a normal man, even one used to drinking tea. To anyone else, it would be lethal.

Dreckitt put a hand into his coat and slowly removed his wallet. He pulled out a wad of notes and tossed them on the table.

The young man counted them. 'Adjusted Sterling,' he said. 'Nice.'

Dreckitt thought about the Hyrax's money, printed with the God Emperor's image three times per note, and largely regarded as worthless.

'It's all yours, man,' the dealer said. 'Knock yourself out.'

Dreckitt collected the Tea of Death and slipped it, and the wallet, back into his coat. He stood up and walked out. At the door the light and heat of the dusk hit him and he slid his hand into his pocket and clenched his fist around the tea. 'One sip from that and you'll never come down.' He felt almost cheerful as he walked back to his car.

Meanwhile, Wainscott was scurrying up the rocky side of Filter Hill, three miles out of Capital City. His boots were quick and agile on the loose ground. Suruk strolled along beside Wainscott, but Smith lagged behind: partially because he was not quite as nimble, but also to look out for Rhianna.

'Ow,' she said, removing another pebble from her sandals. 'This really hurts.'

Being one with Gaia, Smith reflected, was clearly easier on thick grass and flat surfaces. Slightly irritated, he waited until Rhianna had removed the stone and helped her back up.

'Perhaps you ought to wait at the bottom,' he suggested kindly. There was a small camp a mile away, a staging post the Teasmen had set up for the recapture of the Capital. A dozen soldiers waited there, ready for the command to move on the city.

'No!' she replied, and he was surprised to see that she looked annoyed. 'I can manage perfectly well in my own right. I don't need any help, thanks.'

This sounded like trouble. 'Alright then,' he said. 'But I think you'd be better off with walking boots.'

She scowled and he wondered what the hell he was supposed to do. What did she think he was, psychic? Having never quite worked out the limits of her mental powers, he added to himself, If I am supposed to be psychic, could you let me know?

No reply. He slogged on.

They reached the top. Waincott and Suruk lay in the shadow of a dead tree to hide their outlines. Smith and Rhianna crept over to join them.

Wainscott was dressed like a Teasman, with a plantation flag in his belt and a dark cosy on his head. He pointed at the city. 'The enemy,' he said. 'Look.'

Smith took the telescopic scope from his rifle.

He put the scope to his eyes and suddenly the details of the city sprang into view: the gargoyles and nameplates on the warehouses and office blocks, the chimneys of thousands of homes and, biggest of all, the spires, columns and minarets of what had once been the senate-house.

'That's the Hyrax's palace,' Wainscott said. 'The throne of the God-Prophet or some such rubbish. Utter nonsense, all this God Emperor stuff.'

'It's an oppressive patriarchal construct based on false notions of masculine dominance,' Rhianna said. 'The very towers point towards the phallocentric myth at the heart of his so-called *king*dom.'

Wainscott looked at her as if she were mentally ill. 'Right. But that's not the real problem. The Hyrax has his Crusadists, and a crazy bunch they are, but the real power behind him's over there, to the East of the city: the Edenites.'

Gilead's men lurked under a complex mass of sensor equipment and camouflage, their perimeter bristling with anti-aircraft guns. Their base looked like a very large, very plush guerrilla encampment, with more flags and much better TV reception. What Smith had taken for a small building rolled slowly across the perimeter. A hatch opened in the side of it, and three hulking shapes disembarked: motorised combat suits, each seven feet tall and covered in weaponry, puffed out by armour to the shape of teddy bears.

The wind stirred, ruffling the grass around them. A jumble of brassy, raucous sound seeped out of the city and made its way to their ears. Some kind of marching music was parping from the Edenite fortress.

'Imagine dropping an EMP in the middle of all that stuff,' Wainscott whispered. The major's eyes gleamed with excitement. 'You'd close the whole place down in one go. Can you imagine it? Actually *shutting them up*.' He sighed, and the light in his eyes died down. 'Of course, I don't know how. You'd have to get an EMP bomb under the radar. And every vehicle that goes past gets searched . . . goodness knows how it could be done.'

Sounds rose up from the palace now. They were loud and distorted, blasting out of great speakers nailed to the roof. Lumps of plaster must be falling out the ceiling, Smith thought.

'Only the Hyrax is great! All hail the Grand Hyrax! Only the Hyrax is great!'

Seemingly at random, the God-Prophet's voice came on: '– severing the accursed hand from the arm, the wretched head from the neck! The eye that will not see – blind it to make it see! The mouth that will not announce the glory of the Hyrax – fill it with the dentures of faith! The Beast lurks among us, stirring lies against the earthly paradise of the Grand Hyrax – anyone denying the earthly paradise will die! Obey me and live! I hope you're listening to this, harlots of Babylon especially! Crusade!'

With great finality Rhianna said, 'What a colossal jerk.'

'Of course, at the moment he just sounds like an idiot,' Smith said. 'But if they manage to stop people drinking tea, his powers may start to work. And then the people of Urn will be like lambs to the slaughter.'

Suruk had been studying the city in silence. 'I wish I were in the palace,' the alien said. 'Swinging my blade, striking down my enemies, liberating someone from something or other. . .'

'Well, you'd be busy,' Wainscott said. 'Look over there.'

Smith turned the scope on the west of the city, where the spaceport and industrial areas were. They looked dead. Smoke rose from a few chimneys, but otherwise, the place was deserted. The warehouses were locked up, the streets empty – wait a moment. He turned up the amplification on the gunsight.

A column of praetorians turned the corner, three abreast. Light caught their helmets and the leather of their coats. At the front of the column, like the head of a Chinese dragon, was a black banner bearing the antennae'd skull of the praetorian legions. Beside them ran beast handlers, hauling back the ant-hounds the Ghasts used to guard their fortresses.

The main impression Smith had was of bulk. They were taller and thicker than normal Ghasts, more bullish; a blunt, effective tool for killing and intimidation. Smith watched them carefully, feeling a kind of cold readiness run over him. They were bred to terrify, but what he felt now was eagerness to fight.

The praetorians yelled something in unison. A

warehouse door rolled open, the column stormed inside and it slammed behind them. Then they were gone, but for the brief moment that it had been open Smith had caught a glimpse of movement behind the doors: swarming Ghasts, rows of vehicles and weaponry.

'They'll be formidable enemies,' he said. 'Super game, too.'

Wainscott nodded. 'At this range you could pick one of those lobsters right out of its tank.'

'Too risky. Shame, though.'

A thin line of dust crept from the East gates. Light glinted on laser proof armour. Vehicles rolled into the countryside, towards the wilting tea plantations.

'Patrol,' Wainscott said. 'Edenites.'

A sun dragon whirled above the convoy, soaking up heat from the engines. Gunshots popped from the column and it screeched and spun away, tracer fire chasing its tail. No fire discipline, Smith thought. The Edenites had a combination of enthusiasm and paranoia that made them unpredictable when armed – which was always.

'Best get going,' Wainscott said. 'They might get nervy and bung a missile up here.'

Quietly, they turned and climbed back down. The slope was steep and unreliable, and Suruk went ahead to catch Rhianna if she should fall. Smith watched her make a long job of descending and found that Wainscott was at his side.

'Funny bird, that,' Wainscott observed. 'All that "masculine dominance", "phallocentric myth". . . is she any good in the sack?'

'I really wouldn't know,' Smith replied.

2

Many Types of Adventure!

They climbed into the jeep and returned to the main forward camp, by the railway station. Smith was astonished at how busy the place was. Men and women worked ceaselessly: regular soldiers from the Colonial Guard and scouts from the teasmen were unloading equipment from trains, discussing tactics and pouring over maps.

But that was not all. In the fields nearby stood the first of Agshad's skimmers, half-hidden by the tea crop. They were ugly, powerful-looking machines, a mix of hovercraft, fighter plane and tank, covered in armour plates and trophies. Some carried slogans and pictures on the side. Most were red, where the paint had not worn through to show dull metal, greasy with oil. Thin figures moved between them: M'Lak, not quite comfortable here yet, preferring their own company to that of the stubby, pinkish-brown humans.

Wainscott stopped the jeep and Suruk, who was only half-inside anyway, sprang down and looked around, openly intrigued. Smith helped Rhianna out of the jeep – were you supposed to help an enlightened modern woman? Whatever the answer was, he knew he would be wrong – and they headed towards the warehouses.

'They're still poisoning the tea,' Wainscott said. 'They're trying to pressure us into making a bad move.' He looked around. 'We've got six more bases like this one, equidistant from the city. When the time comes, we'll rush it all at once, somehow.'

They found Morgar with Carveth beside one of the skimmers. Carveth waved and ran to meet them. 'Hello all!'

'You seem very cheerful,' Smith said.

She nodded. She was wearing her overalls, and there was already a smudge of dirt on the end of her nose. 'Well, it's nice to be busy, isn't it?' Her voice dropped into a loud, hoarse whisper. 'And guess who's here?'

Smith peered at the fighters, trying to pick one face from the others. Suddenly he spotted a man of average height, handsome in a battered way and wearing a Panama hat to keep off the sun. 'Dreckitt,' he said, as if it were a swear word.

'Eee!' Carveth said, grinning.

Rhianna glanced around and said, 'Where?'

'Don't look, don't look!' Carveth hissed. 'He'll see me in my overalls.'

Smith frowned. Her enthusiasm troubled him. 'Before you go any further, Carveth, I ought to point out that he was sent to kill you last time you two met. It was a miracle that he decided not to.'

She nodded. 'You see? He could have assassinated me but he didn't. That's a pretty good start for a relationship.'

'Well, you're certainly cleared the murder-on-sight hurdle. Next stop, wedded bliss. Honestly, Carveth, I'm not entirely happy with this.'

Rhianna leaned in. 'We'll talk later,' she said.

Morgan strolled over from the skimmers, smiling pleasantly. 'Hello there. Warm, isn't it?'

'As hot as the blood gushing from a severed neck,' Suruk said.

'Quite. Picnic weather. Now, Polly, you must meet my friend Ozroth Bloodaxe. He's quite the auto enthusiast. Ozroth?'

A M'Lak turned from his work and flipped up a welding mask.

'This is Ozroth Bloodaxe, of the line of Drelcor,' Morgan said. 'And this is Polly Pilot, of the line of. . . Pontius, perhaps?'

Smith felt strange, unsettled. His head ached a little. So, this is it, he thought. This is the army that will free Urn or die trying. He had the uncomfortable feeling that he was just about to remember that he had forgotten something.

'Are you okay?' Rhianna said.

'I feel odd. Sort of worried, but I'm not sure why.'

'It's stress.' Rhianna nodded sagely, setting her dreadlocks in motion. 'War is very stressful. Getting shot at can actually put your chi out of alignment. Why don't you have a rest, and then maybe a massage?'

'Really?' he said. The thought of it made him feel quite giddy. 'I mean, from you?'

She shrugged. 'Sure. You need to relax.'

'I need to sit down,' Smith said, still thinking about Rhianna and massage.

'Yes, you do,' said Carveth.

*

Smith walked into the station offices. They were empty. All the men were outside. It seemed oddly quiet here: the eye of the storm.

He pulled out a chair and sat down. He felt slightly ill, as if he had a migrane coming on. Outside, a tall, hawk-like woman was staring into a cup, surrounded by a little knot of Teasmen. She wore robes and seemed to be making some sort of speech. This must be Sam O'Varr, he realised, the Sauceress of Urn. Smith did not believe in tea-seeing: it sounded too much like one of Rhianna's nonsenses.

Bloody Rhianna. He felt depressed, in a dull, placid way. It was better if she didn't massage him. Better not to let her touch him at all, better still to ignore the bloody woman, accept that she was never going to be his and get back to killing Gertie. There was a war to win; the sooner he could forget about sex with girls, the sooner he could get back to bashing the Ghast on his own.

Outside, the sauceress was sharing a joke with a soldier from the Colonial Guard. Smith watched them bang their mugs together and thought: Tea, yes, that's what I need.

He got up. Glancing across the corridor, he saw a small office kitchen. He wandered in, filled the kettle and put it on. Smith found a mug and a small fridge containing a packet of milk. There were no half-decent spoons, so he took out his penknife. It would do. He opened the cupboard and found a small jar labelled 'tea'. It was empty. 'Bollocks,' he said.

Smith turned the jar upside down in case some stray tea had got caught in it. He shook it, but nothing fell

out. It was then that he noticed a single teabag taped to
the base. He pulled it free. Obviously an emergency
teabag, intended for situations much like this. Sensible
chaps.

He put the teabag in the cup and added the boiling
water. He stirred it for a while with his knife, squashed the
teabag against the side of the cup – interesting aroma –
and dropped the bag into the sink. Then he added a little
milk and stirred it again, as per the advice of the United
Kingdom Tea Council.

It didn't taste bad. He was unable to identify the sort: it
reminded him slightly of Kenyan tea, although the rich
aftertaste seemed unfamiliar, as did the purplish tint. Still,
it was refreshing enough. Some sort of local brew,
perhaps, a speciality of Urn.

Hot tea ran into his innards, refreshing him. He felt a
bit better: his head was clearing very quickly. The stuff
was sharpening him up a treat, in fact. In a moment he
would be able to go back outside and help the men get
ready to give some Ghasts a pasting.

Smith opened the cupboard and looked around for a
biscuit. There was nothing. What I need now is some
tiffin, he thought. 'What I need now is some tiffin,' he
said, to make sure.

He left the kitchen. Another door branched off the
corridor; it seemed to lead to a lavatory. He approached
the door. There was a sign on the door. It said, 'Please
leave this toilet in the same state as you found it'.

How absurd. What kind of a fool would find a toilet,
presumably needing a wee, and leave it still needing a
wee? He chuckled at the stupidity of the idea and had

another sip of tea. He stopped chuckling and tried again. This time the tea went inside him instead of down his shirt-front. 'Mm, tiffin,' he said. His nipples hurt a bit from the hot tea.

Smith noticed that no more tea was entering his mouth and checked his cup. It was very deep. In fact, it was one of the largest mugs he had ever seen. Clever thing, technology. He looked down the well-like mug, into its depths. 'Helloooo,' he called. The cup was so deep that a man could fall into it, if he was not careful. Smith would not fall into it. No fooling me, he thought.

'Smith?'

That was his name; he turned around to see Major Wainscott standing in the doorway. Major Wainscott had a beard, which was clever of him. 'Clever beard you've got there, Wainscott,' Smith observed.

'What?' Wainscott demanded. 'What's wrong with you, man?'

'Nothing's wrong with me,' Smith replied. 'I'm the tiffin, you see.'

'You're ill, Smith,' Wainscott said.

'Piffle.' Smith wandered back into the office, reflecting that he needed another sit-down. At the edge of his vision, Wainscott was becoming quite agitated. He had run into the kitchen and was making appalled noises, presumably because there was no more tea.

'Sorry about that,' Smith said. 'I had the last teabag.'

Wainscott peered at him. 'Smith,' he barked. 'Smith, you hear me?'

Smith smiled at the absurdity of the situation. 'Of course I do,' he said.

'Smith, where did you find that teabag?'

'Stuck to the bottom of the pot. Why?'

Wainscott exclaimed 'Balls!' and ran for the door.

Terror struck Smith at the thought of being left alone. 'Wait!'

Wainscott turned around at the door. 'Smith?'

'Haven't got any tiffin on you, I suppose?'

But Wainscott was gone. Smith felt confused and glum. He spotted a magazine sticking out of a small bin. He fished it out. It was *What Ho*, the *Monolith on Sunday*'s colour supplement. The front cover said, 'Azranath the Butcher shows us round his lovely citadel. Top fashion model Olivia Marshing-Purdah tells us her diet secret'. He opened it.

The pictures lunged out at him. He blinked and he was falling, tumbling into the photos of famous women caught shopping and noted actors carrying their babies. The gaudy text rushed around him as he fell into the *Monolith*'s colour supplement. 'It's full of stars,' he gasped, and the last thing he heard was the muffled thud of his head striking paper, and then the floor.

He was in the tea-fields, walking – drifting – through the crop. It stretched on forever, to the horizon and beyond, a carpet of moral fibre under the brilliant sky. He took a deep breath of pure, rich air, that seemed to feed and clean his lungs.

'Allo!'

He turned: a bearded man in ragged robes stood behind him. The man wore a pointed hat, and carried a long stick in one hand. In the other was an ice-cream.

'Alright, young'n,' said the man. 'Time we spoke.'

'Hello,' said Smith. 'I'm Isambard Smith.'

'And I am Merlin!' cried the old man. 'I walk the land, guarding it for the future. And you, Isambard Smith, must hark at me, for there be a battle coming anywhen soon, and it be up to you to win it. So you may ask of me what you will, and I'll guide you best as I can.'

'Ah,' Smith replied. 'This is obviously some sort of hallucination. My brain isn't working right. I'm afraid you'd best come back when I'm feeling better, Merlin.'

'No!' cried Merlin. 'Now is the time, my lad! Ask now, or never!'

'Very well,' said Smith. 'Will we win the war?'

'Nope,' Merlin said. 'Not with what you've got now. You feel it, you know it, but you don't think it. You drink the tea, the tea that grows from the land, but you don't see how truth lies. This is no scrap between two men – when a man wars with us, he wars with the land, see? You turn the land on him, and you'll scag the bastard for sure.See?'

'I think so,' Smith murmured. 'Can I ask another question, Merlin?'

'Speak the words.'

'Am I ever going to get anywhere with Rhianna?'

'Get anywhere?' Merlin's eyes narrowed. 'Are we talking runs, a four, or a six past her boundary?'

'The full trip to the pavilion, I suppose.'

Merlin smirked. 'Keep your pads on and your bat straight, lad.'

'What does that mean?' he replied, but everything was starting to fade.

*

The sky was a bland off-white. There were planes above him, space-fighters, frozen in the air. He blinked. He was on his bed on the *John Pym* and he was looking up at the model kits he had hung from the ceiling.

Heads leaned into his vision. People were looking down at him. 'Hello,' he said.

They crowded in. He felt like a goldfish in a bowl.

'I feel odd,' Smith said.

'You shouldn't do.' This was a gaunt, long-faced man with a thin moustache: W, the spy. 'By rights, you ought to be dead. You drank the Tea of Death.'

'The what?' Smith started to sit up and a hand pressed him back into bed. It was Rhianna. Smith felt pressure on his fingers; she was holding his hand. She sat by the bed, looking both concerned and strangely pleased, as if she knew how to make him feel better again and was looking forward to showing everyone.

'The Tea of Death,' Rhianna said. 'The Tea of Death is a very rare, very potent psychotropic drug, Isambard. You were experiencing a realignment of your consciousness, prompting you to react psychically to both the external world and your inner landscape—'

'In short, you tripped your nuts off,' Carveth said.

'Carveth?' Smith tried to move again, but Rhianna pressed him down, gently but firmly, and felt his brow. He could get used to that.

'Be still, Isambard. Sauceress O'Varr says you're really lucky to be alive. The Tea of Death is actually the product of the blessed crops of Urn that's passed through the sun dragons to rain down upon the sacred land. Isn't that fantastic?'

Smith thought about it. He said, 'Are you telling me I've just drunk dragon pee?'

Rhianna laughed. 'Oh no, the rain part's purely symbolic. It's not literally a liquid.'

'Good!'

'It's solid.'

As Smith choked, W interrupted. 'What you ingested would have killed a man of lesser moral fibre. In fact, we were planning to slip the teabag into the Hyrax's dinner. The very fact you're breathing is testament to the nature of the common man of the Empire. The common man, you understand, who will liberate Urn.'

Smith said, 'Well, can someone get me a straight cup of tea?'

'Right, good plan,' W said, and he stood up in a stiff, awkward way and strode out of the room.

Rhianna leaned closer. 'What was it like?'

'It. . . I saw all kinds of funny stuff. I had a dream about Merlin, and then there were these curious sensations—'

'What were they like?'

He frowned, struggling to remember feelings that, now they were past, he did not have the words to depict. 'Strange. I felt as though I was floating on some kind of magic carpet ride, drifting through purple haze eight miles high above Kashmir. I looked down and saw endless fields beneath me, with some sort of small red fruit in them, going on forever. There was a sign down there. It said, "Pick your own".'

' "Pick your own",' Rhianna echoed, awed. She smiled at him, which made him feel much better. 'Amazing,' she said dreamily.

Smith pulled himself up so that he was sitting. Thankfully, he was still fully clothed. He took a deep breath. 'Rhianna?'

'Yes, Isambard?'

'Thank you for looking out for me. I mean, it's good of you to make sure I was alright. I could have got addicted to morphine or something.'

'Er, yes,' Rhianna said. She smiled again. 'Perhaps I ought to become ship's medic.'

'Well, you've certainly got the most experience of being medicated.' She looked less impressed by this, and he added quickly, 'Look, I've been thinking about things, and I think that—'

'Greetings!' Suruk stepped into the room. He carried a steaming mug. 'Tea,' he declared, setting it down on the bedside table. 'The warm beverage of warriors.' He stepped back and stood in the middle of the room, drinking from his own cup, peering down at Smith. Go away, Smith willed him. Leave me with Rhianna. Just because you don't have any private parts. . .

Rhianna let go of his hand and stood up. 'Well, I'll leave you boys to it. See you later, guys.'

She left. Smith watched her go away – something he seemed to end up doing a lot – and gave Suruk one of his stern looks.

'Is it good tea?'

'It's lovely tea. Thank you very much, Suruk.'

Suruk nodded. He closed the door. 'So, are you a seer now too?'

'I don't think so.' Smith gritted his teeth and strained. 'No, I didn't see anything there.'

'Hmm. Perhaps you have become psychic. I know – can you tell what I am thinking of?'

'Is it war, or cutting the heads off things?'

'Indeed! Both!'

'I think that was just a lucky guess.'

Suruk sipped his tea, a surprisingly difficult activity for someone with mandibles. 'I am glad you are well,' he said thoughtfully. 'We will have every need of good fighters when the time comes to strike.'

'Yes, we will.'

'The city is well-defended. In a fair fight, I do not know who victory would favour – but as we stand now, I doubt there will be a fair fight at all. I fear that the Edenites will simply shoot us down before we come into range. Their guns are large, and armour thick.'

'So we go to our deaths, you're saying?'

'Almost certainly. I personally do not mind – much better to die on my feet, swinging a blade – but I understand that this might trouble you. Especially since you have yet to spawn with the ship's females.'

Smith looked away. He did not want to feel angry and afraid, but he did. 'It's better that we go out fighting,' he said. 'I mean, the bloody Ghasts mean to wipe us out anyhow. Even if they do win, we'll hurt them first.'

Suruk chuckled. 'Well said. The death-screams of a thousand enemies shall be a fanfare to proclaim us to our ancestors!'

'Well, I need to get up. Not doing a lot here.'

'No, Mazuran. Sleep, for it is the evening. I shall help the others; you must save your strength for acts of war. You will need it,' he added, and he opened the door.

*

Smith slept badly, but he did not dream. Soon he woke again, and he lay in the dark cabin for a while, feeling fear stir slowly in his gut. He switched the light on and sat up.

The clock said that it was half-past twelve. He felt clear-headed, but fragile. Smith sat on the edge of the bed for a moment, stood up and put his boots and jacket on. He opened the door and stepped outside.

In the corridor, needles rattled softly in their dials. Even the life-support systems seemed to hum less loudly than before. He walked down the passage, opened the airlock and went out into the night.

His boots were quiet on the metal steps. The *Pym* stood in the shadow of a little wood, where the overhanging branches would break up its shape. To his right the M'Lak skimmers were black hillocks in the dark, like burial mounds. The night was cool on his skin; the air was fragrant with tea and earth.

A voice hissed behind him. 'Who goes there?'

'Isambard Smith,' he said, raising his hands. A small man stood there, a knife in one hand and a silenced Stanford gun in the other. The fellow had crept close enough to touch Smith before challenging him. Wainscott's men had trained their recruits well. 'I just needed some air.'

The sentry relaxed. 'It's you alright. Fair enough.' The man stepped back, and faded into the tea fields. Smith watched him disappear and thought: If all our men are like him, we'll give the Ghasts a run for their money. We certainly deserve to.

He walked into the wood. Someone had cut a narrow

path between the trees and he followed it, not quite sure where he was going. For the first time in a long while, he wanted peace and quiet, to be away from the weapons and preparation for war, to forget about his duty and the fight to come.

Yes, peace and quiet. That would be good. The Imperial Code said that it was noble and right to find peace in the countryside. Being in the country enabled the citizen to reflect on life. Very true, thought Smith. Had not Merlin said something like that? Yes, he'd said that victory would come from being one with the land. Well, this was certainly a good—

He tripped over a root. Smith fell onto his hands. He stood up, said 'Arse!', brushed his stinging palms together to get rid of the dirt, and stopped.

There was a light in the forest. It was a steady, firm glow like an electric torch. It looked like an ember held just in front of him, but there could be no doubt that it came from something further up the path.

He was unarmed. Even his sword was back in the ship. Smith cursed himself for a fool; with a weapon, he would be happy to advance. It would not take five minutes to return to the ship. He could arm himself there, perhaps wake the others. But in five minutes' time, would it still be here?

He reached to his pocket and took out his penknife. Smith opened the blade and looked at it. It was thoroughly blunt. He scowled into the dark, ducked low and scurried towards the light.

The trees were thinning. It was a yellow light, not the blue phosphorescence of Ghast technology. It stayed still, growing as he approached, waiting for him. There were no more roots to impede his progress.

He scuttled closer, bent low to disguise his outline, scurrying from the cover of one tree to the next. The light flickered as something moved across it, and for a moment a creature was in silhouette – a being, perhaps human, perhaps a Ghast with its claws folded down. It looked too short for a M'Lak – but he had seen it only for a moment. He clenched his fist around the penknife and approached.

There must be a clearing ahead; that was where the light was. The figure stayed tantalisingly out of view.

Something moved on the other side of the clearing, high in the trees. It looked like a thin, taut curtain, or the paper in a Chinese lantern.

The figure stepped into view and Smith bit his tongue in shock. His gasp was lost in the rustle of leaves. It was Rhianna.

She was looking at some tall object among the trees on the other side of the clearing, something a little like long poles with a folded sheet hanging between them.

As he watched, the poles moved, and the sheet between them stretched into a colossal wing.

Smith leaped up, hurdled the scrub and bounded into the clearing. In a moment he had shoved Rhianna aside and stood between her and the sun dragon, knife outstretched. Rhianna cried out, and a reptilian head the size of a coffin drew back from them, surprised. Smith brandished the penknife at it.

'Back!' he cried. 'Unhand her, or I'll carve you up!'

The sun dragon peered down at him, mildly perturbed. Smith found that he was panting, and that the arm which was not holding the penknife was around Rhianna's shoulders. There was an embarrassing pause.

'It's all right,' he said. 'I'll protect you. Stay back, by God!'

Rhianna said, 'I'm fine, thank you, Isambard.'

He let go of her shoulder and looked at her. She was wearing a long dress and, were it not for the big shapeless cardigan, would have looked very pre-Raphaelite. 'It's okay.' She held up a plastic bag. 'Look, breadcrumbs.'

'Oh,' said Smith. He looked around the clearing, and realised that there were more of the creatures. They stood at the edge, watching him as one might a tottering infant, their horned heads dipping and tilting like those of birds. Wings rose up behind them and moonlight glistened on the solar panels on their wings and backs. One of the sun dragons yawned, and static crackled around its jaws. They were sleek, lightly-built, and huge.

Rhianna took a crust out of the bag and tossed it to the nearest dragon. It snatched it from the air and gulped it down. 'Beautiful, aren't they?' she said.

'Yes,' Smith said, 'but you need to be careful. They're like tigers: beautiful but dangerous. These must be even more dangerous than that, like. . . like dinosaur-tigers that fly. Like dragons, in fact.'

'They won't eat me,' Rhianna said. She sounded absolutely certain.

Slowly, he realised that this was true. He stared through the moonlight at her. 'You're. . . you're not controlling them, are you?'

'More talking to them. On their own level. They're used

to people being afraid of them. They think we're interesting.'

'My God,' he said. He looked around the clearing, astonished.

'Isambard,' Rhianna said, and he looked back at her. 'Did you just try to protect me from a dragon with a penknife?'

Smith realised that he was still holding the knife. He looked down at it. It looked ridiculously inadequate, as if he had stuck his finger out in the hope of poking one of these monsters in the eye. 'Well,' he said, feeling extremely foolish as he folded the penknife away, 'not really. I mean, I will admit I was concerned, but in the circumstances I felt that—'

'That's the bravest thing I've ever seen.' She moved suddenly and he flinched, instinctively thinking that she meant to headbutt him, but she was too quick and her hands grabbed his head, pulled it forward and she kissed him forcefully on the lips.

Startled, Smith staggered backwards with her still attached. He fell over backwards and she landed on top of him, which bruised his chest. 'Mrpf murn urp,' he said as she kissed him.

She stopped kissing him and pulled back, but she did not get off his chest. Rhianna lay on top of him, grinning. Smith was not sure what one did in situations like these.

'Well,' he said breezily, 'that was jolly. Cup of tea?'

Rhianna did not seem to have heard. 'Oh, Isambard,' she said, shaking her head 'Whatever am I going to do with you?'

'Ah, well, I don't really know, as it happens. Perhaps we

could have a chat, hold hands or something—'

'Rhetorial question. I'm going to screw your brains out.'

'Righto.'

She kissed him again, and because this time he wasn't trying to fight her off, it felt good. He opened his eyes and looked up at the moon and a very puzzled sun dragon.

Rhianna straddled him and started unbuttoning his jacket. He suddenly realised that she meant exactly what she'd said, and terror struck him. His heart jittered and pounded against his ribs. The grass prickled against his hands and neck.

'Wait, wait!'

She stopped.

'I mean, you're not going to do it out here, are you?'

Rhianna had started moving her hips in a disconcerting manner. He tried not to think about it. 'Of course,' she said. 'We're outside, one with nature. . .'

'But they can see!'

'They're dragons, Isambard. They won't tell anyone.'

'I – I just—'

'You're a virgin, aren't you?'

'No! How are we defining virgin here?'

'Oh dear.' Abruptly, she rolled off him and got to her feet. Damn! He wanted to scream. Damn you, Smith! Why the hell did you say that?

But to his surprise she smiled and reached out and helped him up. As he stood up she stepped in close and kissed him again. Her hands slipped around his waist, and she gripped his bottom and squeezed. Pressed against him, she shifted position, and a sort of ripple seemed to move up her body, which got the attention of his old chap.

'Now,' she whispered, pressing her lips close to his ear, 'you're coming in with me, and you're not running away, okay? You wouldn't run away from a girl, would you now?'

'No,' he said into her dreadlocks, and she took his hand and led him back.

The ship was quiet. Rhianna led him to her door and opened it. He felt dizzy.

'Will I be sleeping in your room?' he inquired. 'Because if I am, I ought to go and fetch my pyjamas—'

'Isambard, are you a coward?'

'No!' he said, stung.

'Come on then,' Rhianna said. 'You'll be fine. And forget your goddamn pyjamas. You won't sleep a wink.'

Inside her room it was magical. Suddenly he was in a different world, of drapes and strange smells, cushions, throws and air heavy with the smell of joss. It felt like witchcraft, dulling his brain and sharpening his senses. They kissed and her hands unbuttoned his jacket, and he put his own hands on her bare midriff. She drew back, smiling, and pulled her top off.

As she unfastened his shirt something snapped inside his brain, some restriction broke, and he squeezed her tightly against him. 'You're smashing,' he found himself saying, over and over again. He couldn't think of anything to say other than that.

Rhianna slipped off her skirt. She looked super in her

pants. Then there was more kissing and a bit of difficulty with his trousers and boots. 'Whoa,' Rhianna said, looking at his underpants. 'Polly was right all along.'

She took his hands and showed him what to do, and he kissed her some more. 'You're so beautiful,' he said, knowing as he said it how insufficient it was to describe her, and Rhianna laughed and ran her fingertips across his stomach, just above the waistband of his Y-fronts.

The rest was awkward, and a bit tricky the first time round, but it was *her*, Rhianna, who he would have sworn that he could never have, and that was all that mattered to him. She seemed happy too. It was all wonderful, like a dream, but the best moment came when they were about to sleep. She laid her head on his shoulder and kissed him again and said, 'Goodnight, Isambard.'

'Night-night,' he said, and he felt extremely proud. She's mine, he realised suddenly. Hooray! He put his arm round her and tried to kiss her head through all the dreadlocks, but didn't quite succeed. She fell asleep. So beautiful, he thought, and he did the same.

He awoke to find that it was not all a dream. She was still there: snoring slightly, her cheek stuck to the sheet with dribble. He looked down at her and grinned. He had not been so happy since he was six, when his parents had bought him a book called *Fifty Space Dreadnoughts to Colour and Keep*. It had come with a grey crayon.

Smith did not want to leave Rhianna. A deep, irrational fear told him that if he left her, she would come to her senses and decide that she had made a terrible mistake, or else God, or fate, or secret police would contrive to steal her away. It was one of the laws of physics that Isambard Smith could not get girls: surely you could not break a law of physics. He pushed the thought aside.

Smith could not help waking her as he got up. Rhianna opened one eye and said, 'Uh?'

'I'm going to make some tea,' he said quietly. 'I won't be long.'

He put on his clothes from yesterday and opened the door. 'Cheerio,' he said, and he slipped out into the corridor.

Now, he thought, best do this quietly. Suruk would find the whole business baffling and vaguely shameful – the M'Lak, being neuter, rarely had cause to touch one another at all – and as for Carveth, he could not imagine a single response she could have to the news that would not make him want to cringe and hide. He crept past Suruk's door, stole into the living room in his socks and reached the galley.

It was dark. His hands found the kettle and filled it. He plugged it in and put two teabags in the pot. What a day! Smith thought. What an incredible change to his life the last twenty-four hours had brought! He had survived a massive dose of hallucinogen, seen Merlin in a dream, dis-covered that his ideal woman could commune with dragons and then made love to her. That called for an extra teabag.

He opened the fridge door. There was a piece of paper folded over the milk. He opened it up. It said, 'Nice work, Boss. Give her one from us.'

The light flicked on. Carveth and Suruk stood in the doorway. Carveth had rolled a magazine into a trumpet and blew a fanfare. 'Hail!' Suruk cried.

'Ah, hello,' said Smith, going red.

Carveth ran over and slapped him on the back, then hugged him until his ribs hurt. 'Nice one! You got her in the sack! Whaaay!'

'Shush!'

'Is she weird? I bet she's into all, like, stuff. She'll have you doing all sorts of weird things. You want to watch your arse around a woman like that, literally. But I'm really happy for you.'

'And I salute you,' Suruk said. 'May your seed swim briskly, and a legion of great warriors spurt boldly from your loins.'

'Erm, thanks.'

'But beware, Mazuran! For softness ruins many a warrior, and many times have I been honoured to call you friend. So by my honour, she'd better be good enough for you, or the blade of Suruk will claim her skull!'

'Well, that's very kind.'

'We will still be friends, will we not?'

'Of course we will.'

'Good. You have done well, distasteful as human breeding is to me. Your tenacity paid off: sometimes, it is the longest odds that pay the greatest dividends. Which reminds me,' he added, turning to Carveth, 'seeing that they have finally mated, you owe me five Earth pounds.'

She scowled and fished out her wallet. 'Ah, bloody hell.'

'You had a bet on me and Rhianna?' Smith tailed off, vaguely horrified.

'Well, yeah,' Carveth said. 'More of a sweepstake, really. I thought I'd make some easy money.'

Smith sighed. 'I suppose you want some of my tea, too.'

He returned to Rhianna's room. She rolled over and said drowsily, 'They know, right?'

A muffled whooping issued from the lounge. ''Fraid so,' Smith said.

She smiled, a long, sly smile that he could feel between his pockets. 'Want to give them something to whoop about?'

'Oh, righto.' He approached and put the mugs down on the bedside table. Smith got into bed, fully clothed. Under the covers, he thrashed about.

'What're you doing?' Rhianna said.

'Taking my trousers off.'

'You don't have to keep covering yourself. I've see guys naked before.'

'I'm a bit of a wreck, I'm afraid.'

She sighed. 'That's just negative body image, thrust upon you by the fascist media. Now, come here.'

They made love again. Looking up at Rhianna as she bounced about Smith thought, I could really get used to this.

Fifteen minutes later he sat up in bed with the covers pulled up to his armpits. Rhianna lay next to him on top of the sheets, completely naked. From Smith's point of view, this was a pretty good arrangement.

She was sleek and tanned, with a dancer's body. Her breasts were quite small, her navel a neat dent in the very-nearly-flat expanse of her stomach. She'd once mentioned something about belly dancing; Smith would have liked to see that. Her legs and armpits were, mercifully, shaved, although, he reflected, she seemed a bit fluffy 'down there'. At the moment she lay on her front, revealing a small tattoo between her shoulder-blades. It was probably meant to be a Chinese character, but from here it looked like a stickman. Her legs were bent at the knee and crossed at the ankles, showing him her rather grey soles. The end of her bed, he'd noticed, was slightly grubby from her feet.

'I really feel we connected there,' Rhianna said.

'Well of course,' Smith said. 'I mean, after all, I, ah, don't know how much more connected you can get than that. If you were a space station we'd have swapped astronauts by now.'

'I mean emotionally,' Rhianna said, 'Spiritually. I felt it was a –' she made a weighing-out gesture with her hands, which Smith recognised as a trouble sign – 'I felt that it was more, somehow, than just the ritual intrusion of the chthonic male into the sacred feminine other.'

Smith thought about it. 'You've got smashing boobs, Rhianna,' he said.

3

Preparations for Battle

It was good weather for fighting. A light wind cooled Suruk's skin and the fragrance of tea seeped into his nostrils.

The humans were bringing up their tanks. The task of building them had been farmed out to various workshops and many had improved on the standard designs, giving them cowcatchers, fluted chimneys and extra scrollwork on the armour plate. The tanks had parked up in rows in the tea warehouses, as if for a particularly violent traction engine show.

A little way off, a pair of humans in black gowns were talking to a group of soldiers. Priests, Suruk realised. Suruk recognised the soldiers as the Deepspace Operations Group, Wainscott's men.

He approached. Wainscott waved. He looked slightly more presentable than usual, but still far from ideal, as if he had slept on a park bench instead of under it. Wainscott rubbed his stubbly beard and gave Suruk a hard, friendly smile. 'Mr Slayer,' he said. 'You all set?'

'Indeed. And you?'

'We're ready,' Susan said. She wore a Beam gun across her body, a cumbersome weapon that looked as if it had been improvised from several other sources, including a shotgun and a watering can. A big curved powerpack jutted from the top of the gun. It was ugly and lethal.

'Then may your ancestors guide your blades today, friends. But I must tell you one thing before we make war. Isambard Smith did a thing of wildness last night with the seer Rhianna, and you all owe me five pounds.'

They huffed and produced their wallets. Patiently, Suruk collected a handful of crumpled notes and stuffed them into his back pocket. 'I thank you,' Suruk said, turning to leave.

The elder priest struggled up the hill. 'Good morning,' he said as he passed Suruk.

The alien croaked thoughtfully. 'You too, shaman.'

'Father McReedy, please. Do you need a blessing?'

'I think not,' he said, thinking of the sweepstake. 'I have been fortunate already. Oh, and priest – Isambard Smith's end got away. You owe me five pounds.'

An hour later, Smith ventured out of the *John Pym*. He felt awkward and uncertain after his night with Rhianna, as if he had ingested some powerful drink and was waiting for it to take effect. He wanted to be left alone. The last thing he needed, he felt, was to have to hold hands and introduce her to everyone as his girlfriend. He had left her inside the ship, dozing. He'd felt that it was best to leave her: she looked pretty sleeping. Shame she snored like a pig. Still, you couldn't have everything. As long as their relationship remained private, he would have the peace and quiet to make sure that everything worked out fine.

As he reached the bottom of the steps Wainscott

slapped him on the back. 'Heard you gave the dippy bird a portion. Tidy work there, old man.'

'Hello, Wainscott,' Smith said coldly.

The major's eyes twinkled. 'Reckon we're close to going in against Gertie,' he said. 'Soon we'll move towards the city and give the ant-men a damned good thrashing.'

'Today?'

'Chances are. There's a meeting at eleven: I'll be there along with W, a few captains from the Teasmen and the Morlock chaps. You're welcome to come along.' He stepped away, paused and looked back. 'Oh, and Smith, I'll have the medico look out for you, in case there's any, ah, chafing. I've known a few foreign women myself, if you get my drift. As I always tell my men: avoid rash entanglements and your entanglements avoid a rash.'

He tapped his nose sagely and walked away. Smith grimaced, feeling like a deflating balloon. His delicate romance was clearly as private as a soap opera, and he had a nasty suspicion which smallish android pilot would be responsible for that. Now, if only everyone else would just leave him alone—

'Hey, Boss.' Carveth tugged his arm.

He looked round. 'Hello,' he said, warily. 'Everything alright?'

'No.'

'Worried about the battle?'

'Yes, funnily enough. Boss, this is mad!' she whispered. 'We're going to get slaughtered!'

'Nonsense,' he replied. The sheer urgency in her voice unsettled him. He had always known that she was no fighter, but to hear her talk like this felt wrong.

'I was talking to Susan just now. Do you know where they found Wainscott, originally?'

'In his home, I heard.'

'In a home! He's special forces alright: *bloody* special. We're outnumbered, outgunned and our commanding officer is a bloody crazy nudist!'

Twenty yards away, Wainscott turned from conversation with a tank driver and waved at them. They waved back, embarrassed.

'See?' said Smith. 'Perfectly normal. He's got his trousers on and everything.'

Wainscott took a fruit from his pocket and bit into it.

'He's eating a lime,' Carveth said.

'Perhaps he likes them.'

'So? I like badgers but I wouldn't put one in my mouth.'

'Hmm,' said Smith. 'I don't really think that carries your argument.' He sighed and turned to her. 'Look, Carveth. It doesn't matter if Wainscott is mad or not. He's a nice bloke, and good at his job. At least we know that, with him at the wheel, the need to save Urn will remain the driving force. For now, sanity can take a back seat in the car of freedom.'

'I take it the car of freedom has no brakes?' Carveth looked up suddenly. 'What's that?'

There were specks in the sky – V-shaped things like seagulls drawn by a child. Smith put his rifle scope to his eye. 'Sun dragons,' he said. 'Coming here.'

'Oh, *arse*,' Carveth said.

'Stay here,' said Smith, and he ran towards them.

The forest and the railway buildings hid the creatures. As he ran closer confusion spread through the men:

people were calling to one another, some preparing weapons, others trying to hold them back. A furious argument had broken out among the tank crews. Smith ducked into the shadow between two engine-sheds and suddenly he was in a dark corridor, looking out at a field full of light and dragons. They sat on the grass, clung to the trees at the edge of the field, circled lazily overhead. Their wings rose into the air like unfinished arches, their long necks swaying in the breeze like ropes linking the land and sky.

A few daring soldiers walked between the dragons, awed. They put out tentative hands and felt scales, heard the crackle of static. Sam O'Varr stood between two huge creatures, her shocked gaze flicking from the sun dragons to the empty cup she held as if they had sprung from it. Suruk stood at the edge of the group, eating a biscuit. He looked mildly interested.

Rhianna approached from the middle of the field. A sun dragon stood behind her and, as Smith watched, the great beast spread its wings with a heavy rustle like distant thunder. Turn the land on them, he thought. Well, well.

'You did this, didn't you?' he said.

'Urn did it,' Rhianna replied. 'The planet has declared war on those exploiting it! Nature has arisen to claim back her own.'

'It is true!' cried the Sauceress O'Varr, throwing out her arms. 'As the leaves told it, so it is! Be afraid, oh invaders, for the time of squeezing-out is at hand!'

Smith smiled. 'Then let's squeeze.'

*

Ghasts are not natural individualists. For two hundred generations they had lived like termites, packed close together, each a tiny cog in the steamroller of their race. Their lives – short and brutal – were spent on battlefields and transport craft, close by their comrades, always in packs. What they lacked in individual initiative they made up in group ferocity. They were the best-drilled troops in the galaxy, bar none. Which was fortunate, 462 reflected. Soon the weakling humans would make their move to take back their world. They would fight keenly. It would take elites to drive them back and wipe them out.

As he entered the dormitory, seventy praetorians leaped up as if electrocuted and jabbed their claws into the air: '*Ak nak!*'

'Enough,' 462 said, and they turned back to their work: stripping and feeding their weapons, polishing their antennae, picking their teeth clean ready for mankind.

462 smiled. The Edenites might be fools – more precisely, total fools – but these were state-of-the-brood fighting machines, custom-grown to deal with Earth. To begin with, the Ghasts had underestimated the Empire's will to fight. It had looked like a simple matter of driving a bio-tank over the flowerbed of Imperial democracy, piling out and scoffing Earth's children while mankind's leaders faffed about and muttered, 'Steady on!' Instead, the attack ships had been met with fanatical, demented resistance, and the knobbly-faced, four-limbed, tiny-bottomed little turds had fought back with the ferocity of praetorians.

They dare call us Gertie, he thought, and he hissed.

A particularly huge praetorian stepped over and saluted. 'Great one!'

He looked up at it. 'You are?'

'The Master of Armour.'

462 peered at him. 'What happened to the previous Master of Armour?'

'38,259B? He showed signs of being honourable,' the praetorian said. 'So we had him shot. His number is erased.'

'So there never was a previous Master of Armour.'

'Never was a who?'

'Quite.'

'Is all well, 462? You look. . . distracted.'

462's working eye, already small, narrowed warily. He knew well what this meant. Independent thought was dangerous. In the Ghast Empire, everything was communal. The Ghast that locked itself away from scrutiny was inevitably suspected of treason. He knew well that taking an unsupervised stroll was unwise; taking an unsupervised dump, potentially fatal. 'I was just reflecting on our mission to eradicate humanity. Yourself?'

'We are watching an instructive film later, Glorious Leader, which clearly demonstrates our destiny to conquer the galaxy! Will you join us?'

'Is it the one with the beetles that represent various forms of sentient life, competing to rule the universe?'

'Yes, My Leader!'

'I know how it ends. I won't spoil it for you, but we turn out to be inherently superior and kill everything else. Come with me.'

They walked through the dormitory. At the end of the room, the Master of Armour opened the door and they stepped into a dark, ridged passage that sloped into the earth.

The praetorian followed 462, a pace behind him. At the thought of killing, it had started to drool. 'Leader, will we destroy humans soon?'

'Very soon.'

'Good.' There were scars down the Master of Armour's jaws. Its eyes were tiny behind its battered face, candle-flames behind a screen of melted wax. 'The Deathstorm Legion waits on your command.'

'The humans will be determined.'

'So are we, 462. There is not a man living who could defeat me – nor a M'Lak, either.'

'Excellent. Listen, I want you to look out for one man above all. His name is Isambard Smith, a captain of little value. It was he who took my eye.' 462 flicked a slimy switch sticking out of the wall, and a sphincter door opened before them. 'If you see him, destroy him.'

'I obey,' the Master of Armour snarled, and they walked through the door. They stepped into a lift, and it whisked them down. Marching muzak played and the Ghasts hummed along.

> *Our banner flying in the wind*
> *Spring's joy is all around*
> *We march on through the happy land*
> *And burn it to the ground.*
>
> *The leaves turn green before us*
> *Birdoids sing around our heads*

Lambs and puppies dance around
Then we shoot them dead.

We march as friends together,
Our beloved flag held high
As friends we sing our happy song,
Die, Earthlanders, die!

'That one always puts a goose in my step,' 462 said as the lift stopped. They stepped out into another corridor. 'Now, then,' he said, 'let's see how our allied friend is doing. . .'

There was an airlock at the far end of the corridor. Fans spun in the roof and disinfectant gave the air a sterile tang. A porthole was set in the middle of the airlock. Something stirred behind it. Seen through glass it looked like a creature of the deep ocean, as if it should be moving in water, not purified air.

462 rapped on the porthole. Tentacles thrashed and a huge, soulless eye thumped against the glass.

'Good morning,' 462 said.

A speaker on the wall rattled and croaked. 'Keep back,' the beast said. 'Keep your filthy germs away!'

'And how are you?'

'Better if you keep your disease-ridden head away from me.'

The Master of Armour snarled. 'Shall I gut this insolent pig?'

'There's no need for that. He will have his uses, should the humans prove particularly stubborn. Stay blood-thirsty,' he told the porthole, and he smiled.

*

They gathered at the main local terminal, a hall large enough to hold an army. Like a huge greenhouse, the hall had a glass roof and seemed airy despite the thousands of soldiers who stood in it. Above them, great steel vaults reached out like trees across a country road.

The trains were black boxes among the men. People climbed up on them to get a better view, clinging to the ornamental funnels. Newly-made banners jutted up from the crowd, depicting heraldic beasts, swords, knights, teapots and working men. In the centre of the room one train waited, cordoned off by the army's engineers. This would be going straight for the city gates, packed with dynamite.

Smith walked in and was immediately unsure what to do. People were all around him, as green and numerous as grass in their camouflage, blurring into a single mass like a coating of thick mist above the floor. He stood on tiptoe, looking for a familiar face.

'Hey, Boss!'

Smith glanced up. Carveth sat on a strange, turbine-like device, surrounded by a little group of engineers, both human and M'Lak. Her machine looked antique and purposeless, like pieces torn off a steam-ship and reattached at random. She had salvaged a armoured breastplate from somewhere, which was too big for her. Swinging her legs, she looked less than intimidating.

'What's that you're sitting on?' he called.

'Whopping great vircator,' she replied. Soldiers slipped around Smith, a continual murmur of "Scuse us, mate,' like a stream passing over rocks. 'Had to use some bits from the *Pym*, especially for the, um. . . motor,' she finished, pleased to have remembered the technical term. 'I tell you, one blast from this thing and we'll shut down every computer within five hundred yards. There won't be a calculator within a half mile good for anything other than writing "boobies" upside-down – assuming this thing works, that is. Still, you can't really test a bomb, can you?'

'Barnes Wallis did.'

'You mean you can test a bomb? Ah, hell.' She shrugged. 'Bit late now, I suppose. Hey, what do you think of my body armour? It does wonders for the figure. I've got bigger turrets than a dreadnought in this thing.'

'Very nice.'

She twisted round so as to give him a profile view. Sticking her armoured chest forward she said, 'Like you always say, Boss: up and forward!' She thumped the vircator with her palm. 'With this thing, you'll win the war. Or the Turner Prize.'

Smith wondered if she hadn't been at the sauce. A hand came down on his shoulder and he glanced around. It was Susan, the tall engineer from the Deepspace Operations Group.

'Alright?' she said. 'The boss wants a word with you, matey.'

'Wainscott? Where is he?'

'Follow me.'

She strode off, and Smith waved to Carveth. 'Don't do anything stupid, now!' he called, and he followed Susan through the crowd. 'Where're we going?'

'Up to the front. The others are waiting for you. They won't kick off the speeches until you're there.'

Men moved out of the way in front of them. Only now did Smith realise that the soldiers were all facing in roughly the same direction, watching the far side of the hall. It was like waiting for a concert to begin.

'Speeches?' he said to the back of Susan's head. 'I hope that doesn't involve me!'

''Course,' she replied. 'The bloke who brought the Morlocks here, the one who fought off the suicide pirates of Yull – people'll look up to you.'

'Only because I'll be on a stage.'

'Rubbish. You give the men something to think about, an example.'

'Really? I'm an example to follow?'

'Well, more study than follow, but yeah. Come on.'

Fear and pride wrestling in his gut, Smith followed her. She fished in her thigh pocket as they walked and took out a small metal box. 'Here. Swiped them off a dead Goddie. I gather they'll fit your Civiliser.'

She passed the box to him over her shoulder. It was surprisingly heavy. '*Depleted Uranium revolver shells*,' he read. '*Warning: Radhaz*. What does that mean?'

'Oh, nothing much. Just don't keep them in your trouser pocket. You don't want to end up dressing on both sides. Here we go.'

A fat man moved aside and there was a short flight of stairs before them. Susan climbed and Smith followed, and suddenly, like a mountaineer breaking through a layer of cloud, he stood alone. He turned and looked out across a thousand faces, all looking back.

They stared at him, and he stared back, a rabbit caught in a thousand headlights. Seeing the brave, hopeful faces of the men, he realised that he had passed beyond fear: this was terrified paralysis.

Impasse. Very slowly, like a deep-sea diver, Smith made his way to the microphone in the centre of the stage. It seemed a million miles away, on the other side of a desert. He raised his hand and grabbed the stand as if to choke it to death.

The microphone fell off the end of the stand with a metallic squeal and thumped into the floor. Smith bent down to pick it up. 'Hello?' he asked it.

'Alright mate!' a cheery voice shouted back in the audience, and there were laughs.

'Hello,' he said. 'Unaccustomed as I am to public speaking, citizens of Urn, today we save our planet from—' Someone prodded him in the back. 'From – Major Wainscott?'

'It's not your bloody turn yet,' Wainscott hissed. 'It's my go first.'

'I'm all in the wrong order,' Smith said. 'Terribly sorry, everyone. Sorry.' He walked to the back of the stage and sat down. 'God I'm a stupid prat sometimes,' he told himself. 'I pity the people I lead.'

'You're still holding the microphone,' Wainscott said.

Smith passed him the microphone and looked down the line of people on the stage. He recognised Wainscott, W, Agshad, Sam O'Varr and, surprisingly, Rhianna. Agshad and Rhianna waved at him. The others were unit leaders, captains in the two-week-old People's Army of Urn. They looked smart and tough.

He wondered where Suruk was. Not crouched in the ironwork overhead, where Smith would have expected him to be to get a bird's eye view of the proceedings. The alien had probably gone somewhere quiet to meditate in preparation for battle, to commune with the souls of his ancestors in peace. A sun dragon swooped low over the building and pulled up, looping the loop. For a moment Smith fancied that he could hear wild, cackling laughter coming from its back. Surely it couldn't be – he squinted, puzzled, but it had zipped out of sight.

Wainscott's speech was quick and functional. The first stage of the attack would be the seizure of the orbital missile grid by a crack team led by Wainscott himself and accompanied by a number of sun dragons. The missile array would be immediately launched to cripple any Ghast ships waiting off-world or in the spaceport. Then the main assault on the capital would begin.

There were to be three attack groups, named after the sacred animals of the Empire. Group Lion would approach the city wall around the Edenite sector by dragonback, using the electro-magnetic pulse weapon to weaken the Edenite armour before launching a commando raid. This was to be a small unit led by Captain Smith, who, Wainscott explained, was somewhat better at commando raids than he was at holding a microphone.

The second force, Unicorn, would consist of fast-moving light armour: mostly the M'Lak skimmers, but also jeeps and armoured cars built by the Teasmen. This would approach the walls at speed, striking fast and hard at the Ghast hover-tanks as they emerged to defend the city. It would also include a train, loaded with explosives, which would be used to break the city gates. Unicorn, he explained, was to expect fanatical resistance.

The final force, Common Toad, would be the anvil on which the invaders were to be smashed. This would consist of infantry and heavy armour. Once Unicorn had guided the train into position and used it to breach the city gates, Common Toad was to enter the city and begin the fierce street-fighting needed to drive out the Hyrax and his Crusadists. It was anticipated that the Ghasts would leave garrisons inside the city. These would need to be destroyed.

'None of you will get it easy,' Wainscott declared. 'These are serious, determined enemies, many of them specially created for this very task. You can expect this to be a fight to the death. Many of you will not make it back. On the plus side, it's not raining.

'So, we on this stage can only wish you good luck and offer you the greeting of the ancients. *Rockaturi te salutamus!*' he cried, and he held his Stanford gun aloft.

The hall thundered with cheering.

'Now I'll hand over to Captain Smith. Smith, your go now.'

Smith stood up and looked over the soldiers. Their faces were lifted to him: humans and M'Lak, male, female and neuter, young and old, all ready to face the most ferocious enemies the Empire had ever seen. In their eyes was determination and anger, clear and white-hot, at once full of hope and rage, idealism and readiness to fight.

He realised that he had no idea what to say. What could he say to such people? What was there to say that they did not already know? His experience of public speaking was limited to opening a village fete, when he had been mistaken for a prominent horticulturalist. He remembered the question-and-answer session, and grimaced as he recalled his response to a query about pricking-out in rubber gloves.

Rhianna caught his eye and she nodded urgently at the audience.

He glanced round to her. 'What do I say to them?' he whispered.

'Say whatever's in your heart,' Rhianna said.

Smith thought about it. 'Can you hear me alright at the back?' he asked.

Someone cheered; a thumb was raised.

'It's nice that so many of you have managed to make it here today. Unaccustomed as I am to public speaking, I'd like to say a few words.

'You know, in peace there's nothing so becomes a man as a modest disposition,' he declared. 'But in war–' Smith stopped, suddenly aware that he knew much less Shakespeare than he'd thought. What did happen in war? Brazen it through, he told himself. If you're confident, nobody need ever know. 'But in war, let him get really really angry!

'Gertie wants our stuff. Well he can't have our stuff! Space belongs to the Empire – we saw it first!

'This isn't just a war for Urn: this is a war for civilisation itself. Here is our message to the Ghast Empire: if you will not civilise yourselves, then we will civilise every last one of you, to the last ant-man!

'There are many words that mean a lot to us, words like

justice and freedom. And among those words, one phrase stands out today: "Bugger off, ant-people!" '

Wainscott put his hand up. W pulled it down.

'So now, as Shakespeare would say, we must imitate the action of the tiger, and fight from dawn to dusk and sheathe our swords from lack of argument, because today we take the war to Gertie and kick his big red arse all over the shop, and if anyone asks on whose authority, you can tell them that Shakespeare told you so! That's right! Forwards, men! No longer shall the Grand Hyrax sit comfortably on the throne, for today we shall throw him up and blow him off! And now, without further ado, I declare this army open!'

Hands slapped him on the back as he stepped down from the stage. 'I saw you at the Palladium last year,' a woman said. 'Didn't realise you did political stuff as well.'

They met up outside. Around them, men climbed into machines and the air throbbed with the expectant hum of engines. Carveth watched as a group of engineers strapped the pulse weapon to the back of the dragon she would ride. This is it, she thought, as something like a brick dropped inside her stomach. We're going to war.

Rhianna toured the beasts with a short, dark-haired man who seemed to be some kind of groom, checking the saddles and patting them down. Once they had looked at the sun dragons that the crew of the *Pym* would use, they moved on to the creatures that Wainscott and his men would take for their attack on the missile grid.

'Pass me that gun, would you?' Smith asked Carveth.

She handed him her Stanford gun. Smith looked down

the barrel, peered into the mechanism, made sure that it would work. He passed it back. 'There you go.'

Standing between the dragons, they could not see the army preparing to move out. It seemed as if they were the only people here, surrounded by noise, caught in the eye of the storm. Smith said, 'Going to be a busy day, from the looks of it. We've had quite a turn-out.'

'I wish I had,' Carveth said. 'I'm terrified. One good scare and it won't just be this dragon that drops its payload.'

'You'll be fine,' said Smith. 'We need you with us, Ship's Engineer.'

'Only because I'm the one who bought the Haynes manual.'

'Still Ship's Engineer.'

She nodded. 'Alright.' Carveth pulled her goggles down. 'Let's go. Hey, look!'

Wings flapped on their right. One sun dragon hauled itself into the air, wings battering the sky until it was flying properly, then a second beside it, and a third. Static crackled at their jaws.

'Wainscott's men,' Smith said. 'Want a leg up?'

'Please.'

Carveth put her boot in Smith's hands and he pushed her into the saddle. She reached behind her, where the pulse engine was stashed, and wrapped the starter cord around her hand.

'Just follow us,' Smith said, knowing full well that she would make the journey with her eyes screwed tightly shut.

Two slight, tall figures slipped between the dragons,

light on their feet like dancers: Suruk and Morgar. As Smith looked at them, he felt that he could see a similarity in their strange faces that went beyond them being aliens. 'Hullo,' he said.

'Greetings,' Suruk said. He was eating from a small pot with a spoon. 'Ah, it is a good day for a fight.'

'When did you last have a bad day for a fight?' Carveth asked. 'And how come you've got yogurt?'

'It is not yogurt. It is Vaseline.'

Smith looked the aliens over. 'Joining us, Suruk?'

The warrior shook his head. He carried all his knives, and Gan Uteki, the sacred spear of his ancestors, was strapped across his back. 'No, Mazuran, I shall not. I have come to wish you good hunting. If I do not see you later, then we will meet in the halls of the valiant.'

'Thank you.' He glanced at Morgar. 'So you two are going with Agshad, then?'

Morgar nodded. There was a thick strap across his body and a tube on his back. The heads of a dozen golf clubs protruded from it. 'We will ride together, all three of us,' he explained. 'Just like in the old times. Family day out.'

Carveth looked down from the saddle. 'Good luck, Suruk. May your enemies be numerous, and the battle around you as thick as you are.'

'And may you have a thousand chances to lose your cowardice. Be careful of your steed's dorsal ridges, too. These dragons can be quite uncomfortable – I gather.'

'Thanks.' Carveth sighed. 'You know what I want? I want us to win without any fighting. I don't want to have to fight anyone at all. I mean, look at me. I'm not built for hack and slash – more slack and hash if I had my way. I want us all to be safe and for me to come home without any of this blood and thunder stuff.'

Suruk shook his heavy head, wondering. 'You know,' he said, spooning another white lump of Vaseline between his jaws, 'I always thought there was something strange about you.'

4

Battle is joined

Within the city walls it was still. The Hyrax's thugs patrolled the streets in armoured cars, shouting the curfew from loudhailers. The chimneys were smokeless, the packing factories unmanned.

The Crusadists did not get out of their vehicles. The Grand Hyrax's men had developed a habit of going missing recently: some died, a few defected, others just disappeared. They lied about their losses when they spoke to the Hyrax, and the Hyrax lied some more when he told Gilead, and Gilead lied a little when he spoke to the Ghasts, who trusted nobody, especially not a bunch of disposable humans.

A showdown was coming and everybody knew it.

For most citizens, it would be a chance to get rid of the God Emperor. The Hyrax was now utterly hated. His palace was surrounded by razor wire and every day new severed limbs were displayed on the roof, cut from those brave enough to defy Edenite law. His newest rule had made wife-beating compulsory: even Gilead could tell the difference between a hobby and a legal obligation.

'The man's crazy,' he said, turning from the tiny window. 'I mean, he's holy, yes, but mad, too. He's no use to us. Pious but crazy,' he concluded, shaking his head. 'Who would have seen it coming?'

'He helped destabilise the planet,' 462 replied. 'Besides, his men may soak up a few bullets for us yet.'

They sat in a Ghast bunker, a smooth biological construction the shape of a scaled-up tortoise shell. The aliens had brought it with them. It had some sort of technical name, but the locals called it the Terrapin of Terror. Being inside it was like hiding in a large, armoured shoe.

Number One glowered at them from the dark walls, waving his four arms in a variety of poses. To Gilead the rows of posters looked like the dance steps to a Chinese translation of the YMCA. That made Gilead uncomfortable. Images of the Village People were banned in the Republic of Eden, except for the traffic cop, who was a respectable figure of authority.

Still, the Deathstorm Legion meant business. Whatever rubbish the Grand Hyrax came up with, here was ruthlessness and efficiency to match his own men. When the enemy attacked, his sky-troopers would be fighting beside the Ghasts. The Emperor-Prophet had never been more than a puppet, but the praetorians were. . . well, tough puppets.

The vidcom blasted out a fanfare. With a bio-technological squelch, the screen flickered into life.

A drone appeared on the screen, the sky behind it. 'Strength is obedience!' it yelled, saluting with all its arms.

'Strength is obedience,' 462 replied. 'Report at once.'

'World-Commander 462! We have picked up sun dragons on the visual, approaching the missile defence grid!'

Leather creaked as 462 shrugged. 'So?'

'Normally we would not waste ammunition on mere animals. But these – they are flying in formation.'

'I see. Shoot them, just in case.'

'Yes, Great One! Edenite scum, ready the—'

The drone screamed and shot off the top of the screen as if launched from a catapult. A jumble of noise burst from the speaker – roaring, gunfire, crackling sparks – and the screen went dead.

462 stared at the screen for a moment. 'That drone. . .' he said. 'It. . . disappeared off the top of the screen.'

'It's been ascended!' Gilead gasped.

'Of course it's not been ascended!' 462 whirled and his thin fist thumped a control panel. A siren wailed. 'Ready your men for battle, Gilead! Our enemies have taken the missile silo!'

'But – they'll shoot at the city!'

462 pointed his antennae up and dropped his helmet on over them. 'Rubbish! They are too cowardly to shoot their own city. If they wish to defeat us they will have to draw near, and then – then they will be smashed between my praetorians and your skytroopers! Get your men suited up!'

Twenty seconds later, four missiles from the support grid hit the spaceport. Three Ghast troop carriers were blown apart, two others and an Edenite ship lost their airlock integrity. Wires and gantries hung around the wrecked craft like bunting after a wild party.

It would take days to repair the ships and get back into orbit. The skies were wide open. Both sides were planetbound.

*

Force Unicorn tore across the tea fields, smoke billowing from a hundred buggies and skimmers. On the deck of the family hovership Morgar loaded up a pneumatic harpoon while Suruk drew back the springs that would launch the electromagnets. Around them the skimmer pounded and throbbed. Agshad was at the controls.

'There they are!' Morgar roared over the engines. 'Deflectors up, Dad!'

Suruk glanced round. A black flag had appeared on the city wall, a Ghast skull with two jagged antennae. He nodded and looked at the trophies attached to the front of the skimmer, just above the ram. 'These skeletons are plastic!' he said.

Morgar looked unhappy. 'Sorry, Suruk, it's all we had. I had to go down the Halloween shop.'

'What about the family invisibility device?'

'Now that I do have,' Morgar said, brightening. 'I gave it a test run a few minutes ago. Then I got distracted and put it down for a moment. . .' – he glanced around – 'somewhere. . . Erm, shall we have a record on? It's got quite a sound system, this skimmer.'

For a second, Suruk thought of mocking him. No, he decided. Morgar was at least trying. 'What music do we have?' he asked.

'All our favourites from the good old days,' Morgar replied, keen to show enthusiasm. The wind caught his ponytail and threw it up behind him like a flag. 'We've got Napalm Death, Christian Death, Acid Death, Lawnmower Death, Death and Suzanne Vega.'

Suruk checked the grappling hooks. 'Suzanne Vega. On

second thoughts, that may be depressing. Put on the national anthem instead.'

'*The Ace of Spades? Avec plaisir!*'

On the city wall the Master of Armour saw the great cloud of smoke and dust rushing towards the gates. The Master fastened its helmet-straps and climbed down from they wall, snarling orders as it came. Bio-tanks waited beside the gates. The Master of Armour scrambled onto its personal craft and pulled on a pair of goggles. The city gates opened on great motors. '*Atak!*' the Master of Armour roared, and the Deathstorm Legion poured onto the plain like a black tide.

Carveth saw them first, a spreading black mass leaking from the side of the city like oil from a punctured drum. 'Enemy!' she shouted, pointing.

Smith yelled through his scarf into the head microphone, 'Steer away!'

On the third dragon, Rhianna looked serene. Her dreadlocks waved behind her. 'We'll keep low,' she said, and the sun dragons dipped.

Smith glanced behind him. He could see the cone of dirt following Force Unicorn as it streaked towards the city gates. Already the praetorians were wheeling to face them, picking up speed. Only one way now, Smith thought: forwards.

It was a long, clean hall with an open roof. Against the walls stood seventy battlesuits, like the armour of giants. Men ran and shouted, music and inspiring speeches blared. Ammunition slapped and clattered into place, rotary cannons whirred and spun. Eden was going to war.

Gilead strode down the hall, reading from the Edenite holy book, the amplifiers in his mechanical body turned to full. '. . . turned he to the deniers, and ripped he them a new one, and he said unto them, "Blessed is he who asks how high, for his jumping shall be pure!" '

Yells and cheers from the Skytroopers. A ground assistant ran to Gilead's side. 'Sir! First squad ready to launch, sir!'

'Good.' Gilead lowered the book. 'Turn the music off.'

Someone threw the switch. Suddenly there was silence apart from the sound of humming motors. The soldiers looked uncomfortable.

Gilead put one metal leg up on a bench and rested his hand on his knee. He looked like a robot modelling for a knitwear catalogue. 'Listen up, boys,' he said.

'Let me tell you a few things about our way of life.' Someone at the rear of the room groaned; a voice muttered, 'Oh Hell, not this again.' He ignored them.

'Now listen. Today, we fight the British, a tribe of English people descended from Glaswegians. English people are like insects, hellbound communist insects. When they have tea, or queue up for things, they're queuing to enter their hive, working to make the whole galaxy march to their godless Red tune.'

'This heathen planet is ours now and, twenty-six more captured planets later, your service will have won you the right to semi-vote for our current ruler. Because if you don't fight, you don't vote. Well, kind of vote.

'A man needs to fight to become pure, you see. War makes men out of boys, like it made a man out of me. It takes weak boys and turns them into heroic warriors worthy of Ancient Rome. Some people call me a warmonger. I say No! I am a Roman, and I want boys! You boys!

'And I got you. You are warriors for the New Eden. You are the finest, the most disciplined – no yelling yet, I'm not finished – the most disciplined fighters in the world. You live to defend the pass from apostasy. You are men of Spurta, and I call on you to cover my pass!'

Gilead blinked back tears. 'Go forth and massacre these Urnies in the name of the Great Annhilator, and always remember: when you're on the battlefield, with bullets singing round you and glory in your heart, it was Johnny Gilead who sent you there! Kill these pansies! I love my men!'

The men scrambled into their bulletproof suits and the sound of weapons powering up rose around Gilead like the hum of bees, and his tight, sculpted face managed a smile. His men shouted, banged, stamped on the floor with metal legs. 'Move out!' he called. 'On the bounce!'

'Move out!' a captain barked over the radio. 'Get up to the firing line, damn you!'

The fighting suits clattered across the room. Men whooped and yelled. A dozen bulky, slab-sided skytroopers readied their jets.

Weeping openly, Gilead retreated to the far end of the room. The best men in the world, he thought. The best men in the world. The roaring of jets filled the room like a tidal wave and, with a minimum of collision and unnecessary gunfire, a dozen armoured troopers leaped into the sky.

*

Specks shot out of the city like pips from a squeezed fruit, fragments from an exploding grenade. Carveth peered at them, trying to figure out what they were. Some sort of anti-personnel weapon, fired too soon? Lights flared at the back of one of the specks, then another, and she realised that they were jets. The specks took shape, growing limbs. They looked like jigsaw pieces, now like the silhouettes of toddlers. She realised then that they were men in armoured suits, approaching them in enormous bounds.

'Trouble!' she yelled into the radio.

'Edenites,' Smith replied. His voice was hard and clipped. 'Rhianna, we need air cover.'

'Okay,' she said, and she began to hum.

Smith laid the rifle across the saddle in front of him. The dragon's wings were loud and steady like the beating of a colossal heart. He lifted the rifle, sighted one of the nearer dots, and began to move the barrel up and down in sync with the skytrooper's jumps. Smith held his breath. Up a bit, to anticipate him—

The gun thumped against his shoulder and the bullet caught the trooper on the bounce. The man spun aside mid-jump and ploughed into the ground. A ruffle of fire in the dirt outside the city wall marked his passing.

'Invincible suit, eh?' Smith said.

In response a missile arced out and blew the nearest dragon apart. It burst like a dropped pie. Smith saw it and was sickened: the dragons were beautiful, and he knew for a fact that the cultists would be howling with glee, like apes on a hunt. Gunfire flickered out of the skytroopers, white lights that rushed past them.

Carveth, on the radio. 'Are we nearly there yet?'

Smith said, 'Soon.'

'They're—' A skytrooper bounded up in front of her. Carveth screamed. Her vision was full of camouflaged armour and spinning guns, and her dragon spat at it. A white bolt of static leaped from the sun dragon's head to the wet battle-suit, and the suit fell, shorting. Two missiles arced round to the left and smacked into one of the flanking dragons. The skytroopers bounded forward, hitting the ground and leaping up as if on elastic wires. Carveth clenched her hand around the thin chain that would fire up the EMP bomb.

'Can I pull the chain yet, Boss?'

Smith looked left, at Rhianna. There was something oddly dignified about her, he thought. She looked like Boadicea : upright in her seat, hair streaming out behind her, not quite as clean as she could be—

A bullet flew past his head. Shells sparked on dragonscale. Down below, Force Unicorn was nearly at the city wall. The praetorians were pouring out of the city. Carveth was cowering. 'Now!' he yelled. 'Now, Carveth!'

She had pulled many chains many times, but doing so had never been such a relief.

Force Unicorn tore in from the flank and crashed into the side of the Deathstorm Legion – in the case of the M'Lak, literally. Tank armour buckled, metal squealed against metal, guns and harpoons blasted, vehicles exploded and the two armies tore one another apart.

Morgar aimed the skimmer's main gun, fired and

cheered as the harpoon sank into the hull of a Ghast hover-tank. The wire snapped taut and the skimmer and hover-tank whipped around one another. Morgar hit the controls and the engines reeled them in. He bounded across the deck and slapped Suruk on the shoulder. 'Boarding action, I believe!'

Suruk leaped onto the railing, drove off with his legs and landed with a soft thump on the enemy craft. His brother jumped onto the wire and ran down it, a golf club cocked over his shoulder. A hatch flew open, a praetorian tank commander stuck its head out; Morgar swung his club and number three wood connected with steel helmet – *thunk!* – and the tank commander's head flew into the tea fields below. 'Fore!' Morgar cried.

Suruk sprang to his brother's side and held up a wine bottle. 'Match,' he said.

Morgar lit the rag with a crème brûlée torch. Suruk tossed the bottle into the tank, slammed the hatch shut, and the two ran back to the skimmer. Morgar threw a lever, the electromagnet died and the skimmer broke loose from the stricken hover-tank as smoke began to pour from the hatches. Battle roared around them. The Ghast tank pitched into the ground, billowing smoke as they sped away. Suruk turned to Morgar and chuckled.

'And that,' Morgar said with deep conviction, 'is what happens when we play golf!'

Gilead grinned as his men loaded up. Somehow, the rebels had managed to goad sky dragons into the fight. They would be fine creatures to hunt, especially with chainguns.

'Enhanced vocalisers on-line,' his metal body told him. The long room rang with his hard voice.

'Fly, my brothers, fly!' Gilead cried. 'Once I've finished speaking. Ride out like the angel of apocalypse! Bound into their midst in your special armour and show them your—'

The lights went off.

'Tits!' said Gilead.

Something crashed outside. The lights on the computers flickered out like dying eyes. Around him, in the sudden shadow, he heard the falling whine of a thousand motors shutting down. Gilead stood there, too shocked to move, like a virtuoso silenced mid-cadenza.

The skytroopers stood around him, immobile in their battlesuits. Behind each faceplate, a pair of eyes flicked from side to side, horrified; a mouth opened wide, goldfish-dumb behind glass.

Gilead tried to take a step back and found that he could not. Was something wrapped around his legs? He tried to look down. He could not do that either. Fear broke over him like a wave as he remembered that his body was made of metal too. He was as helpless as his men.

One by one, the skytroopers started to topple over. Gilead watched them fall, the slow wobbling and the inevitable crash, like mechanical skittles.

The emergency systems were working in his chest. He could still breathe, but the less essential parts of his robot body were shutting down. The enemy would be here soon. Terror prickled up the spine he did not have.

'Bladder control, off-line,' his metal body said.

*

The skytroopers dropped out of the air. One moment they leaped into battle, and the next they fell like poisoned birds. To Carveth it seemed as though they had been turfed out of Heaven.

Their armour was strong. A few blew up on contact with the ground, but most just lay there, statue-like. The pulse weapon had worked: every computer within five hundred yards was dead.

Smith pointed to the city wall. 'Landing!' he called, and Rhianna nodded and the flock of sun dragons swooped towards the wall. The city spread and grew details as they came in. Carveth could see the fortresses of the Ghasts and Edenites and the palace of the Grand Hyrax, and crowds spilling out from all of them. Their battle was far from over, in fact the real fighting was about to begin.

From his fortress inside the city, 462 saw the train rush over the horizon and barked out the order for it to be destroyed. He knew the humans needed to get into the city and had expected them to try to ram the gates.

The Master of Armour snarled into the bio-com. Half a dozen tanks split from the battle and pounded the train with shells. In a great bloom of flame it ignited, taking two tanks with it; wreckage thumped the gates, rocked them, but did not blow them open. Force Common Toad and Force Unicorn were trapped on the plain.

The Deathstorm Legion drew back and regrouped. The M'Lak skimmers and Imperial tanks had fought hard and the ground was littered with smashed craft from either side. But the Legion was used to tough enemies. The praetorians whirled and prepared to charge Common

Toad. It would be hover-tanks against civilian vehicles, bio-steel against human flesh. The Teasmen would be wiped out.

Smith sprang onto the city wall. Rhianna slipped down beside him and between them they helped Carveth out of her stirrups. Behind them, the warm air was full of noise: the wrenching of metal, chatter of guns and the steady, constant pulse of disruptor fire. 'Now what?' Carveth said.

'We have to get the gates open,' Smith replied. 'If the others can't get into the city, we're buggered.'

'Is there a key?' Carveth said.

Smith pointed along the wall. The gates stood fifty feet high and almost as broad, locked and reinforced. There were barricades in front of the doors, heaps of objects outlawed by the God Emperor. Every few seconds a head would pop up from behind the barricades and glance around like a crazed meerkat.

'What now?' Carveth demanded. Something big exploded to the west and she flinched.

'We have to get to the gate controls. And I'd put money they're behind that barricade.'

Carveth said, 'Maybe you could lure them away? If they went after you, I could open the gate.'

'Good plan. But what would get them going enough to leave their positions?'

'A bunch of witch-burning, pagan-hating lunatics?' She frowned. 'Tell you what. I'll borrow Rhianna for a moment and we'll think about it.'

*

Like a gunfighter in the Old West, Rhianna stepped into the middle of the street. Thirty yards down the road, the Hyrax's men were reinforcing the barricade, piling up televisions as if making a fort from building bricks.

'Excuse me?' Rhianna said.

They ignored her. One of the main tenets of their cult was misogyny, and it was less effort to ignore a woman than bludgeon her.

'Excuse me!'

A wide-eyed young man nudged his commander, a hoary old madman wearing a sandwich board on which he had chalked the Crusadist edict of the day. The two exchanged a few words, and sandwich waved to his colleagues and pointed to Rhianna. The barricade came to life and one by one forty fanatics turned to look at her.

'Thank you,' she called. 'Now, I'd like to open up a discussion with you all.'

From his vantage point on the city wall, Smith lifted the rifle. So this was Carveth's plan, was it, using Rhianna to get their attention? He'd be having stern words with her later. Smith was new to this relationship stuff, but letting your pilot use your lady friend as cultist-bait was probably not the done thing.

Rhianna cleared her throat loudly. 'I reject your theocratic fascist regime!' she declared. 'The subjugation of my sisters through inane propaganda is a crime against herstory and the false etymology of the so-called God Emperor merely sustains a phallocentric conspiracy!'

Sandwich board was joined by a man wearing a sack and carrying a rocket launcher. He had attached a large picture of the Hyrax to his scalp with a staple gun. Staples looked at Rhianna for a while, shrugged and tapped his temple with a finger. 'Nutter,' he said.

Smith cursed. It's not working. The Crusadists aren't taking the bait. I should never have let Rhianna go near them. Now she's in danger. Dammit, there isn't much time—

Carveth shoved Rhianna out the way. 'Let the expert do it,' she said. 'Hey, wankers!' she yelled at the Hyrax's men. 'Yeah, you, with the thing on his head! You're crap, your God Emperor kisses ant-man arse and I hate you! Oh, and if that doesn't bother you, then get this: Free Speech and Democracy!' she yelled, and with that she pulled her breastplate aside, lifted her T-shirt to her chin and did a little dance.

Smith had known the battle would be tough, but he had not anticipated being repelled in quite this manner. For a stunned second nobody moved, and then a voice screamed, 'Behold! The bumps of Beelzebub!' and as one the whole pack of cultists surged from the barricade. Carveth did not much notice – she was far too busy swaying at the waist to show off her heresies to their best advantage – and Rhianna grabbed her by the arm. 'Let's go!' she called, and Carveth snapped back to reality and realised that a horde of madmen was coming to murder her.

They ran. Bullets clipped past, wild and badly-aimed and, as Carveth and Rhianna passed the gates, Smith got a bead on the man with the picture stapled to his head. Get her into cover, Carveth, he willed, and to his surprise the android seemed to wake up and she and Rhianna ran into a side street, each tugging the other along.

Smith put the crosshairs onto the back of the rocket launcher. Here we go, he thought with satisfaction, and he pulled the trigger.

The bullet hit the launcher and blew it apart. The explosion caught the spare rockets on Staple-head's belt and that, as Smith had hoped, caught the wads of condensed explosive strapped to half a dozen other cultists. The whole horde blew up fifty yards from the city gates. Guns, cloth and scraps of Crusadist dropped in front of the gates.

Smith hurried down from the wall and found Carveth and Rhianna at the bottom, waiting for him.

'Bloody good work,' he said. 'That was brave of you both.'

Carveth shrugged. 'Typical, isn't it? Several million men on this planet and the only one I get to show my bits to looks like Rasputin.' She closed her chest-plate. 'Still, it just goes to show: if you want to get the doors opened – use the knockers.'

462 was studying a holographic projection of the city, collating battle reports. All seemed well outside: the humans were fighting keenly, but the Deathstorm Legion was holding its ground, keeping the raiders from the city gate. Within the city, the Hyrax had sent his men on a mission to kill anyone hindering the righteous, which, 462 expected, would keep the city-folk quiet until the battle was won. The train had been destroyed and without it the attackers could be wiped out in the open. He smiled and took a sip of pulped minion.

The doors opened and a squad of Edenite soldiers ran

in, bulky and pig-faced in armour and gasmasks. The last of them pushed a shopping trolley, and in it stood Captain Gilead.

'What is this?' 462 demanded. 'Get out of there at once!'

'Bad news,' Gilead said. 'They've shut down our systems. The skytroopers are out!'

'What? Out of the city?'

'Out of the battle! They used an EMP bomb on the walls. We – we just stopped!'

'So I see.' 462 took three slow, deep breaths. He stood up and Gilead's guards took a step back, glancing at one another. 462 approached. A nasty smile spread across his scarred face.

Gilead's eyes flicked left and right. 'Look—' he began.

'No, *you* look!' 462's hand shot out, Gilead flinched and the Ghast's hard fingers clamped around his ear. 'Look at this!' and 462 whirled and strode across the room to the bank of monitors on the far wall, dragging Gilead after him. The trolley weaved on its castors and Gilead howled.

462 jabbed a finger at the viewscreens. 'Your supposedly elite regiment has failed! Tell me, Gilead, what have you got to say for yourself?'

'My ear really hurts,' Gilead said weakly.

'Silence!' 462 looked at the screens. 'What's this? The gates are open!' He leaned into the comlink and barked, 'They're coming in! Pull back to the city!'

He turned away from Gilead, snarling. So, he thought. If it's a fight at close quarters that you want, that's what you'll get. Nice and close, our strength against yours. He glanced around. 'You, drone! Take the batteries out of the propagandatron and wire them to this idiot.'

The drone bent to its task. Gilead found that he could move again.

'Send out your remaining troops,' 462 said. 'I want full mobilisation, now!'

'Yes, sir!' Gilead cried, relieved to be mobile once more, and he saluted so hard and fast that his metal arm knocked him out.

As Wainscott reached the battlefield, the Ghasts withdrew. Common Toad had arrived unhindered at the city gate and its soldiers were joining Force Unicorn. Inside the gates men and M'Lak climbed down from a host of vehicles, shaking hands and spreading out. Soldiers ran into buildings, threw up furniture to make strong points, scuttled from home to home.

'Hullo,' the major said, approaching Smith and his crew. Wainscott was dusty and jaunty, and there was a slightly manic glint in his eyes. 'Gertie hiding, is he?'

'The tanks pulled back,' Smith explained. 'Headed west, it seems. They'll be back. Good work on the missile grid, by the way.'

'Thanks. We rather caught them with their trousers down. Which is ironic,' Wainscott added, 'since I often catch enemies with my trousers down. Helps with the air flow,' he added, noting Smith's expression. 'Wind resistance and all. Well done on the gates, Smith. Stick with this chap,' he said, turning to Rhianna. 'He's a good egg. No more than that – several eggs: a veritable omelette of justice. Bear that in mind, young lady,' he added, jabbing a finger at Rhianna's chest. 'Not a lot of girls get to walk out with an omelette.'

Smith pointed and said, 'Look, Wainscott, it's Suruk!'

Suruk, Morgar and Agshad strode through the soldiers. As they approached Agshad gave them all a deep, formal bow. 'Warriors Smith and Wainscott,' he said. 'Fair maiden Rhianna, fair-to-middling maiden Carveth. I greet you all.'

'Welcome back!' Wainscott said. 'Right, everyone, the first and second legs of our attack seem to have gone well. Now, we just need to pull off the third leg and we can all lie back and have a cigarette. But I warn you, it's going to be tough.'

'I believe the phrase is "People's going to die",' Suruk said, and he smiled horribly.

'Let's get going,' Smith said. 'Coming with me, Carveth?'

She nodded, realising that there was no way out of this mess. Once again the swimming pool of life had been tainted by the incontinent toddlers of fate.

From the jeep Susan called, 'Everyone ready?' Soldiers loaded weapons, vehicles rumbled and threw up dust, boots stamped and a low, menacing grumble of determination ran through them all. The fighting up to now had been a preamble. This would be the meat of the battle.

Smith looked at Rhianna. 'I think you should stay here,' he said.

'I can manage,' she replied.

'It's not that. You ought to stay back and talk to the dragons. We still need them.' He patted her on the shoulder. 'You've got incredible powers, Rhianna, just like

Morgan le Fay or Mary Poppins. Besides, I can't make you fight. I don't want to put you in an awkward position or violate your principles.'

'Not in public, anyway,' Carveth muttered. Smith ignored her. She was clearly sulking at the prospect of imminent death.

Rhianna smiled. '*Namaste*, Isambard. Go in peace.'

He cocked his rifle. 'Will do. Follow me, Carveth! To victory!'

5

Forward

From that point on, the battle became a blur to Carveth. They ran into the streets, ducking between houses, a wave of scurrying figures. She ran from one piece of cover to the next, always glancing behind her, always ducking down. At some point someone gave her a plasma gun to carry and then disappeared, so she hauled it behind her like luggage. She could smell dust and burning and the air was full of shots and bangs, crackling gunfire and the creak of machines.

There were incidents that stood out: a car came tearing down the street to give them a message from W that the north side of the city had risen up; Suruk and Morgan spotted an Edenite gunner at a third-floor window and split from the others to creep inside, with the intention of pitching the man out; a soldier at the corner of her vision was struck by some kind of Ghast heavy weapon and turned to red mist. Blinking in surprise, Carveth was very nearly hit by half a dozen disruptor rounds and Smith had to pull her along after him.

They ducked into a narrow street and suddenly everything was as quiet as Sunday afternoon. Carveth half expected wallahbots to roll out of the houses and start scrubbing the front steps. Something loud was going on in the distance. It could have been building work.

'Have a seat,' Smith told her. 'You look like you need a rest.'

'Right, Boss,' she said numbly.

'Back in a minute,' he said, and he patted her on the sleeve and jogged back to the war.

Carveth sat down on the porch and tried to recover some of her composure. She took off her oversized helmet and vaguely considered puking in it, then reflected that knowing her luck she would only need it afterwards. If dying in battle wasn't bad enough, dying in battle wearing a hat full of sick was probably even worse.

Wainscott emerged from the house opposite, a biscuit tin under his arm and a rolled-up magazine in his hand. 'Hello, girlie,' he said.

'Hello,' Carveth felt herself say.

Wainscott held out the biscuit tin. 'Rich tea?'

Carveth said, 'Have you got anything stronger?'

'Hmm. Custard cream?' Wainscott shook the box up. Shocked to find herself doing so, she waved the tin away.

Wainscott looked down at her with a surprising amount of sympathy. 'First battle, is it? Not having any fun?'

She nodded.

'Fair enough. That's understandable.' He shrugged. 'Bad thing, war. I just killed a Ghast with a copy of *Autocar*!' he added, holding out the magazine. 'Ran out of ammo. First time for everything. That said, I once rendered a man unconscious with an issue of *Practical Caravanning*. I made him read it! Cover to cover! Haha!'

Wainscott ducked back into the house, then thought

better of it and leaned around the doorframe. 'Erm, couldn't lend us some ammo, could you?'

'Go ahead,' she said. 'Hell, you might as well have the bloody gun too.'

'You're a decent sort,' Wainscott said, relieving her of her Stanford gun. 'Well, can't stay here chopsing all day. Good luck!'

He plunged back into the building, box still under one arm, leaving her with the magazine. The front cover showed a car driving through countryside, millions of miles away. She got to her feet and picked up the plasma gun. It reminded her of a French horn case.

Sudden movement in the alleyway. Her hand twitched to her service revolver, then she saw that it was Smith. 'Carveth! Plasma gun, quick!'

She bent down and tried to undo the catches on the box. Smith ran over and tried to help her, which resulted in them fighting over the plasma gun. They fumbled wildly in the street as it rolled over and over in its box, their hands scrabbling as if trying to pin down an angry midget. A catch opened, and gleeful with relief they got hold of the weapon inside.

Printed inside the lid were the words: *Leighton-Wakizashi Corp – Plasma, Infantry, Anti-Tank.* Smith slung the gun up onto his shoulder. Carveth took out the instruction booklet from the case.

Smith turned and looked at her. 'Instructions,' he said.

Carveth realised that neither of them knew how to work the thing. A new noise had appeared above the sounds of small-arms fire: the droning of a hover-tank. ' "All please loading shell A," ' she read out. ' "Connecting plasma shell A to main tube D, rewiring C and B as per diagram 6. Make firing pin sad for primer." What?'

Smith thought. 'Depress firing pin to prime!' he exclaimed.

Carveth found a plasma shell – there were three in the case – activated it and Smith bent down so she could push it into the tube. 'It won't go!' she cried. The shell began to smoke alarmingly.

Smith turned the shell around. 'Try that.'

The shell dropped into place. 'Bring up the others, Carveth,' he said.

The alleyway opened into a broad road. Sliding across it, sleek and malevolent as a cobra, came a Ghast hover-tank.

It looked like a colossal steam iron, with a turret where the handle would be. The air wavered under it, and as it approached it gave out a low thrum that made Carveth grit her teeth.

Where was everyone? The road was deserted; the others must have run on ahead. Carveth glanced left and right, increasingly desperate. The tank was swinging round, the skull painted on the front turning to grin at her, and in a moment the turret would be facing them—

'Shoot it!' she cried. 'Bloody shoot it!'

Smith fired. The plasma shell streaked straight into the side of the machine and cracked it open. Carveth threw herself down, felt a great boot of force kick her in the backside, and suddenly she was face-down in the dirt several yards away. Steam hissed in the air. Scraps of armour jutted from the ground like mis-formed, unnatural plants.

The tank was wreckage. Pink fluid coursed from a hole in what might have been its engine.

Smith lay on his front. Carveth ran over to him, felt his pulse and saw blood leaking from a gash in his scalp. He was unconscious but alive.

The blast had blackened Smith's jacket and emptied his pockets over the surrounding area. His rifle and Civiliser lay a little way off. Carveth said, 'Bloody hell,' and there was a metallic squeak from behind and she turned to see a hatch opening on the stricken tank.

Something hideous in goggles was climbing out. Without thinking, she tore the revolver from her side and fired all six shots into it, disgusted, making the same noise she made when hitting spiders with the heel of her slipper. The Ghast fell out of the hatch and flopped onto the ground, made a rattling sound and rolled over, dead.

'Ha!' Carveth said, suddenly very proud. 'Ha! Not so tough now, are you? Haha!' She approached the Ghast and was prodding it with her boot when a long shadow fell over her.

Carveth turned around. 'Oh, heck,' she said.

It was the biggest Ghast she had ever seen. The thing was easily six feet eight. Insignia glittered on its lapels; the flapping coat made her think of Dracula's cape. It clambered from the main turret, shoving the wreckage aside. The face, a mass of scars, twisted into a kind of smile. 'Isambard Smith,' it hissed.

Smith did not move.

The beast took a step out of the wreckage and looked down at Smith. 'You broke my tank, Captain Smith,' it said. 'Now I break you.'

Carveth stepped into the way, raised the pistol and pulled the trigger. *Click*.

The Master of Armour turned to her. 'You, pygmy,' it rasped. 'Step aside.'

Carveth stood there, shaking with fear and anger. She could not move, but nor could she fight back. The Master of Armour took a step closer. It smelt like something that had died behind a leather settee.

'Did you not hear, little man?' The creature pointed at Smith and laughed. 'As if any mere man could stop me now.'

Carveth's helmet had slipped to one side, and she was not quite sure what it was saying. She unclipped the bothersome thing and it fell onto the road.

But lo! Downly did her self-dyed tresses fall, and lone and blonde she stood before the Ghast, and full ticked off and full of wrath was she.

'Then know now,' she cried, 'that Isambard Smith is no man! Wait – no mere man! I'm a girl,' she added. 'Um. . .'

The praetorian swatted her out the way and she fell onto the pavement.

'*Aah*,' it said, baring its teeth, and Carveth grabbed Smith's penknife, pulled open a random blade and drove it into the monster's back.

The praetorian screeched. It stood there, reaching for the tool for cleaning horses' hooves that was now wedged in its spine, and Carveth kicked it in the stercorium.

The Master of Armour whirled around and Carveth darted away. Her hands seized a bent rod, some piece of the hover-tank. The Ghast stumbled aside and Carveth grabbed a handful of leather coat and bashed the monster's back end with the rod like a Mexican child hitting a piñata.

The Master of Armour lurched across the road, screeching and flailing. With a massive effort it shrugged all its limbs at once and the coat fell off, and Carveth fell with it. She hit the ground, rolled over, looked up and it was standing over her with a pistol in its hand.

'Enough!' it snarled, and shot her.

Carveth fell back and the Master of Armour holstered its gun, satisfied. It took a step towards her, grimaced and stopped to rub its throbbing stercorium. '*Ak! Smakt natsak!*'

With a sound like thunder, sunlight blasted through its body from behind. A second thunderclap and half its head disappeared. It dropped to one side in a tumble of limbs.

Carveth could just about see. A man stood over her wearing body armour under a trenchcoat. An enormous pistol was in his hand. It was Rick Dreckitt.

Typical, Carveth thought. I finally meet a decent man and I've got a severe bullet wound. Isn't that always the way?

'Sister,' Dreckitt said, 'you're hurt.' Then he turned and yelled, 'Hey, medic!' He dropped onto one knee. 'Hang on, lady. You'll be alright once the meat wagon arrives.'

Carveth doubted it.

Smith was woken by a Ghast loudspeaker. '– hopeless! We shall ruthlessly crush all opposition! You cannot hope to escape! Your only hope of survival is to completely surren—'

The voice rose into a gabbling squeal and died. Smith

sat up. Behind him was a wrecked alien tank, steaming. Its driver lay next to it. To his right was a huge, dead praetorian, its leather coat beside it. Officer caste, he realised, and he got up.

A familiar figure stood nearby: Susan, the beam gunner from the Deepspace Operations Group. She nodded at him and strolled over. 'Got a nasty cut there, mate. Doesn't look too deep. Better get it sealed up.'

'What happened?'

Susan shrugged. 'Well, your Morlock chums ran off to do over some Goddies, you shot a tank from a stupid range and it knocked you flat, your pilot saved your life by bashing the Ghast headman in the knackers when he was about to shoot you and the enemy are falling back. Um. . . that's about it.'

'Saved my life?' he muttered. 'Bashing the headman? How long have I been out for?'

She scratched her head. 'Five minutes.'

'Where's Carveth?'

'Your pilot? She took a hit. Easy, mate – she's with the medics. She'll be fine.'

'Good.' Smith reached down and picked up his rifle. 'Well, I'd best make myself useful.' Wincing, he meandered down the street and round the corner, towards the Ghast line.

As Smith turned the corner a flapping leather coat disappeared down the road and out of view, followed by a bobbing rear. The praetorians were retreating. Three or four bodies lay in the road: Ghasts, a man and an anthound. Another Ghast hung halfway out of an upstairs window.

There were billboards along the street bearing the Hyrax's propaganda, and the jubilant Teasmen were pulling them down. One showed the Hyrax smiling through his beard and giving a thumbs-up, and read: *Beat your wife – she's probably a heretic.* The soldiers were not actually dancing, but they were not far off it.

A figure stumbled out of an office to Smith's right. He whipped around, gun raised – and saw that it was Suruk. The warrior was badly cut and covered in plaster. In his arms he carried another M'Lak, one that Smith at once recognised: only Morgar could have worn such a horrible golfing jumper.

'Bloody hell,' Susan said from Smith's side. 'That's your fellow, isn't it? He's carrying one of his heavies.'

'He is not a heavy,' Suruk growled. 'He is my brother.' He stooped and laid Morgar down on the ground. Smith saw holes in the architect's chest, four or five of them. Morgar had lost a lot of blood. It looked grim, Smith thought. About the best thing that could be said of the situation was that Morgar's awful sweater was ruined.

'I am dying,' Morgar said.

'Not true, brother,' Suruk replied. He glanced up, and for a moment he looked almost apologetic. 'Gilead's fools ambushed us. I dodged their shots, but Morgar was not so quick, and the cowards shot him many times before I could slay them all.'

'Forgive me,' Morgar rasped. 'I grow weak, Suruk. I have devoured my last canapé, run my final whist drive. I am an architect, not a warrior.' He smiled weakly behind his mandibles. 'I fear I will never go back to the drawing board now.'

'No,' Suruk replied. 'You always were a warrior. You merely took an extended career break. I gather it is often done in the modern workplace.'

'Really?'

'Indeed,' Suruk said, crossing several fingers behind his back. 'On my honour.'

'Then I shall live!' Morgar wheezed. 'I am a warrior of the tribe again! Has anyone seen my glasses?'

Suruk stood up. 'Guard my brother,' he announced. 'Fetch healers for his wounds!'

Other men were pouring in to join them. Smith looked across the square, at the tank he had bagged and the dead Ghasts around it. He felt extremely proud, both of himself and his men. Then he remembered Morgar and Carveth, and he felt guilty for being proud. He looked down at the Master of Armour and a little of the pride returned. Its many limbs guaranteed it a future as an excellent hat stand.

Behind him, Major Wainscott was calling to his men. 'Everyone, make safe the city! Secure the walls and – what was that?'

Smith looked round. The ground had moved, very slightly, but enough to notice. Dust stirred around his boots. He glanced at Suruk, who nodded once, gravely.

'Hell,' said Wainscott, and something huge rose out of the Ghast compound. It came up in jerks like a marionette, buzzing and clanking, looming over the houses like a colossal gallows. An oval cockpit of shining metal, pumping out greenish smoke, and under it a dozen metal tentacles swaying like kelp, flexing and stretching. Vast legs unfolded. In the centre of the cockpit there was a single window, and behind it, in some kind of gas, a horrible grinning face peered over the battlefield.

They gawped as it unfolded against the skyline. For a second it looked down at them, and they gazed back. Then hatches blew open on its flanks, and with a dreadful howl it took a step towards them.

'Walker!' Smith yelled. 'Take cover, everyone! Get down!'

Ch-chunk – bombs sailed from it, cut lazy arcs through the air and crashed into the city. Black mist rose. Men, M'Lak and Ghasts ran, and those caught in the smoke gargled and fell down dead.

'It's a Marty war-machine!' someone cried. 'We're trapped!'

Wainscott was calm and grave. 'Then we must die like Spartans, men,' he said, reaching to his belt buckle, 'nude!'

'Wait.' Smith put his hand on the Major's arm. 'We don't need to drop our trousers to show it that we're men. Leave this to me.'

Wainscott paused, clearly weighing up the attraction of bagging the Aresian compared to de-bagging himself. 'Oh,' he said. 'Well, alright then. What's your plan?'

'I may be able to outflank it, but I'll need you to get its attention.'

'With pleasure!' Wainscott reached for his belt again.

'By shooting, preferably.' Smith turned to Suruk. 'Shall we call for it?'

Suruk nodded and raised a fist. Smith followed suit. They shook their fists three times and held them out.

'Stone,' Smith said.

'Rabbit,' Suruk said. 'Stone beats rabbit. The kill is yours. Good hunting, friend.'

The war machine strode through the city, hooting and bellowing. Poison-grenades flew out of its flanks; its tentacles smashed brick and overturned cars; its desiccator-cannon turned mortar and men to dust.

Smith ran through the back alleys. The walker honked like an ocean liner, drowning the sound of his boots on the cobbles and the pounding of his breath.

He reached the warehouse of the East Empire Corporation and ran inside. It was dark and empty. Marble clattered underfoot. More honking, closer now.

He bounded up the stairs. On the first floor were the tea rooms, sealed chambers where the testing took place. On the second, the storage vats. The third floor was the roof.

He burst into the sunshine and the roar of guns.

Smith ran to the edge of the roof. The walker waded through the city as if through a pond. Plasma shells glowed around its hull. A sort of halo throbbed around it, dissipating the gunfire. Bloody force-field. His rifle would be useless.

How the hell did you stop a thing like that? The only weakness would be the pilot, safe in the cockpit. Think, he told himself. Aresians, horrid blancmange things that they were, lived off blood and had a very weak immune system. For a moment he considered blowing his nose down the end of the rifle barrel, but the pilot would almost certainly be immunised against human germs. Maybe tea would poison it. But how could he get the machine to drink tea?

And besides, what was that little figure on top of the walker, cackling with glee and shaking its fists at the city below? Some sort of Ghast, surely, but one with a metal eye. . .

462 laughed as the walker knocked down one of Urn's civic buildings. A foul smell rose up and the machine's air vents slammed shut to block out dangerous microbes. It stopped and lifted one of its massive legs, looked at the sole and made an angry metallic sound. It had trodden in the sewage works.

462 stopped laughing and coughed into his trenchcoat. Having scraped its foot clean on the remnants of a pub, the walker lurched onwards, gunfire crackling against the hull's force-field. 462 cackled and banged on the roof. 'Turn left! To the orphanage!'

Something glinted on one of the buildings. There was a puny human there, above the word TEA printed on the brickwork. 462 wondered if he ought to climb inside the walker where the force-field would protect him. No, he decided, even British humans would not be stupid enough to try to fight a war-machine of this power. He had only ever known one person idiotic enough to try, and by now the Master of Armour would have dealt with him. He squinted at the figure as it lifted a rifle, and suddenly he knew that the Master of Armour was dead.

'*Ak, fak,*' he said.

The shot hit 462 in the leg and knocked him off the walker. He dropped from sight. Smith smiled – and the walker turned towards him.

The desiccator-beam drew a searing line across the roof.

Smith ran to the door and charged down the stairs, hearing rubble fall behind him.

He reached the second floor, panting. The war machine honked. It loomed up in his imagination, a vast silver thing like a kettle on legs. Yes, he thought, almost a walking urn—

On the other side of the office was a sampling-urn. Smith switched it on, grabbed packets of tea and dumped them in the top. He'd come up with a plan once he'd had a drink.

With a sound like the wrath of God, the walker ripped the front off the building. It dipped its cockpit, and the window filled the hole in the wall as if a helicopter were hovering outside. Floodlights threw Smith's shadow across the urn. Behind the glass the pilot drooled and grinned.

Tentacles wriggled into the room. A hollow spike slid from the tip of each tentacle: syringes, for collecting blood.

A syringe darted out, quick as a snake, and Smith threw himself down and it punched into the urn. There was an awful sucking sound. He drew the Civiliser, raised it in both hands and shot the walker in the vents.

Hot tea sprayed the cockpit. Tea fumes rushed into the vents. The Aresian sucked in, expecting Smith's blood, and got a mouthful of Earl Grey instead. The pilot spat and thrashed with rage, tentacles battering at the glass. Then, suddenly, it shuddered, froze and slowly sagged across the controls. The metal arms flopped onto the floor.

'Blimey,' Smith said.

He staggered outside to the sound of cheers. Wainscott leaped up and down before the war machine. 'There you go, you dirty bugger! What d'you think of that then, eh?'

'I think you should put your trousers back on,' Smith said, and he fainted.

Wainscott looked down at him. 'Strange,' he observed. 'Fancy fainting at a man with no trousers.'

6

A Duel with the God Emperor!

Carveth lay in her bed, her eyes shut tight. 'I'm dying,' she said. 'How crap is that?'

Dreckitt stood next to the bed. There was not much space in her cabin, and he seemed too big, out of scale. 'You're not dying,' Dreckitt said. 'You'll pull through.'

'I feel like a tortoise that's been turned onto its back in the hot sun,' she gasped.

'A tortoise?'

'You know, a turtle? Same thing. It's not fair!' Carveth cried. 'My first battle and this happens to me! I'm not even two and now I'm going to die!' She began to cry. 'You know what? I've seen nothing people wouldn't believe. No attack ships on fire, nothing. Sod all. I got made, I had a few hangovers, got no nookie, and then I died. And now all these moments will be lost, like farts in a hurricane. I don't want to die having seen so little of life and having fat legs.'

'You're not for the Big House,' Dreckitt promised. 'You're only sleeping the little sleep, sister.'

She opened her eyes. 'I'm going to a better place,' she whispered. 'A place with green fields, and ponies, and maybe the odd unicorn.'

Wainscott put his head around the door. 'Hello,' he said, and he stepped into the room. 'Heard you were in trouble. Can't have that. So, where's the patient?'

'She's down here,' Dreckitt said. He got out of the way.

Wainscott nodded sagely. 'Polly, is it?' He leaned over her. 'Polly? Can you hear me, Polly?'

'Yes,' she whispered.

'Good. I want you to open your eyes for me, Polly. Can you do that?'

'I don't think—'

'Try, Polly.'

Slowly, she opened her eyes.

'Good,' Wainscott said. 'Now, listen. You're going to pull through, Polly. You're going to get better, and you won't die, and you know why?'

'No,' she said weakly.

'Because I bloody say so! Die on my watch? You'd be lucky! Now get out of bed before I court-martial you for wasting time, you lazy sod! There,' he said, 'that should do it,' and with that he left the room.

'Nutjob,' said Dreckitt, feeling rather disappointed.

The door opened again and Wainscott looked back into the room. 'I heard that.' He left, closing the door behind him.

'Oh well.' Carveth sighed. 'Suppose I'd better live, then. Don't want to get court-martialled.' She blinked. 'Don't suppose you could check my stitches, could you?'

They met in the palace on the next day. In the Great Hall, where the Senate of Urn had gathered, four hundred citizens waited and talked. Some wore armour and carried guns, others had on their work-clothes. All were Teasmen, free people of Urn.

Light streamed in through the domed glass roof, throwing wedges of brightness across an Imperial flag that hung from the apex, surrounded by motes of dust. A small group of M'Lak chatted with a local journalist. Wallahbots rolled through the crowd, serving tea. The pictures of the Hyrax had been pulled down and burned. The severed heads had been buried decently, the propaganda screens smashed and tossed into a skip.

There was a long crack in the marble floor and bullet holes against the far wall. Nobody had tried to clear those up, and nobody would. It was here that the Hyrax's fanatics had been swept aside by a horde of angry citizens: democracy in action.

As Smith entered he caught snatches of conversation. 'Started the clear-up already,' one of the soldiers was saying. 'Once the drones're done with the city we'll have them help out with the tea harvest. They're only too happy to join in. Thought we'd pulp 'em for surrendering or something.'

A solid man in a cap of office nodded. 'It'll be hard work, but nowt t'British working man can't handle. Have to put it t'guild once new Senate's voted in.'

'I just grabbed the back of his coat and started pounding this big round thing – oh, hello Boss.'

'Hello Carveth. Up and running again?'

She nodded and pulled up her shirt. Her midriff was wrapped in bandages. 'I started to die but I got told off.'

'I came to see you, but you were sleeping,' said Smith. 'You did a lot of good work back there.'

Smith saw Rhianna leaning against the opposite wall. She waved. Where's Suruk? Smith mouthed, and Rhianna pointed. The warrior lounged in the shadows, a sports bag by his feet. Smith tried not to think about what it might contain.

The doors at the far end of the room opened. Wainscott entered, followed by W. 'Alright, no funny business,' said a voice, and behind them filed out a group of Edenite captains, several gaunt, dusty praetorians, and the Grand Hyrax.

They were a battered looking lot. The Edenites looked confused and hurt, and several had red eyes, probably from crying. They looked so woebegone that Smith almost pitied them. Behind them the praetorians hissed and snarled, surly and all the more angry without a means of venting their rage. They still wore their leather coats, although these would soon be taken to make office chairs for the war effort. As they entered Carveth bent over and performed an insulting mime with their death's-head flag.

But the real prize came last. Men and women scowled and clenched fists as the God Emperor of Urn emerged. A nasty rumble ran through the room, a ripple of muttered abuse. 'Traitor.' 'Murderer.' 'Beardy tit.'

The Hyrax wore a long white gown and his facial hair was even wilder than usual. His eyes had a mad, cornered quality quite appropriate in a man named after a sort of feral guinea pig.

'Apostates!' he shouted at the people. He made a sudden break for freedom, but Wainscott grabbed him by the collar.

'No we don't, old son,' Wainscott said.

Someone had brought a stereo into the hall, and they all stood while 'Jerusalem' was played. As the music ended, W stepped forward and coughed into his palm.

'Hello everyone,' he said. 'Good of you to come.'

His long, battered head swung left to right as if on a hinge, taking them in. Under his moustache his mouth pulled itself up into a smile, fighting against the current of his face.

W said, 'Today we are here to receive the surrender of the occupying forces. The whole of Urn will be given its liberty, and power will pass to the Senate again. Once again, Urn will be a free planet under the protection of the British Space Fleet.' He smiled a little more freely, as if satisfied that it would not damage him to do so.

'This is just the beginning, citizens! Today we have boiled a pot whose steam shall be seen across the entire galaxy. The tea must flow, and it shall! The banner of the British Space Empire will be unfurled across a thousand worlds, carried forth by the citizens of Urn, and before them the tea will flow like a steaming brown river of shi—' He coughed violently – 'of shimmering moral fibre.'

Sudden movement at the side of the hall, and the Hyrax broke free of his guards, spun around and snatched a sword from one of the soldiers. He leaped into the middle of the room, brandishing it before him, and jabbed a grimy finger at W. 'Kill this man!' he yelled. 'Kill him!'

Nobody moved. Even the Edenite captives looked unimpressed.

'Your powers are useless here,' W said. 'They always were.'

The God Prophet snarled and waved the sword. 'Curse you to a thousand hells! Well then, which one of you cowards will fight me, eh? One to one, my blade against yours! My god – me – against your decadence! Who'll take me on? You, you wheezing wreck? You, you stumpy blonde Jezebel? Or you, the one men call Smith?' The madman's eyes narrowed. 'Yes, you. I hear you're a good fighter. Will you face me, heresiarch?'

'Certainly not,' said Smith. 'I am a civilised man.'

'I on the other hand, am a demented savage.' They looked around: Suruk stepped forward, mandibles parted. 'Let us get down to business, beard-face.'

'Now wait a moment.' The God Emperor paused. 'Nobody said anything about this – this – what beast are you, devil-spawn?'

'I am Suruk the Slayer – ta-da!' Suruk bowed. 'I fear no enemy in battle, for I am a bold warrior. If you are so keen to be martyred, fool, allow me to assist.'

The Hyrax took a step back. His boots scuffed on the marble floor.

Quietly, coolly, Suruk advanced. 'Or perhaps you wanted someone smaller to kill? Some passers-by who did not see you coming, or a little woman to beat with your fists? Are you afraid, facing an enemy who will fight back? I think so. It is you who is a coward, malodorous one. Now, as the British say, come and have a go, if you think you are sufficiently erect!'

Rage flared up in the Prophet-King's eyes. 'Why, you hellbound infidel scorpion of the four-horned viper in the burning lake of flames of the ninth goat–'

'Ahem,' said Suruk, and he tapped his watch.

'In the name of the all-merciful, all-loving god, I'll gut you alive!' The Hyrax lunged, and Suruk stepped aside, the sword carved the air beside him and there was a flash of steel and blood and the God Emperor fell dead. He lay sprawled across the floor, a mass of white robes, like a deactivated ghost. Suruk wiped his knife and put it away. Someone threw a blanket over the corpse. There was a murmur in the audience.

'Good riddance!' a woman called.

'He's dead!' Carveth cried. 'Yay!'

Smith looked down at the body. He glanced to the right, at the free men of Urn, and among them, his crew. Smith thought: we are more than fanatical. A fanatic has to yell and scream. We simply get the job done, no matter what it is.

W resumed his speech.

'Next week there will be elections for interim counsellors of Urn. In the meantime, Sauceress O'Varr has kindly agreed to help get things going again. The first task will be to get the tea flowing to the other parts of the Empire. Then, fuelled, with tea, we can take the fight to the Ghasts, and make space proper again!'

'Well said!' Smith exclaimed. 'Hooray for tea and dreadnoughts!'

'Silence, scum!' one of the praetorians hissed. 'Our indestructible legions –'

'*Oh, do pipe down!*' Smith snapped back, and the praetorian reeled as if struck. It snarled like a dog hit across the muzzle and shook its head, trying to clear it.

'The Bearing,' Sam O'Varr whispered.

'He knows the Shau Teng way,' Rhianna gasped.

'Well, enough of that,' said Smith, a little surprised by himself. 'But look here, Gertie, if you want a picture of the future, imagine a brogue kicking a big red arse – forever.'

W nodded. 'And on the subject of things kicking arse,' he declared, 'we have recently captured a large amount of rather nondescript Edenite beer and a stack of AC/DC records. Tomorrow, the tea will flow again. But tonight, my friends – disco and barbeque!'

Unlike its inhabitants, the landscape of Yullia was gentle and pleasant.

The country was almost entirely woodland, and the lemming-people lived on the forest floor or in the trees. Status was represented by building height: the Yullian serfs lived in shacks on the ground while the nobility dwelt in fortified treehouses, linked by walkways, from which they occasionally dropped rocks upon the shacks. Greatest of all the treehouse-castles of western Yullia was the citadel of General Zeck.

The ship that collected 462 touched down on the edge of Zeck's estate and a ground-car took him to the citadel. It was early autumn for the Yull and the leaves danced around the car as it slid past. But this was no idyll; there were a dozen furry heads on spikes at the gates and the peasants were furtive and afraid. The Yull knew how to run a planet, 462 thought.

He was led to the treehouse by four axe-wielding guards. The Yull were the same height as him, but bulky in their ceremonial armour. Between them, 462 was skinny and menacing. He had acquired a severe limp. Many things had broken his fall from the Aresian war machine, but most of them had been solid and sharp.

A lift pulled by serfs took him to the highest point of the treehouse. A minion struck a small triangle beside a curtain and behind it something grunted. The servant drew the curtain back and motioned 462 inside.

The room was virtually unfurnished and pathologically neat. Beside the window was an easel, and at the easel stood a figure in a dressing gown and a Foreign Legion-style hat. The figure turned around, nose twitching.

'*Hup-hup*, General Zeck,' said 462.

Zeck squinted at 462. His prim head tilted from one side to the other, the large, quick eyes roving over the Ghast's uniform. 'Humph!' he said. 'A thousand greetings, Commander. I heard of your war with the contemptible British.'

'You did?'

'Yes!' The lemming-man puffed out his chest. 'As we Yull say, news travels fastest when not weighed down by a big red backside. Welcome to my home, Commander 462. Please feel free to stay here until your masters summon you to die for your shameful failure to capture Urn.'

'It will not be failure,' 462 said.

'Not failure?' Zeck laughed, a high-pitched snigger. 'Stupid offworlder, you were beaten by mangy humans and dirty M'Lak. I laugh at your disgrace! Hahaha! See me laugh at you!'

462 reflected that killing Zeck would be a pleasure. Sadly he had no guards to do it, and Zeck, like all Yullian

officers, would be a dangerous foe at close range. He lurched nearer. 'Not when I bring them a billion new allies.'

'What do you mean?'

'You will come back with me.'

The Yull nodded and rubbed his snout. 'Hmm. . . You seek the assistance of the lemming-men of Yull, eh?'

462 ignored the question. His scarred head slid forward on his scraggy neck, and he peered at the easel. 'Interesting.'

'Yes.' Zeck pointed to the picture. 'It is a painting of the clouds above the Aldak Valley, a place noted for its beauty and tranquillity. You could not understand the nobility of such things.'

'And these figures in the foreground?'

'Me disembowelling an offworlder, on top of a pile of limbs hacked from offworlders. Offworlders are cowards and must be destroyed. Stinking offworlders die slow, *hwup-hup*! Present company excepted, of course.'

'Naturally. And it's that which I wanted to talk to you about. The lemming-people of Yull have a legendary reputation, and you stand out among them, General. Even among the fearless warriors of Yullia, you are known as – how can I put this? – a lying, murdering, torturing psychopath.'

The warlord's whiskers twitched with pride. 'Well, one tries.'

'As you know, we are currently engaged in destroying Earth. The Earthlanders are a strange species: the quieter they are, the more fiercely they fight. Several of my superiors underestimated the tenacity of Earth, especially the British Space Empire, and they have been pulped for their errors. Furthermore, our allies the Edenites have revealed themselves as braggarts and fools.'

'So you want them killed, slowly? Gladly!'

'No. I want you to direct your ferocity against the M'Lak.'

'The M'Lak? Despicable scum! They fight like savages, obeying some primitive honour code. They deserve to be hacked to death!' Zeck's eyes flicked to the crossed axes mounted on the wall. 'Hacked to death!'

462 rubbed his antennae together. 'Quite. And they are entering this war on the side of Earth.'

Zeck walked to the window and opened it, taking several deep breaths of fresh air. Down below, a Yullian peasant was driving a plough-team of squol across his smallholding. General Zeck drew a knife from his sleeve and tossed it at the peasant. 462 heard a distant squeak and Zeck closed the window, looking mildly satisfied. Life was cheap among the lemmings.

'So,' he said, 'you are worried that the Ghast Empire will lose.'

462 shook his head. 'We are worried that the efficiency of our inevitable victory may be impaired. We wish to give you the opportunity of sharing that victory with us. You will attack the M'Lak worlds and the humans in the Western arm of the galaxy. In return, you will gain the opportunity to kill huge numbers of inferior offworlders and capture countless sacrifices, whom you can mangle and offer to your war-god at your leisure.

'The time of humanity is over, General Zeck. It is the dawning of a new era: the era of the Ghast. You can be part of that. If you choose, you can guide the lemming-men of Yull towards the cliffs of destiny. All you need do is say yes, and my minions can talk to your minions, and we will sort out the paperwork and then burn it.'

General Zeck snorted. 'Oh, I see. So, you are seriously expecting me to throw away the lives of thousands of my brave kindred, just for the sake of lording it over some bunch of wretched primates who you were going to defeat anyway? You are asking me to send my men to their deaths for the sake of indulging my own petty sadism.'

'Yes.'

'When can I start?'

Suruk held a skull at arm's length, like Hamlet, while he painted glue onto its lower jaw. He stood in the centre of his room on board the *John Pym*, amid the rest of his favourite souvenirs. The banana-shaped head of a Procturan Ripper grinned at him from the mantelpiece.

A knock on the door. 'Hey, Suruk. You coming to this do or what?'

'One moment, little woman,' Suruk said. 'I shall be with you shortly.'

He reached into his bag and took out a large beard, and pressed it onto the gluey skull. Pleased with the effect, he put the skull on the shelf, next to the skull in a chef's hat.

The Empire had never found 462, but it had unearthed Captain Gilead of the New Eden lying unconscious in a Ghast bunker. He seemed to have brained himself with his own arm. Since the Hyrax was dead and 462 appeared to have escaped offworld, they decided to ship Gilead's head to Earth, for trial on grounds of authorising murder and waging a war of aggression.

Suruk had been put in charge of guarding Captain Gilead on the way back home. As Smith had pointed out, it was not a very difficult task so long as Gilead was delivered alive and intact for trial, without any further injuries. Although he might need a bit of a wash.

Suruk took his litter tray down and coughed a pellet into the tray. He pressed a pedal with his boot and the lid of the bin flipped up and he shook the pellets into the bin.

'I'll see you in hell, you hog-faced son of a bitch!' said a voice from the bottom of the bin.

'Undoubtedly.' Suruk closed the bin and left the room.

Carveth was in her cabin, almost ready to go. She wore her blue dress and was checking Gerald's food supply. The hamster's wheel clattered and squeaked. Suruk looked around the room, with its multiple cushions and Shetland pony calendar, and felt distinctly uncomfortable.

'Greetings,' Suruk said.

'Hey, Suruk. How's things?'

'I am well. And you?'

'Yeah, not too bad, all considering. I'm healing up.'

'Good, for we must speak.'

She looked at him a little closer. Her eyes narrowed, suspicious. 'Go on.'

'You saved Isambard Smith's life in the battle, I am told.'

'Oh, well, yeah.'

'Then you did well. You are blooded now,' Suruk said. 'It is the custom of my people not to take a name until one is blooded in battle. When I fought against Smith, I named him Mazuran, which means "The quick brown fox that jumps over the lazy dog". Now I have decided to give you a warrior's name.'

'Wow,' she said, genuinely pleased. 'That's – well, that's really kind of you, Suruk. You know, I thought my military prowess would get noticed sooner or later,' she added, standing up a bit straighter. 'What is my warrior name?'

'Anorak.'

'What? Anorak? You're taking the piss. Can't I be something else?'

Suruk looked as hurt as she had ever seen him. 'Anorak is a noble name!'

'But, Suruk, an anorak is a sort of coat nerds wear. You can't call me that.'

'Then perhaps you ought to reflect on the meaning of the word in my language, not its mere sound in yours.'

Carveth frowned. 'Well, I suppose so. What does it mean, then?'

'It means. . . "piglet".'

'Piglet? That's my name? Bloody hell. Alright then, Piglet it is. But it's Polly to you, alright? Princess Polly, preferably.'

Suruk scowled. 'There are limits, Princess Piglet. But your M'Lak name shall be kept secret, as you wish. Now, we must go to the celebrations while it is dark and all are drunk, or else you shall find no man with whom to conduct your foul ruttings. In which case you would be – wait, I remember the very phrase – left upon the shelf like a big fat sad sack.'

*

The party was in full swing when they arrived. Beer was flowing freely, but the Hyrax's laws had given the cityfolk a new thirst for tea. A huge bonfire had been built under the station's water tank, and the tank had been cleaned out and filled with the precious leaf. Tomorrow it would serve the railway that ran to the plantations, but tonight it was being used as a gigantic pot.

Suruk and Carveth passed down the main street. A vendor gave them sausages from a barbecue. Men and women went by in little groups, drinking and cheering. They had been soldiers until today, but now they were citizens again, Teasmen working for the Combined Horticultural Amenities Regulator.

'Look,' said Suruk. 'Celebrations.'

Figures moved awkwardly in the light of the bonfire, each to his own time. They jerked and lurched like excited zombies, waving random hands. The British were dancing.

Isambard Smith stood at the edge of the dancers, pint in one hand, teacup in the other, talking to W but staring into the fire. As they drew near, Smith glanced round and nodded to them. 'Hello there! How's things?'

'Good,' Suruk said. 'Although the food is a disappointment. This "hot dog" is clearly some sort of sausage. I strongly suspect that there are no notable merchants in the burgers, either. I wonder if there is any spotted dick left?'

'Good luck with that,' Smith said. The alien bounded into the crowd and was lost to view.

Smith sighed and glanced down at Carveth. 'Thanks for looking out for me in the battle back there. You did a bloody good job, Carveth. I'm glad to see you back on form.'

She grinned and shrugged. 'Well, you know me, I was born to raise hell. Oh look – cheese and pineapple sticks!'

W passed her a handful of sticks. 'Come and join us,' he said. 'Smith and I were just discussing our next job. Now that the army has its tea again, I'm thinking of having a crack at the Yull. They've building an empire they call the Galactic Friendship Project. We don't like the sounds of it. Ah, and there's Wainscott,' he added, pointing towards the fire. 'And Miss Mitchell.'

Smith turned back to the figures dancing in the light of the fire. Wainscott might have been a war hero and a fearless leader of men, but he danced like an uncle at a wedding. By contrast, Rhianna was modern and expressive, almost embarrassingly so. Carveth stood next to Smith for a while, watching Rhianna dance.

'So, are you and Miss Wuthering Heights an item, then?'

'I'm not sure,' Smith said. 'You know, I've not really had much chance to talk to her since the battle. It's all been so hectic.'

Carveth nodded. 'Well, you can't hurry love, you know. Bide your time, wait for the right moment to tell her how you really feel, and then bone her.'

'Thanks, Carveth.'

'Happy to help.'

Two tall figures strode out of the shadow and hailed them. 'Smith! Suruk! Anorak!'

'Yes?' Carveth said, immediately making a mental note not to answer to a name that meant 'Piglet' any more. It was Agshad and Morgar who had called. Morgar looked a little uneasy, but quite well, considering his injuries. The

M'Lak healed quickly, and within a week he would be back to normal again. Now there were bandages on his hands, and bumps under his roll-neck sweater that must have been the dressings on his other wounds. He walked with a slight limp.

Agshad had his hands in the pockets of his Barbour jacket. There was a scarf wrapped tight around his neck.

'Greetings, kin!' Suruk said.

'Hello all,' replied Agshad. 'We thought we'd best say goodbye before we go.'

'You're going?' Smith said.

Morgar nodded. 'Indeed. Our work here is done, and, to be honest, it's not quite the sort of party I'm used to. It's a bit, you know, busy. But thank you, anyway. It's been a real education.'

'Yes,' Agshad said. 'You know, Smith, when you offered us the chance to fight beside you, I thought you were an idiot, the kind of fool who thinks "astute" is a sort of weasel. But you have helped me get back in touch with my blood-sodden heritage, and you've taught me to be proud of both of my sons: my useful son Morgar, who brings home a wage, and my atavistic warrior son Suruk, who doesn't. It's been a really good holiday,' he added. 'I will be recommending war to all my friends back at the office. From taxman to axeman, one might say!'

Suruk bowed a little. 'And I know my family is still honourable. Goodbye, father. Goodbye, Morgar.'

They did not embrace: the M'Lak disliked shows of emotion. Fair enough, thought Smith, watching them walk away. Soon he would have to talk to Rhianna. He did not know what to say. Somehow, in fact, sleeping with her had made it more awkward than before. Were they lovers, partners, sweethearts, or had she just made a terrible and naked mistake? Perhaps she didn't want me at all, he thought. Perhaps she just got confused or something. Confused? With what? Stop fannying around, he told himself. Get on with it.

Suruk chuckled beside him. 'And I thought my father had no slight-of-hand. He managed to slip a brochure about law school into my back pocket.'

Smith was not really listening. Rhianna had stopped whirling around – jazz hands and AC/DC really did not go, he decided – and was approaching.

'Hey, everyone!' she called. 'Over here! C'mon, guys!'

They joined her by the vegetarian barbecue. There were some picnic chairs laid out in a rough semicircle and Wainscott and his men were already there, working their way though a box of captured beer. Susan's arm was in a sling. W sat down carefully and helped her open a beer bottle. Even Rick Dreckitt was there, at the far edge of the group, staring into a glass of whisky, the firelight catching on his stubble.

Once they had settled down, Rhianna switched off the radio. They could make out the distant music of other parties across the city, but their group was suddenly silent and intimate. They looked nervous.

'Hey, guys,' Rhianna said. 'I think that it's really important, today of all days, that we express our feelings collectively. I feel that today we've shared something very important, and that we've demonstrated our opposition to oppressive tyranny, right?'

'Yes, super, great,' Wainscott said with evident relief, getting up.

'I'm not finished yet,' Rhianna said, and he scowled and sat down again. 'Now then,' she said, brushing a stray dreadlock out of the way, 'We've had quite an adventure, all of us. And, as anyone who's read the complete works of Tolkein as often as I have will know, an adventure often ends with a party – and a song.'

She reached behind her seat and took out an acoustic guitar. A rumble of unease ran through the group. 'I wrote this myself.'

Smith grimaced. Much as he loved Rhianna, a dark part of his mind whispered 'Folk music – till death do you part'. He found a cocktail sausage and broke it in half. Rhianna fiddled with the strings and made a noise.

'Oh my God, my wounds!' Carveth cried, and she leaped up and staggered off, clutching her head. Rhianna struck a chord. Carveth came lurching back, grabbed Dreckitt by the arm and stumbled away, hauling him after her. 'His wounds too!' she called, and they disappeared into the night.

'Right,' said Rhianna. 'I'll begin. You can sing along with the chorus: singing's always more... *real* if the audience joins in.'

Across the stars and all through space
One thing guides the human race,
Neither politics, nor belief,
Our future lies in the tea leaf.
Yet in our comfort we forgot
Alien eyes turned to Didcot.

The Ghasts invaded, Eden too
Which was a, like, bad thing to do
Hassling people with their hate
They imposed a theocratic state.
Galactic conquest was their plan -
For they were working for the Man.

They took our land, our property
They tried to rewrite history
They held us down with tyranny
But they can never take our tea.

Folk of Urn were its defenders
Brave men and brave other genders:
Women fighting for their future,
M'Lak, who happen to be neuter
And in case there were some, keep in mind
People whose gender has been reassigned.

So we rose against their cruel regime
Destroyed their tanks and war machines
For with some people, I admit,
Non-violence just gets you hit.
And it's hard to use the ways of Ghandi
When you've got a plasma cannon handy.

They took our land, our property
They tried to rewrite history
They held us down with tyranny
But they can never take our tea.

And the moral is that the tea shall flow
And – Guys? Where did everybody go?

As Rhianna looked around, Smith surreptitiously removed the two halves of the cocktail sausage from his ears. The Deepspace Operations Group had used their fearsome powers of stealth to slip into the night, no doubt in search of beer and rock music.

'Just us, it seems,' Smith said, and he got up and walked across to a chair nearer her and pulled it close. He sat down. 'Righto,' he said.

'Yes,' Rhianna said, rather wistfully.

'Right then. Mind if I, er—'

He leaned round, ready to kiss her, and she pulled back. 'Isambard, we need to talk.'

'Talk. Yes, of course.' He leaned back in his picnic chair for a moment, thinking. This must be what they called 'fore-play'. No doubt he was expected to say something to get her in the mood. 'Jolly good song, that,' he said.

Rhianna looked around at him and he was shocked to see that her face had acquired its sincerely-concerned look. Sudden fear gripped him. Something bad was about to happen, and it looked as if instead of rude stuff he could expect a tear-jerking monologue about why dolphins ought to be given the vote.

'This isn't going to work, Isambard,' she said.

'Nonsense,' he said cheerfully. 'I've only had three pints. It's like Carveth says: so long as you crank the handle, an old car can still be a goer.'

'It's not that,' Rhianna replied. 'It's not you, Isambard. It's me.'

'You? If it's about you being half-alien, I really don't mind. It's not like you're Belgian or anything.'

'Very soon you'll have to go again,' Rhianna said. 'And I will have to stay here, with the government, learning how to use my powers. Isambard, no matter what, I won't be anywhere near you. We should part as friends.'

'But – but – what do you mean? We can't just shake hands and go! We – you know – we *did* it. That matters, doesn't it?' Suddenly alarmed, he added, 'That *was* doing it, wasn't it?'

'Yes, that was doing it,' she said sadly.

'Besides, aren't you into free love and all that? I mean, I'm as free as they come.'

'Oh Isambard, if you weren't so new to this, I wouldn't say no. But I don't want to hurt you. I know you have feelings for me, and I know they can't come to anything. That has to end, for the good of both of us.'

'Sod my feelings! I'm English, for God's sake. I don't do feelings. I hardly even have any. Rhianna, this isn't fair. If I was a worse person, you'd be with me tonight. How does that make any sense at all?'

'I guess it's best for—'

'Bloody women!' Smith cried, standing up. 'What is wrong with you people? One of you jumps under a race-horse and the whole world goes knockers-up! Well,' he concluded, 'I've had enough of this. You can do what you damned well like. I'm going to find someone who's sane and decent and actually cares about doing the right thing instead of putting people down and messing around with their heads.'

'Hello,' Suruk the Slayer said, strolling over. 'Anybody want anybody killed?'

'No, thank you.'

'I have just had quite the most disgusting experience of my life. Bounty hunter Dreckitt is being awarded a portion on the kitchen table by the gnome Carveth.' He scowled. 'Several portions, actually. Sometimes, walking silently is not advantageous.' He glanced at Rhianna. 'She weeps, Smith. Not within my ambit.' He turned and took a step away, then looked back. 'Unless you want her killed?'

Smith looked: Rhianna was crying. 'No, Suruk,' he said. 'Thanks for the offer, though.'

Suruk shrugged. 'Merely a thought,' and he sauntered into the dark, whistling cheerily through his mandibles.

Smith hurried back to his seat. Rhianna was weeping. A quiet, annoying sort of crying, like something that has sprung a slow leak. 'Oh Rhianna,' he said, stooping, 'I'm sorry. I didn't mean to be rude. It's just, you know, it seems awfully—'

He did not get to finish. Quick as a Procturan Ripperspawn impregnating a host, she leaned over and kissed him. She stopped before he could black out, and looked at him and shook her head, as if with wonder.

Women, he thought, rum bunch. Distinctly rum.

'Oh, Isambard,' she said, 'Do you really think we could make it work?'

'Can't see why not. I can make a spaceship work, pretty much, and you should see the dashboard.'

She smiled. 'Hey, I've just had the best idea ever.'

'Really?'

Rhianna leaned forward, conspiratorial. 'You know the water tank they've been using as an urn tonight? The bonfire's almost out. The tea'll still be warm.'

'Yes, that's right. Why?'

'Want to go swimming, Isambard?'

'But I haven't got a bathing suit.'

She grinned. 'Nor have I.'

'Well, that won't work. . . Oh my God, do you really mean—?'

'Really.'

To his surprise, he did not pass out on the spot. 'Blimey,' he said. 'Well, I mean to say, bloody hell. Tea's up!'

Acknowledgements

This book would never have been written without the encouragement of my family and friends. In particular I'd like to thank everyone at Red Wave, Myrmidon and Verulam Writers' Circle for all their help. Special thanks must also go to my long-suffering parents, and my friend Owen (even though he doesn't like tea). I raise a cup to you all.

About the Author

Toby Frost studied law and was called to the Bar in 2001. Since then, he has worked as a private tutor, a court clerk and a legal advisor, amongst other things. He has also produced film reviews for the book *The DVD Stack* and articles for *Solander* magazine. The first of his Isambard novels, *Space Captain Smith*, was published in the spring of 2008.

Join Captain Smith and his
crew on their next adventure. . .

Wrath of the Lemming-men!

From the depths of Space a new foe rises to do battle with
mankind: the British Space Empire is threatened by the
lemming-people of Yull, ruthless enemies who attack
without mercy, fear or any concept of self-preservation. At
the call of the war-god, the Yull have turned on the
Empire, hell-bent on conquest and destruction in their
rush towards the cliffs of destiny.

When the Yullian army is forced to retreat at the battle
of the River Tam, the disgraced Colonel Vock swears
revenge on the clan of Suruk the Slayer, Isambard Smith's
homicidal alien friend. Now Smith and his crew must
defend the Empire and civilise the stuffing out of a horde
of bloodthirsty lemming-men – which would be easy were
it not for a sinister robotics company, a Ghast general
with a fondness for genetic engineering and an ancient
brotherhood of Morris Dancers – who may yet hold the
key to victory. . .

Wrath of the Lemming Men by Toby Frost – available
summer 2009!